"If you mix *The Last Samurai* with (With exquisite details and a sweet *When the Ocean Roars* is a refreshingly different story tropes of forbidden love, cultural traditions, and family ties that bind."

—**Lenora Worth**, 2019 RITA finalist and *NY Times, USA Today,* and *PW* best-selling author

"Charlsie is a debut author who is already a master wordsmith. If you love romance in exotic locations, prepare to be swept away by *When the Ocean Roars!*"

—**Janet W. Ferguson**, best-selling author of the Coastal Hearts novels, Christy Award finalist

"Charlsie Estess offers an elegant voice in the vibrant landscape of contemporary romance. She hooked me on page one, and the story held my attention until the end. I loved the pairing of a prizefighter and a Japanese socialite set in Japan. Keane and Ami's love story of faith, hope, and perseverance tugged at my heartstrings. If you enjoy moving stories of strength and resilience, this book is for you."

—**Carmen Peone**, author of *Captured Secrets* and *Broken Bondage*, Seven Tine Ranch Romance

"Author Charlsie Estess's debut book, *When the Ocean Roars*, is a masterful story that takes us to Japan and draws us into a controversial romance amid a championship martial arts fight. Estess does a superb job of creating tension between the characters as they deal with choosing sides. Despite the challenges of public and private identities, the hero discovers a fight that is not the one he planned for, but a different kind of battle in a life-and-death situation where the victory is greater than a trophy. I highly recommend this new, exciting story.

—**Marilyn Turk**, award-winning author of *The Escape Game*

WHEN THE OCEAN ROARS

A NOVEL

CHARLSIE ESTESS

Birmingham, Alabama

When the Ocean Roars

Iron Stream Fiction
An imprint of Iron Stream Media
100 Missionary Ridge
Birmingham, AL 35242
IronStreamMedia.com

Library of Congress Control Number: 2023941659

Cover design by Hannah Linder Designs

ISBN: 978-1-56309-676-1 (paperback)
ISBN: 978-1-56309-677-8 (ebook)

1 2 3 4 5—28 27 26 25 24

For my lion-hearted boys.
Stay strong and courageous.

God is our refuge and strength,
a helper who is always found
in times of trouble.
Therefore we will not be afraid,
though the earth trembles
and the mountains topple
into the depths of the seas,
though its water roars and foams
and the mountains quake with its turmoil.

—Psalm 46:1–3

Chapter 1

"Midas? Are you lost?"

No one ever called him Midas.

Keane Temple blinked, his eyes long since glazed over, straining to make sense of the Japanese characters flashing across a digital display board. The petal-soft voice came from behind but couldn't be speaking to him. No one should recognize him. Not yet.

He rubbed the back of his neck to loosen up tight muscles—not that the ultramodern train station with its broad spans of spotless glass anchored in polished steel brackets overwhelmed him. Still, he drew in a deep breath, inhaling the smell of hot metal tracks mingled with citrus-fresh window cleaner.

At ten past six in the evening, he'd been waiting on a train in the luxury shopping district for far too long. He turned and surveyed the platform to put a face with the alluring voice. But the lady must be speaking to someone else.

The backlit display cases along the station's exit wall sparkled with designer accessories. Prada pumps. Diamond-studded Cartier baubles. Vuitton handbags. And in front of that exorbitantly priced glitz stood a bald, sandal-footed Buddhist monk, speaking with a young girl with fuchsia hair and surgically shaped Barbie-doll lips. Japan was an island of extremes. But no one else on the platform passed for Midas with his golden touch—not even remotely—except him. Fair-haired with a towering build, Keane must stand out in this crowd.

The fighter in him bristled. He pretended *not* to hear and regretted taking directions from Hans after practice. A long walk to the train station had sounded like a great idea. Fresh air should combat jet lag and boost his mental game, so he'd passed on his usual, a chauffeured Bentley SUV, and headed out. Big. Mistake.

Never take tips from the guy you just face-planted. His sparring partner knew better than anyone how Keane relished control and hated the unexpected, and given Keane's supreme dominance in the ring, practical jokes let easygoing Hans get in a good jab. It lightened the mood in the gym, especially during the stressful days leading up to the World Championship.

Nevertheless, that joker was going to pay on Monday. Keane could have been back to his Westin suite by now, unwinding in the steam room. Definitely no more trains.

"Midas?" The sweet singsong stroked his senses again before a string of giggles chased it.

The muscle in his jaw twitched. He wadded the fake directions in a fist, scratched through his unruly lion mane, and spun to face the schoolgirls swarming the base of an escalator. In stylish skirts and designer pumps, they must be the college variety. But with all those high-end shopping bags, they sure weren't struggling through university the way he had.

"Are you lost?" the young woman repeated in flawless English. And did that honeyed voice carry the slightest hint of a British accent? His gaze landed on the exquisite creature at the center of the pack. She had the strong presence of a ballerina, and the way her bamboo-green dress showcased her figure brought a warm tightness to his chest. Dainty fingers covered a timid laugh, but her unflinching gaze leveled on his with enough heat to keep him staring far too long. Her chin gave a defiant tip, breaking his hold over her and letting him know she wasn't about to be ignored. "Are. You. L—"

"Maybe." The admission came out huskier than intended. His irritation melted, and despite efforts to veil any interest, a lopsided grin tipped his mouth.

"You are the American fighter, yes?" The lady adjusted her purse straps on her narrow shoulder, glided forward, and unleashed an unforgettable smile.

"Yes. And you know me?" He was well-known in the States— but Japan? He hadn't expected the prefight publicity to be out for another week and had hoped to ride a wave of anonymity until then. With a long stride, he closed the distance between them and extended a hand. "Keane Temple."

As she took it, she dipped in a bow, and a waft of perfume drifted in his direction. He breathed in, trying to identify the tantalizing spice. A note of pepper. And perhaps mandarin?

"My name is Ami." A rose flush bloomed across powder-pale cheeks, her lips easing back into that lovely smile. He was all too familiar with his effect on women. Most he encountered weren't of the keeping sort. But the fine-boned fantasy before him—a sleek cascade of obsidian hair flowing to her trim waist—stirred something long latent.

How long had it been since a woman affected him with such swift intensity? Drawn him with such ferocity?

She chuckled again, slid back a step, and turned to her friends to fire off a series of phrases in Japanese. After questioning glances and awkward waves, the other girls rode the escalator. "So"—she faced him—"I will take you home now."

"Pardon me?" He half coughed at the brazen statement. Still, a wave of dark amusement rolled through his mind.

"You are lost." She waved toward the exit. "The Japanese do not give directions. Our way is to help someone find his destination. What is your address?"

Come to think of it, hadn't he read about that hospitable custom in his *Fodor's Travel Guide* on the plane ride over? He searched her kind face. But was a twinkle of interest lurking in her eyes? "Ichibancho. The Westin."

She swiveled to examine a nearby map of the train lines and then studied the flickering schedule board. "Sendai Station is closest—not far from where I attend university. We should wait here for the next train."

"You seriously mean to come with me?"

"Of course." Those dark eyes were unreadable, but her body swayed toward him as naturally as a flower craning toward the sun. "You could get lost again."

"And you're sure you don't want to keep shopping with your friends? I'm pretty good with directions."

"No. I want to help."

The heat of her perusal rolled over him again. Her gaze reconnected with his. Her pupils flared under his intense scrutiny. With four US Championships to his credit, he had maneuvers that could break the fiercest men, let alone takedown moves that could level a woman to her back with finesse. And yet, this woman—some rare species holed up in a glass-and-granite jungle—remained undaunted.

"I'm done shopping. My mother used to say life never fails to deliver the unexpected." She arched a delicate brow. "I've always preferred the unexpected."

"But . . ." He swallowed the rest of the words, a broad smile stretching out his mouth. Were all Japanese women this feisty? "I can't argue with that, and company would be nice. Thank you."

The tracks began to hum, and wind wailed through the station as the next train approached. "This is it." She caught his elbow. The automatic doors hissed apart, and she slipped onto the train and anchored herself to the support pole nearest the doors.

He followed, dipping his head through the entrance, his body skimming hers as he cut past a tangle of travelers to grip the floor-to-ceiling steel rod beside her. "Is it far?"

The pneumatic doors sighed shut, and the locomotive began to whir along. He made small talk to staunch his restlessness. Since childhood, he'd hated confined spaces, and friendly banter helped bury the unwelcome claustrophobia.

Ami only shook her head as she bit at her lovely lower lip. And he suspected he knew why. A heady charge infiltrated the cramped compartment, making him aware of how his stature dominated it and pressed into her personal space. "What are you studying at the university?"

Her face relaxed. "Geophysics. The graduate program is well-known here, but my undergraduate work was at Oxford."

She must have been older than he'd pegged her but still five or six years younger than he. Oxford explained her proficiency in English. But geophysics? Wow. "So, what, you study the earth and gravity?"

"Yes, but I have a particular interest in seismology—plate tectonics and volcanism."

He scratched at the stubble on his chin, likely failing to hide his growing fascination as she gushed about her studies and passion for earthquake awareness. "What can I say? You impress me. And there must be plenty of research opportunities around here."

Her gaze dropped at the compliment. Gorgeous. Accomplished. Caring. *God, is she real?*

"This is it." She pointed, her words hauling his thoughts in a different direction. As the train eased to a stop, she braced against the steel pole with the control of a ballerina back at her barre. "See, there is an ocean mural on the station wall. It might help you remember."

Outside, Keane paused to admire the cityscape, shifting from the flashing lights and jingling payout noises of a pachinko gaming parlor to the more serene street scene. The mild tension from the train drained from his shoulders as he absorbed a blend of street smells—wet concrete, ripe apple from a corner fruit stand, and rich roasting coffee carried on the breeze. An early sunset lit fire in the vibrant blue sky, gilding the scattered rain clouds and turning ordinary street puddles into shimmering mirrors of nightlife. Short-trunked trees, heavy with spring buds, oversaw the bustle of Sendai's avenues and infused deep-green life into the sea of boxy office buildings.

"You like the greenery?" She cocked her head, one well-sculpted brow rising again.

Man, she was something. Grinning, he hooked his hands on his hips. "How'd you guess?"

"In your green eyes. So bright now." She shifted her purse. "Did you know this is The City of Trees?"

"No, but it lives up to the name." He raked a hand through his tousled hair, appreciation guiding his line of sight. "Which way?"

She aimed a finger at a street sign and ambled toward the damp sidewalk. "That is Ichibancho."

A flicker of recognition registered. "We'll have to cross. My place is there." He motioned toward a luxurious building complex wrapped in glass. At the intersection, they scuffled in lockstep with a mass of professionals making their evening exodus.

On the opposite side, two office towers bookended a row of traditional Japanese structures with tiled hip-and-gable roofs. A tea emporium. A noodle restaurant with the standard waving fortune kitty. A booklover's bookstore. A fine stationery shop. A European coffeehouse. All in all, Sendai was a charming city.

He shortened his stride to swing with hers as they meandered through the crowded block, letting her lead when necessary. But when she glanced over her shoulder, her dark irises drifted over him. Was she interested in being more than hospitable? Perhaps going out?

The restaurants would be filling up soon. He could invite her to dinner, even though going on a date was against his better preflight, stay-focused judgment. But then again, he was shot and sore after a full training day. A cold shower and sleep were musts before heading anywhere.

"Keane?" Her voice drew him out. "This is it. Do you think you can find your way inside?" Her easy laugh bolstered his courage.

"That's debatable, but I think I can manage." He flashed a smile, and she nodded, her foot inching back as if she were turning to leave. On instinct, he reached out to touch her elbow and stepped toward her. "Hold up." The sudden proximity produced some maddening chemistry that made his words come out low and husky. "Look, tomorrow's my only day off from training. I'm no good at finding my way around here. Spend the day with me."

"I already have plans." She wasted no time in responding, but the glint in her eyes betrayed her interest.

He slid closer, his gaze never wandering from her face. "Change them." As she weighed his proposal, he sent up a silent plea, praying she'd agree.

She scrunched her dainty nose, but then her mischief evaporated. "I will, but staying in town is not good for me. I could show you one of my favorite places, just outside the city. I will pick you up."

Oh, you already have. For the first time in years, a hard, hot bullet of anticipation pierced him deep. "Sounds good. But allow me to arrange for a car."

"Okay. Eleven o'clock?"

"Eleven it is. Where are we going?"

"It's a surprise," she said with a bewitching blush, then pivoted.

After watching her leave, he crossed the wide street, hustled through the Westin's swank lobby with its polished marble floors and plush furnishings, and rode the mirrored elevator to the top. Then the penthouse's thick mahogany door clicked shut behind him, and his steps echoed in the cavernous room. With the curtains tied back to frame the floor-to-ceiling windowed wall, the remaining glow of sunset filtered through and silhouetted the low couch and table. There was no television, per his request. Just furniture. A simple kitchen with a well-stocked fridge. A grand bedroom reduced to a no-frills space with a Japanese futon and a marbled bath. Sumptuously Spartan.

He preferred bare-bones living. Like it was when he'd been an angry kid learning karate at his local church. Without karate, where would he be? That after-school program—not only the healthy outlet fighting provided but also Pastor Ray's steady encouragement—pulled him through his nightmare childhood and gave him faith, a sense of purpose, and a profession. No distractions, especially women, had always been his fail-safe standard before a championship fight. And he'd come to Japan for one reason—to win the Ultimate Fighting World Championship.

God, help me stay on the narrow path.

He steeled himself against the mind-consuming chemistry still lingering like an unshakable fever. Didn't want it. At least, not right now, if he were honest.

After a reheated dinner of broiled chicken and a broccoli-rice blend, he stripped, showered, and slid into the futon. He tried to read but just stared at the pages. Huffing, he traced circles around his temples with his fingertips and attempted to visualize sparring drills.

Counting down, less than two weeks remained until *the* match of his life. He'd spent decades pushing his body and honing his mental game. And he'd need to bring it all to take down Niko Ono, the fire-fisted Japanese giant approaching legendary status. But try as he might, there Ami was, an irresistible angel, appearing against the backs of his eyelids. Where she was concerned, going cold turkey was the sole way to defeat distraction, but this distraction would be showing up in the morning. Why had he asked her out? He didn't even have a number to call and cancel.

One day with her. That's it.

"You should have seen him," Ami crooned. Even in black performance joggers and a matching hoodie, the broad-shouldered build of a man in his physical prime was evident. She'd recognized him in the station but never imagined he'd be so striking. So golden. Undefeated all year. The serendipitous nature of their encounter summoned an old Japanese saying: *seiten no heki-reki*, a thunderbolt from the blue. The devastatingly intense attraction struck just like that, electrifying her. Their meeting was no coincidence, right?

Even so, she was playing with fire. But why should that stop her? He didn't need to know who she was. Some things were better left untold, especially when the man would be in the country only a short time.

"What happened?" Knees hugged to her chest, her roommate curled up on the couch. "And do tell all."

Ami hooked her purse on a peg by the door, breezed across the marble-tiled foyer, and sank into the cushion next to Mika with dramatic flair. "I will give him a tour tomorrow."

"Did you tell him who you are?"

Ami shook her head, her lips pressed into a hard line.

"But honesty—"

She waved away the reproachful glint in Mika's eyes. "Keane only knows me as me, not because of my family. And I want to keep it that way."

"And what about Ichiro?"

Ah, Ichiro. The man her father expected her to marry. Ami

fiddled with the thin ruby-studded ring she'd inherited as a young girl. "What about him?" She cringed at the flippant-sounding words. "Keane is here a few weeks at most."

"And then?"

"And then, Father's plan. Just not before I have some fun of my own choosing." She tucked her long legs underneath her. "He. Is. Magnificent."

"It's true. That sandy blond hair and those jade eyes. Ami, he is *gorgeous*." Mika giggled, making her angled bob bounce along her jawline. "You missed the evening entertainment news. The anchorman said Keane fights like a brute and has the staying power of Methuselah." Her eyes widened before she clapped a hand over her mouth to stifle another snicker. "Even your father would be pleased."

"I beg to differ." Drumming her palms on the charcoal suede seat, Ami shot Mika a think-about-it look. "You're like my sister and know me better than anyone. Why would you even say that?"

"His net worth is pushing three billion yen. But there's more. I am *the* queen of recon." With a playful grin, Mika wiggled her shoulders. "You're welcome."

"Thank you." Ami winged out her elbow and gave Mika's arm a chummy poke. "So, what did you find out?"

Mika picked up her phone and let her index finger swirl back and forth over the screen. "Between his prize purses and sponsorships over the past five years, he's done really well and achieved more-than-fighter status to become one of Houston's richest and most eligible bachelors. He's heavy into real estate investments, like your father. Sits on a start-up's board. Last year, he organized a huge fundraiser to benefit military families in honor of his friend, a fallen soldier. There's not much on his family or personal life." Mika glanced up. "But—you'll love this—he puts on a monthly karate tournament for up-and-coming fighters at the place where he learned."

Ami absorbed that. She pulled the length of her jet-black hair over a shoulder, twisting a long lock. "*That* would get Father's attention. Most women, too. But a man's net worth isn't my concern." A long beat passed. Staying at the top of his fighting game, coupled with that kind of business success, would take serious acumen though, as well as incredible initiative and grit. The news didn't get everything right, but if even half of what Mika said turned out to be true—well, a surge of respect filled Ami. "Keane was inquisitive on the train. I liked that, but it also made me nervous."

The span between Mika's brows furrowed. "Because he might find out?"

"You mean about *my* family's net worth?"

Obvious disappointment crumpled Mika's expression. "You know what I mean."

"He won't." Ami grinned and nudged her friend's shoulder. "Not where I plan to take him."

A closing bell's distinct clang rang through the quiet. Drenched in a cold sweat, Keane jolted off the downy futon, arms thrashing.

The sound came again.

He fumbled with a light switch and spotted the source. He punched a button and jerked the phone to his ear.

"Not funny, Mark," he chided his longtime coach and manager. "You messed with the ringtones again, didn't you?"

Muffled laughter crackled in the receiver. "I remember you, Keane Temple, requesting a comprehensive battle strategy extending beyond the gym walls. That ringtone serves as your reminder of the task and should keep the sense of urgency real for The Golden Lion."

"The what?"

"Japan already has a literal Golden Temple, so that's what they're calling you here. The Golden Lion. Ha. It's all over the papers. The women love it. And here I thought you needed a haircut."

Keane ignored Mark's ramblings. "What time is it? And why are you calling me?"

"Half past ten. We need to get a fresh publicity picture of you now that that adored mane of yours is messier. And pronto."

"Hasn't that already been done?"

"No, it hasn't already been done."

Great. He could *hear* Mark rolling his eyes. "But someone recognized me last night. I figured—"

"Get used to it. You've hit the international big time. Try enjoying it. Does three work?"

"Can't today."

"Why not?"

"Personal plans."

"Personal plans?" A lengthy pause buzzed. "Keane Temple, Mr. I Don't Date While Competing, has plans during the day?"

Keane clenched his teeth at the heckling, refusing to bite. "Yes, I do. And, no, they can't be changed. Work out the photo shoot for some night this week."

The sound of papers shuffling popped through the phone line, followed by a groan. "I'll see what I can do. But behave yourself."

Right. This time he rolled his eyes. "You just said to enjoy myself. So, which is it?"

"Sure. Savor the local cuisine. Don't let it spoil your long game. Especially with all the endorsements on the line. Rumor has it Ono's in town as we speak. And you've come too far to—"

Keane jammed the red End Call button, tossed the phone on the chair, and dropped to do a set of push-ups. He didn't need Mark to repeat the concerns already lashing his brain. Unwavering physical and mental discipline drove his success, converting him into a powerful man. But how often had he made sacrifices over the years? Driven by a bold belief that human limits can be pushed, transforming man into the realm of something greater? He sidelined his last serious relationship, and while he felt extraordinarily blessed, a dull ache radiated through his chest. Could it be longing?

Of all times, why did a woman drop into his life now? Terrible timing to ponder heavy thoughts when he'd just met the girl. And yet, thinking of Ami made him want more. The chemistry warmed his blood, pounded through his body, knocked at the door of his heart. But with two weeks till the biggest bout of his life, he'd keep that door shut.

One day of fun to get her out of his system. Nothing more.

Eyes on the championship prize.

Simple, right?

Chapter 2

Keane slid into a hot shower. He didn't have much time, but he stood long enough to loosen his knotted shoulders. He toweled off, wincing as he patted over tender ribs. Hans had landed a solid roundhouse kick yesterday, and the purple outline of a good bruise had begun to surface.

While he brushed his teeth, he worked through proper attire for the day's outing. Ami hadn't hinted at her plans or the locale, so he'd go for a dressy casual ensemble. Graphite-gray jeans, designer but still rugged. Black V-neck sweater. Suede ankle boots. Midnight jacket. He'd have to thank his personal shopper when he got home.

A glance at his phone. Only a minute to spare. He summoned the elevator and rode it to ground level. Pale morning light hazing over quiet streets replaced last evening's bustle. The salty air smacked of the nearby ocean. A sidewalk-span away, Ami waited at the curb, arms folded across her chest, chin tipped up, eyes closed, and chest rising and falling in steady rhythm. For all he knew, she could have been praying. And he soaked in the sight as the nippy breeze rattled young leaves into a frenzy. A twinge struck him.

He stopped spying and tapped her shoulder. As she startled and spun to face him, he quirked a grin. "Morning."

"Hi." A rose flush rushed her cheeks. "Are you ready?"

She inspected the black Bentley SUV idling at the curb. The private security chauffeur in his woolen newsboy hat and leather driving gloves reclined against the side, awaiting Keane's signal.

"Almost." He widened his grin. "Have you had breakfast or, given the time, brunch?"

She shook her head.

"Me neither. Let's grab a bite over there." He pointed at a European-style coffeehouse. "And eat on the way. Then I'm all yours."

He arched his brows, seeking verification the plan worked for her. When she shot him an encouraging smile, a deliciously unwanted expectation filled him. But why did *unwanted* feel like a lie?

Sunday traffic was light. They checked both ways and crossed the street midblock. With the scent of fresh-baked bread seducing the nose, he caught the door handle, ushered Ami inside, and warmed at the grin she tossed over her shoulder as she stepped ahead of him in line.

Tastefully decorated and somewhat crowded, La Patisserie enveloped them in its quaint environs. Dark wood paneling. Amber-glass pendant chandeliers. A well-stocked community bookcase. Carrara marble-topped café tables along a cleared aisle leading from the door to the counter.

The glass display case featured the most decadent and artfully prepared pastries he'd seen since last year's European Championship in Paris. A hardworking barista tamped fragrant coffee grounds and steamed milk into clouds of froth at a shiny La Marzocco espresso machine. "*Irasshaimase*," the barista called, not breaking to look up from the assembly line of mugs.

At his questioning look, Ami shrugged. "It means 'welcome to the store.'" Her posture conveyed confidence, and her eyes spoke of hunger, devouring the sight of buttery croissants. "What do you want?"

"A cappuccino and one of those almond things you're staring at."

Her nose crinkled up. "You can't eat those, can you?"

"Of course. Why not?"

The space between her brows furrowed. "Are you not on a special diet?"

"I am, but I eat whatever I want on Sundays. Sundays only. It keeps me sane."

Shelf by shelf, she stooped to peruse the pastry options. And as she deliberated, his gaze shifted over her slim curves. An ivory cashmere cable-knit. Dark blue jeans. Expensive handbag. Camel-colored driving moccasins. She appeared as comfortable dressed down as she was stunning in that unforgettable green number she'd been wearing at the train station. She must have thought he wasn't looking, because she peeked back at him out of the corner of her eye. They both flashed guilty grins.

After a stretch of silence, she took the liberty of ordering for them both, glanced across the roomful of patrons, and spun toward him. "They are watching you, Midas."

He pursed his lips at that nickname. "And?"

"Does it not make you nervous?"

He tilted his head to the side. "Not really." After checking the cash-register display, he pulled out his wallet and paid in yen. With the white paper bag of croissants pinned under an elbow, he worked his wallet into a back pocket and confessed, "But you might."

She gathered the steaming to-go cups and led the way out. It felt like an Epcot journey from one country to the next, leaving France for Japan.

Keane knocked on the Bentley's hood and startled the uniformed driver into action. The chauffeur stood and jerked open the rear door, flourishing a hand toward the back seat. One foot in, Ami paused to address the driver. "Matsushima Bay."

The driver circled the SUV, engaged the engine, and raised the privacy partition as the tires began to whine over the asphalt.

With an elbow propped on the door's armrest, Keane leveled his full attention on her. It took no more than the draw of a breath, and everything turned awkward and intense. Keane, then Ami, released a string of uneasy laughs before he tried to ease the moment. "So, what is Matsushh . . .?"

"Matsushima Bay is one of my favorite places."

"It's pretty?"

"Very pretty. Very ancient. *Matsu* means pine, and *shima* means island. You'll see why." Her dark eyes danced as she spoke. There was some familiar spark in them, but he couldn't place it. A tiny bell sounded in his mind, but he brushed it aside. "But it is not far, so eat up."

He draped a napkin across her lap, handed her a warm Danish studded with fresh strawberry slices, and dug his Sunday indulgence out of the bag. One bite of the plate-sized croissant and golden flakes sprinkled down his chest and across his thighs. He released a contented groan. "Incredible. How's yours?"

"Delicious." She set the food down and held the coffee, perhaps heating her palms, and examined him with an equally warm expression.

"What?"

She chuckled and shrugged off his question, redirecting her gaze to track the horizon through the glazed window. "That's Sendai Castle." She pointed into the distance where historic ruins overlooked the city, but some amusement still shone too brightly in her face.

He sipped cappuccino to wash down the bread. "What?" he repeated, arching a brow. "And don't change the subject, or I'll have the chauffeur head back."

She shifted toward him and traced his lips with her thumb. The sensation made them tingle. "You had a small beard of these." She laughed, showing him her thumb, now coated in croissant flakes. "Golden, like your mane."

His lips curled into a half grin. Yeah, just golden. He finished his breakfast and brushed the crumbs into the paper bag. "Ma–stew–she–ma Bay." He tried out the word, sipping his scalding drink. Sure, it wasn't liquid confidence, but its rich smokiness sent comforting waves of warmth throughout his body, giving his spirits a good jolt. And he needed that today. He needed to bring his game and make good on his promise to himself.

"Good." She clapped, bouncing in her seat.

Unconvinced his pronunciation was anywhere near intelligible, he rolled his eyes but found no hint of teasing in her expression. "Thanks." He let his cynicism go. "I don't get to see much when I travel." *And I'm determined to make the most of this day.*

He could be in the company of a woman. Just spend the day with her. See the local sights. Nothing more. Right?

"Then you will enjoy the bay and its family of islands." She waved with her drink toward the window. "It is one of Japan's most scenic places, and the drive is amazing."

And he could see that. The stone-and-glass buildings sprouting from the city's tree-lined avenues yielded to a countryside patchwork. Rich brown earth tilled into irregular rectangular rice-paddy fields. The occasional roadside home. A smooth black ribbon of asphalt climbed toward a string of stair-step mountains. Against the blue-gray sky, the peaks were dark, overlaid by a threadbare cloak of evergreen hooded in white.

"You're right. The mountains look ancient. Constant old giants."

"Mmm." Ami agreed with a nod.

He swiveled in the seat and relaxed, propping an elbow against the headrest and resting his head in hand. He glanced from the vista to his visitor. "So, tell me about you. Do you have any brothers or sisters?"

Just a basic, no-pressure question. But a flash of something, maybe panic, ripped across her face before settling into some semblance of composure. What was up with that?

"Six brothers. No sisters," she said in a tight voice. A rosy glow highlighted her cheeks.

Quite charming. Probably first-date jitters. What else could bring her blushes on so often? "Seriously? Six brothers?" He rubbed a free hand over the day-old stubble along his jawline. Six brothers might explain a lot about the bold beauty. "Must've been rough."

"Very. I was a bit of a tomboy growing up." She chuckled and crossed her legs, bumping her toe into his calf, knotting hands in her lap to still them.

"And where are you in the lineup?"

"Last." Lips tucked together, she looked up from under a fan of lashes.

"Wow. Guess I better be on my best behavior, then." He shot her a playful smile and cocked a brow. "I'm not bad at what I do, not bad at all, but taking on six guys at once might prove a challenge, even for me."

Despite the mild amusement lighting her face, her eyes widened. "I don't know. You *might* be fine. But . . ."

"But what?" he encouraged, seeing something darken her features. Surely, it wasn't real doubt. What was she thinking? What was she hiding? "Is there someone else?" The words rolled out before he contemplated the wisdom in asking. Great. Hardly first-date—only-date—material. Wrong line of thinking for his don't-get-too-involved mentality. But hey, why not?

She shook her head. "No. No one significant, anyway." The fire in her eyes burned low, making them darker, somehow gentler. "And you?"

He sat up straighter, his chest swelling. She might be a keeper, but as much as that satisfied him, something about her unattached status didn't add up. "No."

And he'd been fine with that for ages. It made life easier. Much less complicated.

"And what about siblings?"

"Only child." He sipped his drink. "Tell me about your parents."

"Father develops real estate. Mother died when I was seven. She was in the wrong place at the wrong time."

She rested her forehead against the chilled window and stared out. Not wanting to push the subject, he waited, but when she fell quiet, he said, "I'm very sorry." How many times had he feared his mother's death? Prayed for her protection? She'd been his biggest fan and sole source of love for so long.

Ami nodded, her somber gaze drifting to his. Time to slow down with the questioning. His line of sight traced along the delicate curve of her neck up to her flawless cheek and beyond.

A multilingual sign on the roadside displayed Mount Otakamori in English. From the heights, a glorious view unfurled. A sapphire bay shimmered like a jewel notched into the eons-old mountainside. Sunlight sparkled off rippling waves. Harbor waters speckled with innumerable rock islands. The bleached-bone islets poked out of blue depths like iceberg tips capped by wind-gnarled pines with a life-grip on the stone.

His body perked up. It was the kind of place you could breathe, a still kind of place, set apart from the world's pace. A sanctuary. This had to be it.

Had the bay's serenity charmed her too? Perhaps he'd imagined it, but it seemed that the weight of dark memories drained from her posture, her eyes regaining their twinkle. "I come here sometimes on weekends. There's a fishing harbor, but the shore park is so peaceful. Walking there helps clear my head." She soaked in the distant sight before finding his eyes again. "What do you want to do? Zuiganji is a nearby temple. It's worth a visit, or—"

"Let's just walk. Is that okay with you?"

"Of course." She leaned forward, tapped at the privacy partition, and waited while it hummed open a few inches. "The harbor," she instructed the driver.

The Bentley snaked down the hill and purred to where the pavement ended. Under the bright midday sun, the island-studded harbor dazzled. When he stepped outside, the ocean air slapped his cheeks. The chain of ancient mountains covered in black pines extended from land into the Pacific, forming a horseshoe around the bay and guarding its far reaches. Tidy rows of fishing and pleasure boats bobbed along the pier. The oyster shells blanketing the water's edge stretched to the horizon. Chattering seagulls. Scurrying ghost crabs. Rollicking waves.

Her feet picked a seemingly familiar route down a staircase to the uneven shell-covered shore. He slid alongside her, attempting to will away his blossoming fascination. *Nip it in the bud, man.*

The steady breeze stirred her perfume and pushed its cool fingers through the nooks of his woolen sweater. He picked up a flat oyster and whizzed it like a Frisbee across the water. It skipped twice and sank. "How far do you go?"

"Depends." She tossed her hair to the side, pursed her lips, and flashed a smile as inscrutable as the response.

As a gust blew her hair into an asymmetric fan, he clasped his hands behind him, resisting the temptation to capture one of those long, glossy locks between his fingers. Were they as silky as they appeared?

"How many days will you stay in Japan?"

"Let's see. I landed on Thursday. Fight's on the eleventh, and my flight departs on the thirteenth." He frowned, working the mental calculations. "So, fourteen more days."

"Fourteen days," she repeated, whispering to herself as she crouched to pick up a spiraling seashell, though he couldn't make out what else she said. She stowed the trinket in a pocket and doubled over again, rummaging for a smooth oyster shell. With the flex of her elbow and the flick of her wrist, she gave her own shell-skipping technique a try. It pecked at the water past the wave breakline, hopped thrice, and vanished into the vacuous depths. She didn't gloat, but as they resumed their stroll, he spotted her repressed grin and held back his chuckle. He knew a competitive spirit when he saw one.

Her recognition of him at the train station and her line of questioning . . . She must have done her homework. What man wouldn't be flattered? And working with such a schedule somehow upped the ante, compressing their time together into something bordering on intense, despite his reservations. And the necessity of sticking to his one-date rule.

"You must know you're all over the news for your unrivaled skill. The Golden Lion has become a household name even amongst the ladies here." She gauged his reaction from under a veil of coal-black lashes.

"You heard that?"

She released a breathy, almost dismissive laugh. "Hard not to. It has a strong ring to it, but I still prefer Midas."

He risked a glance at her pretty lips before finding her eyes again. "You know, so do I."

She grinned. "What drove you to study karate?"

He freed a hand and scratched along his jawline. "My mom's doing. Our church had a martial-arts program, and she signed me up as soon as I could walk."

"You fight for her?" Sounding surprised, she swiveled toward him.

"Something like that." He let out a breath, his chest deflating.

Head cocked, she slowed her steps. "What is it?"

"What is what?"

"That sad look."

He almost laughed. A stupid show to hide how on-point she was. He pressed his lips together, stretched his neck from side to side, and focused on where the ocean fed into the mouth of the bay. Only the scatter-crunch of shells underfoot competed with the steady lap of water on the shore.

He stopped. Ami's draw was powerful, and her patient silence compelled him to tread on a topic he rarely discussed. "My earliest boyhood memories aren't of the happy sort. My father was . . . rough. Learning to fight was necessary for survival for me and my mom. A plus B equals C. And I turned out to be pretty good at C. It's that simple. My passion turned into a profession." He checked her face for some hint of shock, maybe judgment.

Instead, her slender fingers found and twined into his. The gesture sent a swell of comforting heat up his arm before radiating throughout his body.

"I see," she managed.

Inching closer felt natural, but his better judgment surfaced to remind him it'd do him no good. One day—that was all. With pensive eyes, he gazed over her shoulder at a gull shaking water from its wings. What must she be thinking?

"So, you learned. But why continue?"

"It clicked with me. I'm a rather physical guy." His eyes narrowed in on her. "And fighting makes me feel fully alive." It sounded silly, even though it was the truth. His eyes locked on hers, and her blush deepened to an appealing shade. After a breathless beat, his tone shifted, intentionally less personal. "But everyone has some fighter in him—or her."

Her expression twisted, and her chin lifted. "How so? *I* have no desire to do what you do."

"Maybe not in the sense of battling in a ring for sport. But we all contend with our own demons." His eyebrows arched. "Give people the right reason, hit the trigger that motivates or maddens them, and they'll come out swinging every time."

"But what about that saying—lovers versus fighters? What will you do when you're too old to fight?" Something sparked in her eyes again. Her lips parted as if she had more to say, but she quieted and pulled her hand away from his as an older couple passed on the beach.

The blush on blush mixed with her intellect and natural allure were becoming a serious temptation. "I hope I can manage both," he muttered, his resolve weakening. His stay-detached tactic of *not* touching her failed when she slipped a silken palm back into his. His pulse thrummed, and like fighting, she had awakened some snoozing part of him. *Just today. Make the most of it, then get back to training. No women from here on out.*

Riiight.

Like a lofty cedar before a quivering blade of sea grass, he faced her, trailed his fingertips up her arms, feathered over her shoulders, and raked his hands through the length of her waist-long hair. He'd wanted to all day, and the movement released that fragrant citrus scent, scrambling his thoughts.

Her focus shifted to his mouth. "I think—"

"Don't think." With an iron grip, he captured her wrist, hauling her hand toward him, wanting to feel it against his chest.

But with stunning swiftness, she planted a foot back, grabbed the seized fist with her free hand, and jerked her arm backward. The move strained his thumb while her front foot snapped a playful kick at him.

In a tense moment of appraisal, he glowered at her, almost as if he didn't see her. Fighting was as natural as breathing for him. Muscle memory activated in response to her move, transmitting the signal to counterattack. But a whimper and the flash of dark hair swaying slammed the brakes on his momentum, reminding him she was no enemy. Just. In. Time.

"Keane. Say something." She rested her palms against his chest.

Who would have guessed she'd know, let alone use, an escape technique? Darting through the air like a hornet, she spoke his physical language. The honed instincts of a prizefighter teetered on the narrow edge of a blade, and several long beats passed before the cadence of his heartbeat slowed.

"Very risky." He inhaled, working to rein in the heat she'd unleashed.

Under his scrutiny, she gulped hard, broke free from his unyielding stare, and glanced out over the bay. Her expression glowed with rebellious triumph. "Yes."

"What were you thinking? I'm more than twice your size."

She threw him a look. "House of brothers."

"That's all the explanation I get?" He plowed a hand through his mess of hair. He'd suspected it, but Ami proved her recklessness. And why was it so appealing?

She shrugged with a vague grin and laced her fingers through his. A buzz of electricity cycled between them, but he fell speechless as day slipped into a sunset nothing short of divine. Copper-penny sun. Molten-mirror bay reflecting fiery heavens.

"This view soothes my soul," Ami said at last.

A moment passed. The harbor pier was no longer visible. The low-lying string of stores—an artsy ceramic shop, a teahouse, a traditional restaurant—was now a distant sight. After the late, butter-laden breakfast, they'd long since missed the lunch hour as they drifted up and down the shore, landing by a stand of pines backed by an impassable sheer cliff.

"Agreed. A view to soothe the soul." But his gaze fixed on her.

Perhaps Ami's reasons for pursuit extended beyond mere intrigue. So what? Keane Temple was a potent force. Like a black hole, he was drawing her in, closer and closer. Most men were predictable. And she knew more than one thing about fighters. But he was unexpected. Attentive. Patient. A fleeting opportunity for the taking.

With a glance, she admired him, head to toe. One second, her wild imagination was rushing in a treacherous direction. The next, she was flying through the air. Her toe had snagged a chunk of driftwood. As the rough beach raced toward her face, a strong arm darted under her to break the fall. Keane toppled beside her. But she wasn't complaining.

Chapter 3

"Ugh." Keane groaned, shifting on the jagged shells now jutting into his already tender ribs. "You okay?"

Even at dusk, Ami's irises bored into him before her gaze drifted over the cross tattooed on the underside of his right wrist. After a moment of disorientation, she nodded and sat up.

The neediness in that look surprised Keane and teased the hollow ache in his heart. Measured breaths came and went, even as his heart stammered in his chest. He had allowed himself one day. But to do what? He hadn't been specific in his mental prep work. The too-good-to-be-real day now felt too real to ignore.

He leaned forward until her breath tickled his neck and her exotic scent floated over him. The mere dip of his chin, and his lips would seal hers. He hooked an arm around her waist while the fingertips of the other feathered cool strokes up a cheekbone. Just a quick kiss. Nothing more. He primed himself for that initial rush of electricity. His lips parted, preparing to tease hers, when the horn of a passing ship blared over the water and echoed against the mountainsides.

They jerked toward the sound and squinted at a crew of waving fishermen. A kiss incomplete, ruined by an audience of men in waders.

He huffed a throaty chuckle, stroked the scruff along his chin with a hiss, and pushed to his feet. Rosiness lingered in her cheeks. A gentle fire smoldered in her eyes. Despite his initial annoyance, maybe the bellowing horn was a blessing. Anything more was a risky step toward distraction, and distraction was dangerous before the upcoming bout.

He stretched in hopes of flinging off the excess energy. "I'm starving."

She matched his grin. "Me too." She clasped the hand extended to her, not releasing it even after standing by his side. Then she pointed out a freestanding building down the beach overlooking the bay. "There is a good restaurant over there."

The evening breeze was heavy with the scent of sea salt and wet shells and purred with unfulfilled possibility. A steady lap of water over shore ticked away time. Hand in hand, they backtracked along the deserted dusky beach. The fifteen-minute amble delivered them to the upscale restaurant with an ocean-blue tile roof, over-sized picture windows facing the water, and exterior walls matching the oyster-strewn beach. Inside, the foyer bled into a smoky bar area. Tugging him along, she suggested one of the private dining rooms common in Japan.

"Sounds perfect," he agreed.

Chin tucked and eyes averted, the hostess in a kimono-style dress embroidered with colorful fish shuffled halfway down a hall of rice-paper walls. She paused to nudge open a sliding *shoji* door. Both elegant and comfortable, the intimate dining area featured a low table decorated with an artful flower arrangement of plum blossoms. Mounds of crimson silk cushions. A *tatami* mat floor. Water trickled down a wall of rough-hewn stone into a basin of flashing koi while beyond the door a massive window displayed the bay glittering under the last shreds of sun.

"Your server will arrive soon." The young hostess tried her English on Keane before backing out of the space and nudging the door shut.

Ami gave off a breathy laugh as she knelt on the mat and sat on her heels.

"What?"

"You made the girl blush."

"She's not the only one." Ami's cheeks bloomed a charming shade of pink under the spotlight of attention. His head wagged in the direction of the foot-numbing position of her legs. "So, am I supposed to sit like that?"

"No, Midas." She let out a teasing giggle. "Royalty can sit cross-legged on their golden–"

"Whoa now. No need to get sassy." He pretzeled long legs under himself. "You're not going to stop with the Midas bit, are you?" When she shook her head, he chuckled. "Fair enough."

He shifted sideways onto a plush pillow and reached to tuck an unruly tress of hair behind her ear. The waitress appeared at the sliding door carrying menus, a steaming pot of green tea, and hot towels to clean and thaw their cold fingers. "Oysters are out of season. Our specialty on today," she described in unfamiliar English, "it is grill beef tongue. We also offer finest Wagyu beef."

Keane wrinkled his nose, snapped the menu shut, and handed it back. "Wagyu for me."

The recognizable guitar riff from Michael Jackson's "Beat It" screamed from Ami's Vuitton purse. She stood, dug through the purse, and unearthed a phone. In rhythm to the blaring background music, she ordered and turned to Keane. "Sorry." She raised the phone to her ear. "One of my brothers. I must take it."

Trying not to be nosy, he leaned against the pillow mountain and retied a lopsided shoelace as she carried on in Japanese. After several groans, the phone conversation evolved into an exchange of quiet hostility. Clipped whispers. Angry eyes. Tense shoulders. Standing in the room's back corner, she pounded the End Call button.

"What was that about?" he asked.

She spun around and dropped onto the *tatami* mat. "My oldest brother arrived in Sendai. He was . . . displeased . . . when I was not waiting at home."

"O–kay. Were you supposed to meet him?"

A pause as she seemed to weigh her words. "No. My brothers, like my father, are traditional. Domineering. He assumed I would be there. Now, he's angry." She shrugged out a single sharp laugh and peered out the window.

Was she hiding her face? Searching the seas for composure? His thoughts tumbled as long beats passed. Then he exhaled in a questioning hiss. "Is that why you brought me all the way out here? To keep me away from the city, so your brother wouldn't see me?"

Ami wheeled around. "Yes and no." Her gaze never drifted from his until he knew she offered the truth. "It's more complicated than that. I wanted you to myself today. Collectively speaking, my brothers keep a constant thumb on me. They lead their own lives but still try to manage mine. This was my choice. For once, I wanted a chance to carve out what is *me* in life, and having distance helps. Without their interference. Without unwanted opinions."

A whistle almost escaped as he glimpsed her wisdom, well beyond her age. "Would they be upset about you being here with me?"

The sliding door rolled open and the waitress entered, scuffling over the mat on her knees. She retrieved sectioned lacquer trays of food from a cart, set them on the low table, and poured more tea, then backed away.

Ami met his stare with an air of challenge. "Does it matter? I want to be here."

He tilted his head from side to side. "I enjoy your company. Probably too much." He donned a naughty schoolboy expression. "But tread lightly where family is concerned."

"What do you mean?"

"Family dynamics are always complicated. Using someone to make a statement—I would never want to be a dividing line." He coiled a lock of hair behind her ear. "Especially when they mean well. I could've used a few big brothers to keep me in line when I was younger."

"You are much like my oldest brother." She gave a humorless laugh and slanted a sly look his way.

"Does that mean we'd get along well?"

Avoiding eye contact, she dropped her chin and tinkered with a string at the cuff of her sweater a tad too long. "You have much in common, but you would not get along." Serious eyes flicked to his. "Shall we eat?"

"Absolutely." A tad deflated, he stroked his chin. Some air of inevitability lurked in the conversation, and though he couldn't pinpoint it, it bothered him.

"Wait. Before we eat, the Japanese put our hands together like so." She captured his plate-sized palms between hers. "And say *itadakimasu*."

He shook his head. "Yeah, I'm not going to butcher that one." He copied her gesture, taking her hands in his. "But before I eat, I say grace." He dipped his head, offered a simple prayer, and pressed grinning lips to the silky backside of her hand. "This could get interesting." He plunged the *hashi* into a ceramic bowl of rice. A clump of sticky white rice hurled through the air. Great. "I'm terrible with chopsticks."

"Well done." She gave a light chuckle, repositioned his fingers, and demonstrated the proper technique. "Try holding them like this."

The touch buzzed him with an electrical jolt.

"Why did you decide to train in Sendai? It's an odd choice. Why not Tokyo?"

"I wanted to distance myself from Tokyo's chaos. Fame can be a curse, and I figured there'd be less chance of being distracted and recognized. Of course, that didn't pan out." He hoisted a morsel of delectable steak to his lips.

"No. Massive, blond-headed men stand out anywhere in Japan. But you said you like Sendai's trees too, right?"

"There's that. And the country's other views. The bay for starters. And . . ."

For a heady moment, he stopped eating to appreciate Ami's fine features.

"And?" she prodded, her expression softening.

He winked. "And the dojo's great."

"Yes, one of the best."

The comment unsettled him. "Do all Japanese women know so much about dojos?"

She took a long sip of the amber-hued tea, peeking over the rim. "Maybe. But remember—six brothers." Her gaze flew to the window before finding his face again. "Do you like the attention?"

"The attention?" What a quick topic change. His career was his passion and necessitated he respond to instinct. Reading people was a key to his success. And something had gone askew, tucked behind a poker face. Why was she diverting? What was she hiding?

He inhaled. "No, not the attention. I try to avoid . . ." He hesitated, uncertain where he was headed, but if he shared something, perhaps she would too.

"What?"

Supported by an elbow, he shifted on the pillows and traced

tiny shapes on her palm with his free hand. "Getting swept up in the hype. I love the sport. See—"

She stilled his wandering hand by weaving her fingers around his.

"When I'm in the cage, the spotlights are blinding. But beyond the cage, it's pure darkness and roaring noise. The starting bell clangs and triggers what I think of as machine mode. It's all physicality and instinct. Driven on by the crowd's cheering, I get lost in the moment. Life in the cage is distilled into . . . inescapable intensity. Everyone but my opponent vanishes. Crushing him is the only exit.

"Reading his eyes, the dance of his feet, the rhythm of his movement to find hiccups in body language. Striking at his mistakes. The adrenaline rush. The smell of blood and sweat, the pain, means I'm still alive. It's real." Water trickled down the rock wall like sweat down his body in a fight. "It's present. Kind of like being with you. And it's difficult to deny the present."

He flashed his most charming of grins. Had he inadvertently given himself advice?

"You really *don't* like the attention, do you?" Her glossy hair slipped to one side as she angled her head.

He shrugged away her surprise. "People talk about the fat prize purses. And the publicists are always crafting some new spin to sell out. Sure, money serves a purpose. And don't get me wrong, I love what I do, but there are nonmonetary costs to winning. The loss of privacy, lingering aches and pains, the disciplined diet . . ."

His eyebrows arched suggestively. Fans believed fighters, the alphas they are, were the wildest of the wild. Many were, and he wasn't proud of, even felt deep regret over, his past flings. No heart or mind attached. Never soothed the God-given ache in his soul. Left him searching for something more to build upon—one lady who didn't want counterfeit fame and saw past the sports icon to him, just a simple man. A woman with values that matched his own.

After fumbling with his chopsticks, he captured another sliver of tender steak and shot her a proud grin.

Fighters weren't supposed to believe in one true love. It was hardly gym-talk. And the notion of soulmates clashed with memories of his mother being bloodied and bruised by the hands that were supposed to care for her. His gut wrenched. He swore he'd never be that kind of man. But instead of letting a spark catch fire over the years, carving out a life devoid of real intimacy had been far easier to bury the aching hope for a woman he could treasure, pamper, and protect.

A wave of selfishness surged through him. He wanted to explore those things, see where they might go with Ami, and understand why she dodged discussing her family. There must be more to her boldness, something steaming beneath the beautiful facade. But could he manage a relationship and still achieve what he'd come to Japan to do?

He set his *hashi* on the chopstick rest and reached out, dragging his thumb across her collarbone. His fingers slid beneath her thick curtain of hair and raked up the back of her neck. She shuddered, and her face regained its glow. The effect of his touch on her satisfied him. "Would you like to watch me fight?"

Ami tensed, dropped her gaze, and forced a bite of tempura-battered eggplant past her lips. A cautious quiet carried on several awkward beats.

"What's wrong?" he pressed. "Why are you stalling?"

She shrugged, gulping down the bitter guilt rising in her throat. Why did he have to be so observant? And why should she feel guilty? It didn't change the way he made her pulse skyrocket. She hadn't expected the attraction to be so . . . uncontainable. Still, this intrigue was anchored in something deeper than mere heat.

"You're right. I . . ."

He squeezed her hand. "You can tell me."

She'd wanted to close the gap between them all day and nudge their intimacy forward. The brush of their lips on the beach didn't count as a full-fledged kiss. Keane took an interest in her past and future. His supreme confidence and iron-wrought physique made her feel secure. His gallant ways enveloped her in a storm. Could it be the makings of a real relationship?

As good a chance as the sun rising in the west. The second he found out who she was, *if* he found out, his interest would evaporate. Mika's reprimand echoed in her head, grating at her conscience. She held his gaze with lips parted to speak the truth. "I've enjoyed today, but I need to tell you more about my family."

"I'm all ears."

At his encouraging nod, she swallowed hard, knitting her restless fingers together. "My oldest brother—"

Keane toyed with a tress of her hair. His full attention leveled on her, even though the waitress had reappeared. Good thing he disregarded the intrusion. He'd been hesitant to touch her, but now that he'd started, she did not want it to end. And she needed to tell him.

"You were saying . . .?"

She sucked in a deep, shaky breath and blew it out in an audible rush. "On—"

"Ami?" A bass voice came from the hallway.

Her attention snapped toward the door, and adrenaline-laced panic flooded her, leaving her feeling as if her spirit had separated from her body.

When the waitress shifted to the side of the room, an older Japanese couple lingered in the hallway, displaying the conservative and classy attire of a pair married for a life in politics. A Rolex watch glittered under his cuff. A choker of marble-sized pearls gleamed at her throat.

Ami bowed toward them, even as they eyed Keane. Their stunned expressions unnerving her, she struggled to show them the customary politeness.

Heat tingled up her neck. Ugly ruby splotches must be blotching her face. She gestured to Keane, spoke in Japanese to her father's old friends, and attempted to keep her composure.

As Mr. Yamada inquired about her father, Ami winced at the precise moment Keane's body stiffened. He had recognized the name Ono. How foolish to have operated with a sense of invincibility and hope. Did anyone who toyed with fire plan to get burned? Not smart. Not smart at all.

"*Sayonara.*" At last, Mr. and Mrs. Yamada bowed.

Ami repeated the farewell, her posture sagging as the couple left. But the damage was done. A pregnant silence stretched as the waitress finished her work, left the bill, and exited the private room.

"Friends of yours?"

She cleared her throat, feeling shaky. "Friends of my father."

"I want to know what they said about Ono."

Unshed tears blurred her eyes as they locked on his. She pressed her fingers to her forehead and averted her gaze. "I was beginning to tell you before Mr. and Mrs. Yamada arrived." But that was beside the point now, wasn't it? "Ono. Niko Ono is my brother."

His mouth ripped open. He dragged a hand over it and scowled. "Your brother is Niko Ono?"

She nodded. Niko Ono, Japan's national karate champ five years running and the man he was contracted to fight in mere days. "My oldest brother."

He gritted his teeth. His eyes narrowed. "You have to be joking."

She shook her head, managing to keep her chin up and her gaze on his.

"*Fantastic.*" He slashed a hand through the air, then jabbed at her as if adding it all up. "Your familiarity with the sport, quick karate skills, even the similarity I couldn't place about your eyes."

He exhaled in a steam-releasing burst. "This is bad."

He straightened and began pacing, looking anywhere but at her. No doubt he needed a release. If she'd been a man, he might've punched her. Strange how she knew he wouldn't hurt her, even angry as he was.

She didn't budge. "Please, I did not want it to matter that he is my brother."

He stopped, the full weight of his green eyes assessing her. "Maybe you mean it. Maybe not. You look remorseful." He pivoted and resumed pacing. "But looks are dangerous. Deceiving."

He grunted. "A father in construction. Ha, humble intro for one of Japan's premier commercial construction empires." He stretched his neck from side to side, muttering something about blushes and chemistry.

She leaned closer, catching the end. "You didn't imagine those, and they couldn't have been fabricated."

She froze, bracing herself. She didn't want to crumble, but she felt broken, as if even the gentlest of breezes would scatter her unrealized hopes for miles. Crazy how hope was such a powerful feeling. It was too soon to feel such, but she did. She couldn't fathom what he was thinking. What could she say? Her stomach floated to the heavens the moment she'd spotted him. And the first time he'd touched her, something in the world shifted. She wanted to be mad at the Yamadas, but this was *her* doing. She just hadn't planned on getting caught. Her gut plummeted from those heavenly heights.

"Does he know you're with me?"

"No."

"Why did you do this to me?"

A boulder jammed in her windpipe. "Never have I been so

drawn to someone." The barefaced admission cost her. More heat flooded her face. "I had to try."

"What's that supposed to mean? Never mind. Don't bother." Keane dug his phone out of a pocket, punched a series of buttons, and tossed a wad of yen notes on the table—enough to cover the check and make the waitress's night. "We need to leave. Now."

He hooked a hand around her elbow. Even upset, he ensured his grip was gentle. She made no attempt to pry away as he barreled through the short hall and out the front entrance.

An indigo sky had replaced the sunset, and nightfall drained the air of its warmth. His driver waited by the back door. So she cut across the sidewalk and slipped in and across the seat, making room for Keane. The door sealed with a click. The driver hurried around the SUV, pausing at the wheel for further instructions.

"Please tell him your address."

At Keane's instruction, she mumbled the details and stared out the window in a stupor, playing connect-the-stars. Even the crescent moon looked sad.

The tick of Keane's wristwatch measured out the forty-seven-minute drive back to Sendai, the monotony broken only by his irritated exhalations. She wrapped her arms around herself. The backseat confinement punitive. The silent treatment torture. But his masculine scent—some sultry blend of bergamot, sandalwood, and something sweeter—paired with the residual angry electricity still circulating sent her in a hopeless free fall straight to hell.

As much as she wanted to justify herself, she'd gotten what she deserved.

Chapter 4

When the SUV door cracked open, Keane jerked his head up. Oh. They'd stopped on a residential street by a two-story stone condominium of European inspiration. Steep slate roof. Tall arched windows peaked above the cornice and pushed into the eaves. Classy place. Pricey. Probably one of Ono Enterprises' countless properties.

Curtains swayed in a second-floor window. Someone had been waiting and now retreated. Ami hesitated on the edge of her seat. Brows arched, he prodded her with a no-nonsense expression, and she exhaled long and low.

"Keane Temple, you surpass the hype." She kept her chin tucked, displaying none of her usual poise. "Maybe one day a lucky girl will wow you as much as you have wowed me. I wish I could undo the strings attached to me. I *have* tried, but I am an Ono, like it or not."

She straightened and walked across the shadow-strewn sidewalk to the building.

The charge of attraction dissipated. Cold air hit him as the door shut. The driver hustled around the Bentley. The high-performance

V-8 engine roared. Three minutes, tops. Just blocks, and the SUV stopped.

He headed toward his suite, her diplomatic words unsettling him—words far too cool for the heat crackling between them.

He jammed a key into the tumbler, knocked the door back, chugged a bottle of water in the kitchenette, and dropped a trail of clothes to the bedroom. With the comforter heavy and silky-smooth on his bare skin, darkness enveloped him. He flung himself sideways and put a choke hold on the pillow at the memory of that momentary brush of lips. Good thing it had gone no further. He was in Japan to win the world title bout, not wrestle with that memory.

Keane closed his eyes, sent up his nightly prayer, and then surrendered to a hard, dreamless slumber until light soaked through the curtains. He stirred awake and pushed to a sit. Monday. Eleven days until Fight Day. Keyed up—anxious to get to the dojo and hit something. That'd brighten his day.

Travel cup in hand, he took the lobby stairs two at a time. The Bentley was idling at the curb when he hit the sidewalk. The driver hopped into action, efficient and observant but not talkative. Perfect.

Keane settled into the leather seat, a flickering blur of green and gray passing the window. Fifteen minutes through the heart of downtown to the western fringe, he drained the coffee cup and was wide awake.

His fists clenched, ready for action at the sight of the nondescript metal dojo. Soaring ceilings. Concrete floors. Four garage-style doors opening to a rear loading dock. Security guards posted to each side of the dock to keep the press away. Emptied of its machinery, the industrial space was as solid, steely, and rugged as its current occupants.

Rolled up, the garage doors allowed a steady breeze to cut across four sparring areas—two octagonal cages and two traditional matted rings. All but one of the cages were in use. Piped-in music pulsed at twice the pace of the human heart. The wordless trance track made the fighters' feet dance around the rings. This was home, and he breathed it in, feeling more like himself at the first whiff of sweat, rust, and menthol-infused Icy Hot.

This was what he was in Japan to do.

"—ey. How's it going?" A voice, thick with a German accent, boomed from the right.

Keane glared at a platinum-blond titan known as the Swiss Striker. "Fantastic. And thanks for the fake directions, Hans. Your little prank—"

"You like that?" Hands on his hips, Hans smirked.

"Actually, yeah." Keane winked. "I landed a date at the designer shopping stop."

Hans's nostrils flared. He hated having his tricks foiled. Keane's longtime friend met his fist bump. "*Ja.* Well, that's nice. Always the overcomer, you are. But how did you pick up a girl that fast? Is she ugly?" Hans cocked his head, eyeing the approaching Brazilian, Paulo Da Costa.

"What can I say? *She* picked *me* up. Escorted me all the way to my place."

"*Ja*, the Japanese do that. Very hospitable." Not impressed, Hans crossed his arms and leaned against the wall.

"Yeah, yeah. I guess he took her home all right." Paulo's eyebrows shot up as he elbowed Hans.

Ignoring the crude bait, Keane dropped to the mat and worked through his warm-up stretches.

"Don't let her see you stretching like that." Paulo pointed as Keane's hips shifted through deep splits. "Gumby. You know Gumby? That's what they should call you."

Hans gave a hearty laugh. "You're scared Keane will steal your prospects, but you do not understand how this man ticks. You, Paulo, are one hundred percent trouble, but I am a family man." His hands thumped his chest before gripping Keane's shoulder. "And I know one when I see one, even if Keane does not yet. What's her name?"

Who needed to disclose what had become a dirty little secret? "It was just a date. There won't be another." Why did he even share that? It sounded defensive. "But her name's Ami."

He flattened his spine over his outstretched legs, resting his forehead on his kneecaps.

"Ami. Does she have a last name?" Paulo prodded.

"She does." He'd never pull off a lie. Heat flashed through him, igniting the fuse.

"Are you going to tell us?" Hans pressed this time. "I am happy to see my friend dating after a long dry spell."

Keane released the stretch, straightened his back, and glared at Hans.

Cocking a hip, Hans crossed his arms over his chest. "What is it?"

"Ono." *Whew*. Bomb released. Confession did feel good.

"What's an Ono?" Paulo's brows pinched together.

Keane shook his head and stood. "Ami's last name is Ono."

Hans's jaw dropped. Uncomfortable seconds passed. Then he flipped a sweat-drenched towel over his shoulder. "The stress has gotten to you, hasn't it? Are you insane?"

Keane only shrugged. "It was one date. And I didn't know."

"I've seen this Ami of yours." Paulo whistled. "On the cover of one of those fashion magazines. I remember well her short robe." Whistling, he gestured to the mid-thigh.

Keane gritted his teeth. Was that jealousy burning at the back of his throat? He swallowed hard. "Care to elaborate?"

"Was this mini-kimono of white feathers like a bird or an angel with *very* long legs. Well done." He waved. "Maybe Temple seeks a death wish, but he's not insane. He has excellent taste."

Hans's critical eye bored into Keane. "This is not like you."

"You're right about that." He scraped a hand through his messy hair. "Like I said, I didn't know who she was until the end of the evening."

"See, I told you." Hans clapped Paulo on the back. "That is the look of a man rethinking his youthful ways."

Paulo poked a finger against his chest. "She rattled your cage that quickly?"

"Nah." Keane chuckled, knocking Paulo's hand away. Oh, man. Did his voice sound as flimsy to the others as it did to him? He'd have to work on that. "I'm here to fight. Nothing more. I *will* finish what I came here to do."

With his stretching sequence complete, he rubbed the cross on his wrist, his ever-present reminder, and climbed into the cage to begin sparring.

"'S good thing you're a praying man." Paulo scrubbed his hands together.

"Yes, it is." Hans followed Keane and clambered into an elevated octagonal ring. "Better pray Niko Ono never finds out."

"Finds out what?" Mark, emerging from the front office where the coaches' Monday morning meeting had wrapped up, must've caught Hans's teaser.

Hans jammed a silicone mouth guard into place and shrugged, his eyebrows jumping suggestively.

"Think you're a wise guy, Hans? Temple's relentless. Brings the ferocity of one of the all-time greats. I'll be here when he drops you." Mark's cackle cut across the ring.

Hans mumbled something unintelligible around the wad of plastic sheathing his teeth and began taunting Keane from his corner with a dance of alternating jabs and kicks.

Keane assessed Hans with laser-sharp focus. There was the standard glove-touch to show sportsmanship. The referee yanked a cotton cord, and the official starting bell gave a loud ding.

He prowled toward Hans like a fearless lion. Slow, methodical movements. Gaze locked in astute appraisal of his opponent's body language. Could people have an extra sense? Could he? If he had a superpower, scenting strategy in the air—pinpointing how a foe would attack and counter—was it. No doubt it set him apart.

Hans's stride shortened. Keane took note of the subtle change, tracking his every movement. When a smug look surfaced on Hans's face, Keane's jaw clenched tight, and his battle spirit roared to life. He charged and went to work.

Hans shuffled close enough to receive a swift double punch followed by a low kick.

Gloves up, Keane continued his stalk around the ring, falling within earshot of Paulo's and Mark's sideline anecdotes.

"'S going to be a long day." Paulo moaned.

"For you. Long and bloody." Mark gave an amused laugh.

Hans's fist whizzed past Keane's right cheek. Keane's core tightened as his shoulders angled away from the blow. Even in his fighter's trance, his ear tuned in to his coach's commands.

"I love it, Temple. Maintain the intensity," Mark said.

"You are a sick man," Paulo said. "One or two scars is okay with the ladies, but more . . . and Paulo may not get so lucky anymore."

The comment whistled by his ears. Luck had nothing to do with his success. He stepped toward Hans with a feisty jab, but the boxer shifted and managed to land a rapid series of punches to his rib cage.

"Bring it," Keane taunted, wanting Hans to go hard. Hard work stoked his success, and cross-training through disciplines elevated everyone's game.

Keane eased out of reach. Hans's feet shuffled side to side. Each fighter reevaluated his next move. With the slight turn of his body, Keane seized his moment of opportunity, pounced with lightning speed, and corralled Hans against the cage. Managing to catch

Hans's head in a Muay Thai clinch, Keane kneed him repeatedly in the gut until Hans tapped out. At the submission signal, the bell rang to end the practice bout.

Mark pulled a pad from his pocket and scribbled a page full of notes. "Man, you are my dream made in heaven. Can you taste the win now?"

"Absolutely." Keane flung his arms across his chest and then wide as he moved around, cooling down.

A woman appeared from one of the side therapy rooms, carrying towels and water bottles.

Ignoring her flirting, he kept his focus on business, pulled off his gloves, and eased down the ring's short flight of stairs. With a terry cloth draped over his shoulders to sop up sweat and stave off a post-fight chill, he headed to the weight room.

The blended scent of Dry Erase markers and Clorox lingered in the iron dungeon. He skimmed through the day's strength-training exercises. The bout with Hans had gone well. Better than expected. The Ami situation *hadn't* rattled his cage. His game was still intact. Better than solid, in fact. What a relief.

Now, he had thirty minutes of private time to pound through the barbells, followed by an in-gym lunch break and a deep-tissue massage before his late-afternoon jujitsu session with the Brazilian.

A barbell gripped in each fist, Keane faced the far mirrored wall and started a set of curls, counting off repetitions until his muscles spasmed. Wrapping up the first round, he activated his watch timer and settled on one of the flat padded benches, elbows to knees and head bowed while his breathing slowed.

The door creaked open, but he didn't budge.

"You're mighty riled up for a Monday," came Mark's gravelly voice.

When the one-minute alarm beeped, Keane stood, nodded his

acknowledgment, and moved to a machine meant to strengthen the back.

"Care to share why?"

Arms overhead in a wide *Y*, he began pulling a weighted bar on a cable down behind his head. Arms high, then down to his shoulders to fortify the lats, he inhaled and exhaled in controlled hisses, Mark's gaze boring into him. For a heavyweight, Keane was leaner and more ripped than he'd ever been and had the stamina to rival most pro marathoners. But what were devotion and discipline without desire?

Once the exercise had stopped, his manager's eyes were shining like a prideful father's.

"Had a run-in with Ono's baby sister," Keane said. No reason to elaborate.

"That's . . . strange. Coincidental, I guess. But people do cross paths. Anything else I need to know?"

"Nope." He moved to another muscle-building machine.

"Okay then. I'm not sure what lit you up this morning, but you were on fire."

"How's Hans?"

"Banged up. No doubt you want the win. Stick with the program, but next time, try not to crack any more of the guy's ribs. I thought you were going for a knockout."

"Anything else?"

"Good grief." Mark slumped. "Look who's Chatty Cathy. That attitude—take it out on the weights."

Keane finished the workout and headed to an adjoining therapy room. The magic-handed masseuse spoke little English. While she kneaded a tender knot in his upper back, his mind went to work. He tried to feel some sense of satisfaction. Mark had given him an unexpected compliment, but deep down, he knew what—or rather who—stoked his firepower. Sleek and steely, Ami was a pistol. Bold.

Competitive. Perhaps even fiery when you hit the right trigger. Images ricocheted around his skull, but that was the wrong direction for his thoughts to flow. He cursed his weakness and, beneath the cotton sheet, flipped on the therapy table.

"The feet, please," he instructed the masseuse while pointing at his toes.

She placed a warm towel on his face and rubbed his feet until his taut muscles melted into pliable mounds and his mind blanked.

"You roll in five." Hans dropped onto a neighboring table with a hard thud. "Take it easy on Paulo. He's young and values his life, especially his manhood."

Still dazed, Keane sat up and pulled his T-shirt back on. He could smell himself. Sweat mingling with a hint of peppermint from the massage oil. "But it's *his* specialty."

"Your jujitsu has improved and . . ." Hans winced as he yanked his shirt over his head. Knee-shaped red welts bloomed over his torso.

"Sorry." Keane inspected his handiwork. "And what?"

"And—I haven't seen you fight with so much passion in years. Don't write the girl off so quickly." The corners of his eyes crinkled with meaning. "But win the big fight for our House."

Ami awakened to a riot of birdsong. She lay in bed, replaying her nightmare as light pushed through velvet darkness. Would she ever experience such a powerful connection again? Her stomach knotted, her body registering the painful loss all over. Bittersweet memory or not, she was still an Ono, and her swirling feelings amounted to crushed hope.

She had taken a risk . . . and lost.

Something must've startled the birds because their lively

chatter ended. She sat up in bed. Hmm, six o'clock. After months of collecting and analyzing data, her graduate project team was finishing a research paper due Friday. She'd better get moving.

She hopped in the shower, streams of liquid heat cocooning her. When she returned home, Mika had been waiting with Niko. They'd had that tense phone conversation during dinner, but why'd he think he could drop in and out of her life? He never called unless he needed something in return.

To build buzz about his upcoming fight, she'd done a photo shoot for *Silk*, speaking adoringly about her big brother to smooth out their friction. The article portrayed him as a preeminent power in the sports sphere and one of Japan's sexiest bachelors. Despite her being the cover model, *Silk* portrayed her as little more than a lovely swan, the female figurehead of a high-profile family. No mention of her studies and academic research. Or her year volunteering in Chile while the Ono men expanded their empire and banked more yen.

As she raked shampoo through her hair, the mandarin blossom scent joggled her. Could her brother still be in the apartment? Too shaken after the fallout with Keane, she hadn't given much thought to her roommate sitting snugly by her brother. They looked *too* comfortable. And what about that takeout for two on the table? Ami had refused to talk to him, but Niko was never the type to be dismissed.

She rushed through her daily routine. As she cracked her bedroom door, two voices came from the kitchen. Great. Niko had spent the night.

She took a deep breath and padded down the hall.

"Are you okay?" He sat at the Western-style breakfast table.

Mika sipped coffee without meeting her gaze.

Ami stilled. "Excuse me?"

He craned his neck toward the television on pause.

Wait. She was on the screen, climbing into the sleek Bentley. The video material must've been shot after Keane discovered her identity. "But how—" She motioned toward the television. She'd told Mika she was leaving town but not where she intended to go.

"Are you okay?" Niko repeated. "You looked upset. Did he hurt you?"

Niko was on his best behavior—totally out of character where she was concerned. Upset? Where should she begin? With Keane's conduct or with her brother's sleeping arrangements? Had he seduced Mika to get her to snitch? Ami's stomach gave an unsettling roll. "No, he was nothing but a gentleman. But what is this between you two?" With both index fingers, she pointed between Niko and Mika, crisscrossing her hands back and forth. "And how long has it been going on?"

Mika flushed, but Niko ignored her inquiry. "The video doesn't look romantic, but people speculate."

"Let them. He just got here. Why would people automatically speculate 'something'"—Ami's already upraised fingers made air quotes—"is going on? I showed him the bay. That's all."

"Nothing more?" Mika spoke as a longtime friend, not the latest toy to fall prey to Niko's seductive powers.

"Nothing more." Ami swallowed the disappointment down hard.

Niko's intensity chilled her. "You're supposed to be the brilliant scientist. What were you thinking going out with a man like that? You know better."

He was being too respectful. Put on edge, she ground her teeth and fisted her hands at her sides.

"It could have been disastrous for me and especially for Ichiro. It is good that it is nothing more."

She moved her hands behind her back, clenched and unclenched her fingers. "You had me followed, didn't you? *You* had us filmed." She snatched up the remote, pushed the play button, and watched the miserable end to last evening. "Why?"

"Not followed. I stopped by. Mika said you'd gone out of town. It didn't take much creativity to guess where you'd go. So, I called in a favor with a friend. Incidents are best managed from the get-go. Feed the press, and they can't devour you." He leaned back and crossed his arms over his broad chest. Smugness softened his square jaw where a deep bruise had begun to bloom purple. "My friend made it in time to catch the end of your sad little excursion."

Angry heat rushed to her face. She surged forward and braced her hands on the table as she leaned into his space. "You sold me out? Fed the press using me as bait? Seriously, did I get that right?"

"It wasn't like that at all." He batted her words away, then grabbed her sleeve and toyed with a pearl button. "You know you're a vital part of the team."

Her throat felt tight. He viewed her as his personal chess piece. She drew in a long breath, willing her blood pressure down, considering how to take the upper hand in Niko's game. Given Keane "The Golden Lion" Temple was contracted to fight Niko "The Flying Dragon" Ono . . . Well, pitting a dragon against a lion was a surefire thriller from any marketing angle. "Okay, then, how do *we* spin this?"

"Ah, there's my baby sister talking. Always a good team player." His arms uncrossed, he planted his forearms flat on the table. "Promise me, one more time, there's nothing real between you, okay?"

With the black tunnels of his irises fixed on her, she suppressed a twinge of sadness. She met his scrutinizing gaze and prayed her thrumming pulse wouldn't betray her. "Nothing real."

At least not now.

"Good." He gulped his black coffee and relaxed back, as much a top-tier businessman as a trained fighter. Niko's business mind was as shrewd as their father's, and an all-too-familiar strategizing look sharpened his eyes. "For press purposes, you are now Temple's official ambassadorial escort during his stay."

Hope sparked deep in her core. "So, you fed the press, releasing the footage and assigning me as his ambassador, to make you look gracious to the public before you go for the knockout. Did I get that right?" Playing the Good Samaritan card, so he didn't look like the womanizing playboy.

Mika must have felt uncomfortable because she stood, cleared the table, and busied herself in the kitchen.

Preening, Niko sat back in the seat, pulled down his tee's hem, and ruffled a hand through his glossy black hair. Just long enough to pull into a ponytail, it gave him the bad-boy appearance that drove women wild. And he was bad, just in ways no one expected. "Of course. My ratings jumped after your spread in *Silk*. This will keep the spin visible and let the public see Ono Enterprises' nice side." He winked. "By the way, that stern look on your face is priceless."

She didn't bother asking why he tracked her down. If he saw an opportunity to tip the public scales in his favor, he'd grasp it despite the cost to anyone, including her. But she'd get to see Keane again, Niko's blessing and all. If her brother only knew. He wasn't the only one seeking to align the stars. She folded her lips together to hide a grin and sighed out an appropriate note of resignation. "What comes next? A photo op during the prefight press party?"

"My PR team suggested we arrange another outing to maximize hype. Perhaps you could show him the harbor." He waggled his brows.

Her lips stretched in a smooth grin, but she didn't try to hide it this time. "Trying to make him look like he's sightseeing while you're training hard?"

That was only part truth. Niko was far too vain to be seen sporting a sizeable bruise. It made him look battered and vulnerable. Unchampion-like.

"Bingo." He saluted her with his coffee cup. "I knew you'd get the angle."

He might be confident with his strategy, but his unconventional approach could backfire. Man plus woman, especially one with a sad face, made for juicy romantic drama. "I get it, but I can't help until the weekend. I have a project due on Friday. Assuming Keane's people even agree to your—"

"They will. Keane's talented, but he knows how to play people better than just about anyone. That's why the press thinks he's such a game changer." Niko pushed away from the table, having accomplished his business. "I'll have Ichiro talk with his people and let you know."

"And what about your manager? Do you think *he'll* go for this?" Ami dropped the question before he reached the door.

"Manager?" Niko pivoted. One side of his thin mouth quirked. "I like that. I'll make sure he's on board. Glad you're beginning to warm up to the idea of him."

Heat flared in her cheeks. "You know that's not what I meant."

He slipped on a jacket. "You may not like him yet, but Ichiro *will* handle you well one day. And when that day comes, it's your job to make sure he doesn't get bored." A warning darkened his eyes. "Until then, you said there was nothing between you and Keane. Make sure that continues to be true."

The door shut with a metallic click. Alone, she sat, trying to rein in her fury. Niko had left for college when she was barely fourteen and had somehow missed the woman she'd grown to be. No doubt he discounted her intellect. That got her fired up on a good day. But she couldn't let him get to her. The anger must morph into something productive.

And he'd offered her a golden ticket to The Golden Lion, so she'd make the most of it. When Mika tiptoed back into the dining room, looking rather sheepish, Ami unleashed a broad grin, and the tension melted from her roomie's shoulders.

"Why the smile?" Mika busied herself at the coffee bar.

Ami shot her a knowing look. "Some things are better left unsaid."

"Are we speaking about you? Or *me*?" Mika handed over a steaming coffee mug.

Indulging in a careful sip, Ami glanced at Mika over the rim. "Both. But please be careful where Niko's concerned. How about I won't ask you what happened last night—for now"—her index finger punctuated her sentiments—"but if, and only if, you keep my feelings for Keane private?"

Chapter 5

Endless sparring sessions. Punching drills. Sprints. Strength conditioning. Performance eating. Eucalyptus-infused therapy baths to unwind muscles. Training days bled into one another before tapering off in the anxious days leading up to fight night. But Friday was a day Keane wouldn't forget. He dipped a respectful bow to the largest sparring partner he'd ever fought and exited the arena with an ear-to-ear grin.

The sports management office employed attractive female trainers—Mark said their presence was proven to boost performance—and a cluster of trainers now hovered ringside. For the first time all week, Keane had gone shirtless, sporting only black training shorts during the intense sparring session. A shimmering sheen of perspiration covered his muscled torso, and more than one of the ladies ogled at the view. He could hear them buzzing. The word *sexy* needed no translation from their flirtatious Japanese banter. But that's not what had him wired.

He sifted through the crowd toward Mark. "A sumo?" Keane ran a hand towel across his brow, chuckling at the giant across the ring. The *rikishi*, his hair in a topknot and his manhood covered with a white cotton loincloth, appeared dazed until a lovely assistant attended to him with a water bottle and towel. That brought a smile to his round, boyish face.

"I promised unparalleled cross-training, did I not?" Mark beamed. "Gotta prep for the unexpected."

"Yeah. That was interesting. He was so big I could hardly get a hold until I managed to snag his belt." Keane wrinkled his nose. "And he smelled like baby powder."

"Well, grabbing the belt followed by a leg hook—genius," Mark cooed. "I didn't think he'd ever get up after a massive take-down like that."

Paulo whooped as he rushed forward and gave Keane's backside a chummy spank. "You are one slick stallion, a thoroughbred."

Keane glared at his friend. "Never do that again." It came out as a light scold, but he glanced over his shoulder at his sculpted backside.

"What? I compliment you, and you get snazzy at me."

"You think I'm snazzy?" Keane let out a groan and waggled his brows at Paulo. "Come on, man."

Hans approached. "Think you meant to say *snippy*, amigo."

"Snazzy. Snippy. Whatever." Paulo flushed as a round of guffawing played out. Then they strutted to Mark's office. "It was insane."

"He's right. We should've filmed this and used it in the ads. Speaking of—you got a little press time already." Mark's eyebrows arched, and his lips curved to complement them.

"When?" Keane sank into one of four club chairs in Mark's office.

"A day—no, two days ago."

"And you're just now telling me this? Where was the footage taken?"

"Not sure. I didn't catch it all, but you were getting in the

Bentley with a woman. They called her your ambassador." Reclining in his chair, Mark laced his fingers in his lap. "Care to share?"

"My *ambassador*?" Baffled, Keane looked from Mark to Hans, who now leaned against the doorframe.

Hans shrugged. "I didn't see it either. I must've been at the airport picking up Ella and the kids."

"Long hair?" Keane's eyes bored into Mark. A lump formed in his throat. "Pretty?"

"Beautiful."

Paulo laughed and, despite Mark's protests, shuffled through a stack of papers and magazines until he found *Silk*. He showed it to Mark before tossing it into Keane's lap.

"Yeah, that's her," Mark confirmed.

"Your bombshell swan." Paulo winked at Keane. "I saw the footage too."

Before he could consider whether it was wise to peek at the magazine, his line of sight landed on *Silk*'s February cover girl. His heart jerked toward his throat, and it must've shown in his face.

"You know her?" Mark scooted forward, moving his hands to his desk.

"I do," Keane mumbled, angling the glossy magazine cover to catch the light. "Remember, I ran into Ono's little sister." A long beat passed. Tension had his shoulders riding high. His gaze cut to Mark, and disapproval tightened the guy's mouth. "What? You didn't make the connection?"

"What connection?" Mark pressed without thinking, his voice loud. Then understanding restructured his face into something troubled.

Even Hans snickered.

Exhaling, Keane tipped his head back, ran a hand through his unruly hair, and tried to clear the lump from his parched throat. He had allowed himself one day with Ami Ono and then, with the self-control of a proven champion, forced his mind back on the title-belt track.

Fighting was both his passion and, where other things were concerned in life, his diversion. In the ring, he had to be fully present, mind, body, and soul. That intentional kind of diversion—or was it an excuse?—insulated him from Ami during the day. Nights were different. Every. Single. Night.

Just as he bowed his head before each fight, Keane prayed in the dark. It had become routine. The repeated words too automatic. But, since he'd met Ami, he prayed to forget their perfect chemistry. That connection had done a number on him, threatened to intoxicate his thoughts, and consumed his sleep.

Paulo called it. Ami Ono rattled Keane's cage. When had a woman ever captivated him so? Even when he tried to deny it, his body betrayed him. Five days later, her pull remained. If he let her get close again, he knew how it'd be. He was fiercely protective—possessive, even—where loved ones were concerned, and her effortless charm had rubbed off on him like some irresistible magic residue.

"Yep. Think you got it now, Mark. The woman on the news, *Silk*'s swan, is Ono's little sister." Still studying the cover, Keane exhaled, letting out relief at the confession until Mark snapped to attention and sprung to his feet.

With his hands pressed to the desktop, his cheeks reddened. He opened his mouth to speak, but only a string of groans and exhalations came out. "Well, goshgollygee, makes sense she's the one, then. Ono's manager called 'bout this ambassador deal."

"What are you talking about?" Keane jerked upright in his chair.

"Ono wants to do a joint meet-and-greet fan event. It'll air on the local news leading up to the fight. Your backstory. Some poster signing in Sendai. You get it."

Keane opened his mouth, but before he could protest, Mark

thumped the magazine. "Hear me out. If you have any objection, you won't for long, 'cause that tasty little morsel will be your guide."

His pulse thrumming faster, Keane did a double take at the cover, admiring Ami in a custom-fitted swan dress of silk and feathers that skimmed her thighs. Satin-smooth lean legs. Innocent pink lip gloss. Obsidian cascade of hair fanning over the feathered fringe.

He crossed his arms, cocked his head. "Niko won't be there?"

"Apparently not. Strange strategy if you ask me, but that's the deal."

A crooked grin stretched his lips so wide they hurt. "First a sumo. Now this. I can't imagine why Ono would want his sister to be my guide, but—whatever the rationale—I'm in."

But what exactly might that mean?

Ami set a leather school tote on the foyer table and hooked her favorite jacket, a powder-blue walking coat, by the entrance.

"It's been one crazy week. We should celebrate," Mika declared the second the door snapped shut.

"What are you thinking?" Ami crossed the Italian tile. "Dinner?"

"Dinner. Dancing. Anything, as long as it's merrymaking." Mika's shoulders bounced in a happy jig. "You need to get out. All week, you've lived, breathed, probably even dreamed your stupid research project."

Ami braced against the couch arm and sighed. "It isn't stupid, Mika. It's important, brain-draining work that somehow energizes me. You can't help but feel something at the lab. The whole project team has this . . . this collective hunch we're on to something."

Mika rolled her eyes. "Sure. I'm also sure you're shooting for an A. You'll probably get it, but that's all you guys are on to."

"Maybe. Hopefully." Ami crossed her arms. "But wouldn't

it be something?" A British rock star of a geologist oversaw their work. He'd spent most of his adult life in the Pacific Ocean's Ring of Fire, studying earthquake evidence to predict risks better. And he'd needed help doing the analytical legwork. "Professor Newman is fantastic. In these last six months, the team and I have learned more than we ever imagined."

Should evidence of a geological event serve as a predictor? Would people take notice of the work? Accept or challenge the evidence? Put the team's scientific findings into practice? Chill bumps rushed up her arms.

"Yeah, well, whatever." Mika dropped onto the couch and smoothed her short bob. "Apart from sneaking in trips to the aquatic center's pool to do whatever it is you do there—"

"Practice diving and underwater breath-holding techniques."

"—you've spent every minute with your team. Tell me that's over now. Today, you finished your final research paper."

And the eyebrow-raising results stunned even her. Ami pushed away from the couch, shifting to face her roomie. "Mika, we think—"

"Spare me." Mika held up a hand. "It's on the Brit's desk. Leave it. And let's go out for some girl time. *Please.*"

Her fate now in his decisive hands, it was time for a break. Dinner. Dancing. Merrymaking. Anything where her mind could take a plunge.

"You're right." Ami sank back into the plush sofa with a sigh and a contented grin. "I'm up for any or all of that."

"I'll text Sora. Should I call Niko?" A flush came with Mika's question, but her tone stayed light.

Ami hadn't heard from her overbearing brother since Monday. He'd probably had one of his lackeys following her all week. "No, I should." She made her way to the foyer, dug through her purse, punched Niko's number into the phone, and stiffened with each electronic *brrrring-brrrring.*

"Baby sister." His booming voice broke through the receiver. "I've been waiting for my little ambassador to call. Guess you didn't even see yourself on the news, did you?"

"Of course not."

"Always so studious."

His pandering made her stomach flip. "Mika and I are going out with some girls tonight. You probably already know that." She winced. Yep, Niko brought out the worst in her. "But you're welcome to join."

"I have plans tonight, but don't stay out too late. You and Temple are on for tomorrow morning. A fan event."

"Oh?"

"Didn't think I could make the ambassador deal happen?"

When it came to romance, she'd always yearned for a choice, a chance to pursue a man who drove her wild. Who wouldn't want that? But in the Ono family, things—especially romantic things—never went her way. At least, her brother couldn't see her beaming. "Oh." Good. The word came out neutral, devoid of emotion. "What time?"

"Ten sharp. He will be at Lakeside Park with the video crew. Introduce him. Take pictures. Show him around. Be a hospitable *ambassador*."

"I can manage being hospitable." Less than a week ago, she'd been afraid to appear in public with Keane. And unless she'd imagined it, their chemistry—their profound connection—had been more earthshaking than the stats she'd buried herself in. By the time Niko figured that out, it would be too late. This was his doing, after all. Still, she couldn't squash a spark of hope—a hope that surpassed the unwanted life her family had arranged with Ichiro Wantanabe.

Chapter 6

Like a school of exotic fish riding a stream of liquid energy, a crowd had already queued outside the exclusive club, the girls shimmering along a flow of concrete sidewalk in their jewel-toned party dresses, the guys cruising like sleek sharks on the hunt. But since the building belonged to Ono Enterprises, Ami waved to the bouncer and bypassed the wait. One of the few perks of being an Ono.

The entrance dipped through a short, torch-lit tunnel before emerging into an expansive circular room under a star-studded dome. It was a celestial adventure for the eyes—an indoor version of the city's Pageant of Starlight, one of Japan's biggest winter festivals. The inky indigo ceiling featured a blinking constellation of Orion, and a moon phased across the man-made sky. The polished stone flooring created a black lake edged by carved mahogany booths resembling sailboats hauling rich purple velveteen pillows. Shooting-star pyrotechnics. Honeysuckle-scented party fog. Spellbinding music. Steam pouring into a rolling sea of high-spirited dancers. All insanely over the top.

Ami's troop found an empty booth. Sora tossed her jacket onto a padded bench and coaxed everyone except Ami and Mika to parade straight into the dance mix. Under the winking spotlight, Ami sank into a plush feather bolster as her friends gained the attention of a pack of men. Several had lost their ties and platinum cuff-links. Having come straight from the office, they must have needed to unwind as much as Ami.

Spotting a waitress, Ami lifted a hand. In a showy silver-white rabbit ensemble, the young server smiled. "What can I get for you?"

"Diet Coca-Cola for me and—" Ami waved to Mika.

"Ditto."

The girl punched the details into an electronic handheld device, made something of a curtsy, and backed into the current.

"You never said. What was Niko doing tonight?" Mika coated her lips with shimmering gloss.

Ami toyed with the bolster trim, sinking into a more supported position. "He said he had plans. Nothing specific." With her gaze roaming over the festive crowd, Mika must have been struggling to keep her face from falling. Ami squeezed her friend's cold hand. "I'm sorry."

Mika shrugged. "It's fine." She sucked in shallow, shaky breaths. "And you look happy. Is that because of the completed paper? Or does it have anything to do with seeing Keane Temple again tomorrow?"

The waitress delivered drinks. Ami accepted hers, the dark liquid reflecting starlight. She wouldn't be able to hide the truth from Mika. "Both."

"You're lucky—super lucky—Niko didn't figure out your interest in Keane. But he will, right?"

Ami shrugged before nodding. Her friends were enjoying themselves, especially Reiko. Lanky with caramel-hued curls, Reiko landed a rather handsome dance partner and began shimmying like a sunflower in the wind.

"But after all this time, you've stopped caring, haven't you?"

Mika pressed deeper, scooting right up to Ami's side, her words shooting right to the heart.

Ami let her smile widen at her friend's mild astonishment. "Niko's rules make me miserable. Sticking my hand in the fire makes me feel alive."

Mika gave Ami's hand an understanding squeeze, finished her drink, and scooted off. A wounded heart likely drove her to the dance floor, but Ami was in no rush. Entertained by the crowd, she began to relax and let her memory rewind to *the* excursion. With Keane, she felt an unexpected gravity underscored by a zing, and it was too strong—and rare—not to explore.

Then the masses parted. A real-time exhibition of nature's rules of attraction played out. That inexplicable force. Women flocking to powerful men. Cocky. Brawny. Fearless men. Practiced protectors. Imagination awakeners.

Professional fighters strutted through the crowd, but not Keane. She scooted forward on the seat, bracing for the dance floor, when movement stirred the air and filled her nose with a masculine scent. One breath of that bewitching cologne roused her memory, knotted her stomach, and rushed electric tingles all the way to her toes. Keane Temple was behind her.

She swiveled, face-to-face with a glorious smile. Its wearer hovered over the bench back, and the angle at which she'd turned brought their faces close to one another—so close her breath hitched. Music drowned out the pounding of her heartbeat, but the rapid thrumming within her rib cage raced to outdo its tempo.

Breathless, she bobbed forward, drawn in by the magnetic force until her brain reined in what felt so right. With a gasp, she snapped out of the trance, straightened, and swallowed hard. "Hi."

"Miss Ono." Low and husky, his voice shivered over her. He motioned toward the vacant bench. "Mind if I join you?"

She worked to organize her jumbled thoughts. "That depends. Is this about business? Or of a personal nature?" She glanced up from under her lashes, fought the smile twitching at her mouth, and cocked a questioning eyebrow.

"Strictly business, of course." As he took a turn around the booth, he ran his fingertips along the bench back, letting them brush over her hair.

She shuddered, her gaze drifting over the length of him, doing a double take on his tailored black cashmere trousers. A black crew-neck sweater showcased his rock-hard build and created an alluring contrast to his golden complexion. But there was more to this man than just good looks. The talented Keane Temple moved with the confident swagger of Midas.

She rubbed her lips together to contain a hot mess of jitters. After the bay, what could he be thinking? The playful glint in his eye somehow bolstered her outward poise. "Then business it is. What do you have on your mind?"

"Marketing, specifically." He slid onto the bench across from her, shifted a glass out of his way, and clasped hands on the table.

"Marketing."

"Sure. If we're to be partners, we need to decide how to leverage tomorrow's rendezvous."

Heat flooded her face. Did he seriously want to discuss business . . . in a club? Maybe he was as astute a businessman as he was a decorated fighter. Niko intimated as much. Had she been naïve? Like a direct glance at the sun, could the dazzling attraction have blinded her? Or should she read between the lines? "What do you have in mind?"

Somewhere in her periphery, white lights pulsed in time to the music, but his iron-hard gaze gripped her. Several beats passed in a stare down before he responded. "Shock value."

Ami loosed a surprised cough and attempted to swallow the cotton caught in her throat. "I beg your pardon."

"Let's level-set expectations." His commanding voice overpowered her, and his bright eyes cut straight to her soul. "What happens in the ring is only part of this business. So, I had to ask myself: What's in this marketing arrangement for Niko? Does he always involve you in his work?"

"Often. But never like this. Niko knows how much I dislike fighters." Oops. She trudged on with a shrug. "Guess he figured I'd be a safe bet, and you both could leverage the exposure from the bay."

The low lights softened the grin widening his lush mouth. "And here I thought you might like some fighters." He paused, seeming to wait for her reaction before surveying the glittering crowd.

Good. She needed a break from his jade eyes. She hadn't lied about being an Ono, but she had withheld that detail too long. And regretted it.

As Keane chuckled, her discomfort over his teasing faded, his easygoing nature hard to resist.

"Part of my appeal has always been my . . . enduring eligibility. Niko knows that. My being seen with you, sightseeing while he trains. The smoke-and-mirrors tactic will fuel his image and make me look like some pleasure-monger. Unless I'm wrong. Or unless the plan backfires on him." He ran a hand over his five-o'clock shadow, looking far too contented.

"What are you getting at?"

"I suspect Niko missed the real connection between us. He doesn't know you *like* me, does he?" The way his voice rumbled made Ami's pulse jive.

"Who said I like you?" *Like* was not an adequate word.

The blaring music transitioned from a techno-trance song into a moody slow number. The faux starlight shifted from silver-white to warm amber. Keane pushed his sweater sleeves up and rested muscular forearms on the high-top table.

She dragged her gaze from his prime build but couldn't drag her imagination from snuggling close in such a safe embrace.

The eagerness in his expression made her heart twinge. His mouth spoke of business, but his body language said otherwise. His eyes shimmered translucent green under the ambient lighting.

"My time here is too short to pretend." He drummed his hands on the tabletop. "For this filming deal tomorrow, we can put on a respectable show. If the audience sees something friendlier than a business relationship, so be it. No doubt it'd add to the hype. But between us, I don't want to pretend. And I don't want to waste time."

Such inclinations had plagued his thoughts each evening, but until he'd seen her again, he'd buried them. The past week of sparring had been his best in years. But was she a weakness to his fighting, as he'd always believed a committed relationship would be? Or an unimaginable blessing? He couldn't resist the urge to find out, even if it cost him the championship. And that freed him.

His palms felt hot as they inched forward on the cool marble tabletop. His fingertips grazed over hers, switching on that electrical current. "In less than a week, we've run into each other twice. What is that? Coincidence? Chance—in a city of more than a million? This isn't the way I do things, but it also doesn't seem right not to explore whatever *this* is."

Ami's brow arched and lips pursed. Then her eyes twinkled. "But you said you came to speak business."

"Miss Ono, I'm suggesting we mix business with pleasure."

"And what benefit is there for me, Midas?"

A spark of playfulness energized him. "How about a trade? Your cooperation for . . ."

At his pause, her brow arched higher toward her ebony hair. "For what?"

"Hmm. In-kind services . . . incredible companionship." The proposal came out throaty.

A rowdy whoop erupted tableside, preventing him from discussing what that might entail. "'S Mr. Temple, girls!" Paulo, Igor, and John approached with newfound lady friends—Ami's friends.

"Have a seat, Paulo." Keane thumped the bench as he slid to make room.

Ignoring the gesture, Paulo stole the seat beside Ami. She opened her mouth to say something but stopped when the flirtatious Brazilian sat far too close for Keane's comfort. Even from across the table, Paulo's strong cologne and party sweat intruded.

A blast of impatience—it *wasn't* jealousy—burned through Keane. "Man, what are you doing?"

Paulo swiveled on the bench to face Ami. "Why are you not dancing with my friend?"

She shrugged, the twinkle still lighting her dark eyes. "We were talking business."

"Business? Really, Keane? Shame on you. No business tonight. Just dancing." Paulo threw back someone's drink and, feasting his eyes on Ami, jerked his head toward the crowd. "You must dance, pretty swan."

In the span of a breath, her gaze drifted to Keane. His jaw twitched as he rose. "Excellent idea. I'll make sure she has a good time." He gave Paulo's shoulder a squeeze, pressing him back into the seat, and then captured Ami's hand. "Ami, are these ladies your friends?"

She cleared her throat. "Yes, Sora and my roommate, Mika."

"*Gentlemen.*" Keane emphasized the word, tugging Ami toward the dance floor. "Make sure these ladies have a phenomenal time tonight."

Linked by fingertips, she trailed through the swirl of dancers. A sassy Latin song reminiscent of Rio's infamous hip-swaying Carnivals played over the loudspeakers. The party fog changed to a tropical scent. And the stars receded for an impressive firework light show.

Under the colorful blinking, Keane halted and spun toward her, never releasing his grip with one hand, catching her trim waist with the other. He pulled her in close, leading the movement of her hips with his own in a fast-paced salsa step. Rocking back and forth. An occasional spin. An air of festivity. A steamy crowd.

"You obviously do some dancing." She flicked her hair back as he led her. Was appreciation warming her tone?

He chuckled and spun her out and back into a confident embrace, more tightly now, making every skin-to-skin contact point sing with sensation. "Paulo taught us."

"Really?"

"Yep, rainy day. We couldn't run, so we had an impromptu . . . cardio session." He glanced down. A rose flush now painted her fair cheeks, and her peep-toe pumps triggered a memory of *Silk*'s cover-girl swan—those long lean legs adorned by opal- and crystal-bejeweled strappy heels. "Killer shoes, by the way."

With a contented smile, the gliding swan continued to follow his lead. Perhaps it was a trick of the light, but he could have sworn her flush deepened. The music blended into the next song. With the petite swan in heels, their bodies aligned, their hips brushing together. He liked the feel of her in his arms. He had to clear his throat to distract himself. "You're not a half-bad dancer yourself, Miss Ono."

The reverberation of her giggle tickled his chest. "Thank you. So, does dancing qualify as *more* than business?"

"Mmm. This is nice, but not what I had in mind."

With an abrupt flick of his arm, he twirled her outward before reeling her in, guiding her with one warm hand pressed to the small of her back.

"Then tomorrow will be interesting." She smiled.

Chapter 7

Too edgy to sleep any longer, Keane pulled on a microfiber half-zip and joggers, a baseball cap, and his running shoes. He stepped into a brisk breeze carrying the aroma of brewed espresso and baking bread from the café. A quiet street. A glowing predawn skyline. A run before the traffic got heavy would ease his nerves and loosen his muscles.

Five miles and a brilliant sunrise later, he dropped by the café for a steaming cup of coffee and a bowl of hearty oatmeal before heading back for a shower. Fan days were fun days, and excitement sped up the morning routine. He had donned a pair of camel-colored Italian wool trousers and a forest-green cable-knit when an electronic closing bell echoed.

He located the phone on the kitchen counter, answered, and pinned the slippery device between his ear and shoulder as he tugged on socks.

"I'm waiting at the curb."

"Didn't realize you were coming, Mark. Think I need a babysitter?"

"Absolutely."

Keane laughed. "You might be right, but I'll try to be on my best behavior."

"Good. Hurry up, champ."

Keane grabbed a herringbone topcoat, slid his wallet and phone into a pocket, hustled downstairs, and hopped into the SUV.

Too quiet, Mark inspected Keane's face.

"What?" Did Mark know Keane had had a second run-in with the black-headed swan? Paulo might have mentioned it, but he'd seemed too preoccupied at the club to have outed him so soon.

Mark shrugged and scrubbed a hand across his lips and chin, sparks lighting in his eyes. "Nothing. We're meeting the film crew at Lakeside Park."

"Is it far?"

"Not too far. They wanna get footage of you and Miss Ono on a stone bridge, and then the fan event is at eleven near the entrance."

"Got it." Keane snapped on his seat belt. "Why aren't we driving?"

"We're waiting on Hans. Both of you will do the meet and greet. Sign posters. Shake hands. Smile pretty." With a belly laugh, Mark thumped Keane's left biceps. "Ono's manager said to be ready. The Japanese haven't earned their picture-taking reputation for nothing."

Keane glanced out the window. In the Westin Hotel lobby, Hans shared a tender kiss with his wife. His knee-high twins tugged at his pants. A peck on the cheek for each of the little girls. A fare-well wave. A brisk walk to the vehicle.

"Anything else?" Keane ignored a tiny twinge of envy—must be nerves—as the security chauffeur opened the door and Hans slid in.

"Nope."

"And Niko Ono won't be there?" His gaze cut to Mark. A public confrontation would be disastrous.

"I confirmed. His manager's a real turd, and he said no. Just the sister."

Keane chuckled at Mark's colorful description and settled into the leather bucket.

Ami Ono. If news of their arrangement—or was it a relationship?—leaked, the salivating press would hound them. He'd better be on his best business behavior at the park, but sometime, he'd have to deal with her big brother, in the ring or out.

For now, he let his mind drift through the prior evening's party fog, replaying memories of the woman who managed to get close enough to shake up his world. That made her a rarity. The drive to Lakeside Park passed in a happy blur.

But "park" was an understatement. Manicured lawns flowed into rows of cherry trees covered in buds. Hedgerows pruned into artistic swirls merged with sweeping displays of multicolored flowers. Water lilies lazed in scenic koi ponds. A meandering path led to a low-lying stone bridge. Gurgling fountains competed with giggling children.

"I should've brought the girls." Hans climbed out before the driver could circle to get his door and stood stiff-legged on the sidewalk. "They've been pretty cooped up."

Keane paused a beat before pivoting toward Mark. "Can you arrange for his girls to join the fun? Maybe treat them to an afternoon at the amusement park and ice cream on me?"

"You two get started walking that way." Mark pointed toward the bridge and squirmed out of the back seat after Keane. "I'll send the car back for Ella and the girls and be over in a minute."

"Thanks for that, man. We've been friends for many years. And today, you are quiet." Hans's elbow winged out to nudge Keane's arm. "You like her?"

"I like her." Keane cringed over the admission. "Am I a fool?"

"*Ja*, there is no wisdom in liking your opponent's sister, but the heart can lead us on an unpredictable journey."

Keane nodded as they ambled toward the bridge where the film crew readied cameras and set up portable lighting equipment. On the bridge's high point, Ami stood facing the mountains that rose in deep-green rolls. Her dark hair was a glossy black fan overlaying a fitted winter-white coat. Her posture exuded strength and feminine poise, but even in profile, she looked forlorn. Until she turned her head and spotted him. A wide smile broke across her face and brightened her eyes before she contained it in a thin-lipped, businesslike grin.

Keane and Hans made the remainder of their walk in unspoken understanding, but before falling within the film crew's earshot, Keane idled and swiveled toward Hans. "I saw her again last night." With his right hand thrust into his pants pocket, Keane jangled the chain of his lucky pocket watch. "But this deal today . . . She and I agreed—our relationship is professional. 'Kay?"

"Okay." Hans swiped a hand over his mouth, failing to erase his amusement.

"Good. Tell me something though." Keane's hand stopped jiggling, and he took a step closer.

"What's that?"

"Was it intense with Ella? Like, mind-consuming?"

"Was?" Hans cocked his head, his grin widening. "Still is."

"But—"

"No buts. Ella drives me insane. Has since day one. There has to be more than the physical stuff to make it last. She makes me think, you know, and pushes me when I'm stubborn." He rolled his eyes and reached over to squeeze Keane's shoulder. "Just go try. You never know what might happen."

Keane nodded, gave Hans a friendly jab to the ribs, and faced Ami. She was watching him. Laughter glittered in her eyes. He flashed her a private wink and tried to rein in his racing pulse as he strode toward a man who appeared to be in charge of the production.

"Wantanabe-san." The gangly stone-faced man, Niko Ono's manager, bowed. "Ichiro Wantanabe." He repeated his full name and shook Keane's extended hand.

"Ichiro, nice to meet you. I'm Keane, and this is Hans."

"We are glad you could join us today. The cameras are arranged. We will first get some footage of you, Mr. Temple, with Miss Ono on the bridge, and then we will move to the park entrance for the fan event. And I coordinated with your Mr. Mark concerning social media posts. Your and Master Ono's pages were updated yesterday with news of the event, so we expect fans to show in significant numbers."

Man, this guy was dry as dirt. "Excellent. Shall I go ahead and visit with Miss Ono?"

"Ah, yes. Yes, that would be good. I have a call. . . ." Ichiro was already pounding numbers into his phone.

Despite her efforts to appear uninterested, Ami must have been tuned in to the conversation. Her posture was a tad too perfect, primed to respond to his arrival. So he paused by the serene pond, making her wait. As white-and-orange koi glided through the water, he mumbled familiar words, a brief prayer, under his breath. But before she could get irritated, he hustled on.

"Miss Ono, it is my great pleasure to formally make your acquaintance." Feeling the weight of the onlookers' eyes, he bowed in a show of good etiquette.

A sequence of rapid-fire clicks cut through the brisk air. Ami returned the gesture with a professionalism that hid the undercurrent of attraction. Her cool smile left him wanting more. "The pleasure is mine. And welcome to Sendai."

A blue-haired photographer and his film crew stood on a crescent-shaped platform around the pond's edge. "Face me," the photographer shouted. "Good. Hold it. . . . One more second. Now, Ami, hand him your *omedeto*."

From an interior jacket pocket, she retrieved a palm-sized package bound by a vivid red ribbon. "A token to welcome you to Japan." She presented the gift and dipped a bow. "We hope you enjoy your stay."

Keane accepted the package, pausing for the photo op with his fingertips lingering on hers. The physical contact paired with his lack of an expected gift for her hijacked his pulse. On the flight over, he'd read about Japanese etiquette and the ritual of gift-giving. Panic snagged his speech until he grasped his sole option to reciprocate. He dug deep into his pocket and unfolded a clenched fist. Resting on his palm was the gold pocket watch he always carried.

A rosy blush bloomed on her cheeks. She stared a moment too long. He caught her hand, pressed the watch into her palm, and echoed her sentiments. "A small token."

"You are too generous." With her chin lowered, and silky hair cascading across her cheeks, she started to pull her lower lip into her mouth but stopped before smearing her ruby lip gloss.

"It is *my* pleasure." He let a finger trace a line on her palm, his voice low and secretive. Just for them.

A sharp whistle drew glances toward the film crew.

"The footage is good." Ichiro's bombastic tone rang out over the pond. He stormed toward the bridge, an air horn in hand and Hans in tow. "The crowd is very, very large size. The park entrance has become congested. We must hurry."

Festive energy pulsed through the park. An infectious back-beat came into earshot, and an announcer's distant voice pumped up the crowd. Large screens projected fight scenes. A raised platform resembled a mini-arena surrounded by fans with posters and pens. And when those fans sighted Keane rounding a bend, a lion-worthy roar surged through the crowd.

Ichiro ushered Hans, Ami, and Keane up a step into the mock arena and motioned toward a trio of captain's chairs. Hans settled into the chair on the right. Keane shifted to the left, giving her the center seat.

She dawdled, pulling off her jacket, letting her gaze linger on the massive video screen serving as the stage backdrop. He glimpsed himself on the screen locked in a fierce battle. He remembered that night well. His first US Championship.

"Welcome," came the announcer's shrill voice. He spoke in English before rattling off the greeting in Japanese. Jet-black hair formed a helmet of porcupine spikes on his meticulously groomed head. Gripping a microphone, the wiry man wove through the fans and bounded onto the stage to introduce the celebrities. Keane managed to decipher their names, championship titles, and the mention of *Silk* before the mass morphed into an endless queue of people.

The swan image might be eye-catching, but the woman seemed so different from the one who'd ambled alongside him around the bay. Ono's marketing ploy sold her short. She was beautiful. No one would dispute that. But she was also a kind woman of science, and Keane had only begun to delve into her intellectual depths.

Ichiro unlatched a side rope, and the influx of meet-and-greeters began moving from Hans to Ami to Keane.

"Hello. I'm Sakura." A young woman handed Keane a palm-sized autograph book. "May I also get a picture?"

"Absolutely." He signed the book and posed for the camera. The girl and her friend wandered away, tittering.

Where did the brutal warrior hide in that gorgeous golden exterior? The raw masculine power of his public life coexisted with a protected private side. He'd allowed Ami close enough to see a glimpse of that, and it pricked her heart, sending a warm rush throughout her body. What else was yet to be uncovered?

A stream of people and time slipped by in a dizzying blur of signatures, smiles, and flashes. Sitting side by side, outward attention directed toward the fans, she still sensed the electric awareness buzzing between her and Keane and savored her front-row ticket to witness his crowd-pleasing skills. A natural charmer, he somehow counteracted the anxiety posed by his chiseled physique. The girls' hands trembled when they faced him, but every single one left with an easy grin.

"Keane?" The lady spoke in English too good not to be that of a native speaker.

Everyone's gaze snapped up to catch a striking blonde with sky-blue eyes. A strong pang swept through Ami. Was it envy?

"Yes." A beat passed. Keane tipped his head, narrowing his gaze. "Have we met?"

"No, I'm Mary. Mary Dubois. Ray Highbridge is an old friend of mine."

"Ah, a mutual acquaintance."

"Ray saw the publicity tweet yesterday and said you'd be here." The American woman gestured to the Japanese teenagers clustered around her. "These are my students. I'm on mission in this area, teaching English as a second language."

"I see." Keane stood to shake her hand. "Any friend of Ray's is a friend of mine."

"You'll have to tell him we met."

"Of course." Still clasping her hand, Keane pulled her in for a half-hug before signaling the students up onto the platform. "Ami, please let me introduce you to Mary, a friend of my pastor."

Their gazes locked before his brow arched. What did her face give away to get such a . . . knowing look? Whatever it was, the way he ogled her appeased her.

Ami took a deep breath and dipped a graceful bow. "It's a pleasure. Would you like your group to get a picture with Mr. Temple? It can be arranged."

Mary agreed, and the students formed a semicircle around Keane for the snapshot.

"Before you go, please get my number from Ray," Keane said. "If it works with my schedule, I'd be honored to drop by one of your classes. Maybe let the kids try out their English."

The corners of Mary's mouth twitched into a genuine grin. "That would be awesome. I'll be in touch." She waved farewell and hurried down the sidewalk to catch up with her class.

When the event ended, Ichiro reappeared with that outrageously cutting-edge phone shoved against his ear. His head bobbed as he clipped off orders and then, without hesitation, punched the End Call button and hopped onto the platform.

Her gut wrenched at his proximity.

"Good event." Keane stood to shake Ichiro's hand.

"I agree." Ichiro spoke in English only in front of his guests. "Hans, your wife and daughters are waiting for you by the bridge. Thanks to you, and you, Mr. Temple, for helping promote the fight. I regret Mr. Ono couldn't make it, but his sister is a special woman."

With the polite dismissal, Hans lifted two fingers to his brow in a farewell salute and took off toward his family.

Then Ichiro shifted closer to Ami and let his fingertips trail down her arm in an intimate gesture, making Keane's skin crawl and his fists clench. "Ami," Ichiro said. "I have a business conflict for this afternoon. Keane's manager and I need to wrap up planning details for the press party. Can I arrange a cab for you?"

Her nostrils flared. When she retreated from Ichiro's grasp, Keane bristled.

"Thank you, but no. I have business too. I'll handle the cab. What is it you always say, Ichiro? No harm, no foul." Quite unlike the fireball with whom Keane was familiar, she now spoke with a cool demeanor. Ichiro's face went white at being written off so easily, even before she waved a hand. "Oh, good luck with your meeting."

Her unrelenting eyes fixed on Ichiro. Keane stifled a chuckle. His little swan was staring the man down. What prompted the non-verbal challenge? Something was off.

Ichiro dropped his gaze. "I wish you the same." He bowed, spun on his heel, and walked to join Mark at the front gate.

The moment no one was within earshot, the angry fire in her eyes faded into an expression both confusing and smoldering. Head tipped down, she fiddled with her jacket cuff. "Are you hungry?"

"Yes. But what was that?" He inclined his head toward the gate.

"You mean Ichiro?" She met his gaze, waiting for his nod before responding. Her tight throat worked to swallow before any words came. "This morning, sitting by your side, all I wanted was to spend more time alone with you. I promise to tell you about Ichiro, but right now, I just want to be with you and not talk about him . . . not even *think* about him."

Her comment coaxed a grin from Keane. He sidled closer and smoothed a windswept lock of her hair behind her ear. "How can I argue with that?"

He snagged her hand, kissed its silken back, and tugged her toward the parking lot.

"What do you have in mind for lunch?" she asked as they strolled hand in hand.

"Anything. Something quiet. Private. Is there anywhere we could go to unwind?" He pointed toward his black Bentley.

"I know a place." Her footfalls snagged a beat as she scanned her surroundings to ensure no one was near. Still, uncertainty squinched her eyes while she waited for the driver to catch the door, then slid across the butter-soft leather seat.

Keane climbed in behind her, feeling the thrill of being alone with her in a confined space. "Where to?"

Her eyes gleamed. "It's a surprise."

"Another surprise?" His brows flew up. "I'm not sure I—"

She rolled an innocent shrug, shooting him a look that turned his mouth desert-dry. "Don't worry. I promise you'll love it."

Maybe, but could he handle another after what happened at the bay?

Chapter 8

The chauffeur followed her instructions. Then the Bentley halted outside a historic inn overlooking an undulating green river. With its blue tile roof, the structure was traditional, yet timeless, and its abundance of windows promised peaceful views.

"You brought me to a hotel?" Keane gave Ami a sideways glance, scrutinizing her flawless face.

Steadied by a doorman's gloved hand, she stepped out and turned as Keane stood. "Don't get too excited. It *is* a hotel." Her slow grin rounded her cheeks under her twinkling eyes. "There's also a fantastic restaurant. But we came for the *onsen*."

The caution came too late. He'd been keyed up all morning, but at the risk of sounding like a sweaty-palmed teen, he withheld *that* comment. "An *onsen*?"

"Hot springs. They're therapeutic, and you said somewhere you could unwind."

Ha. His pulse skittered as they entered the pristine lobby. "Miss Ono, are you flirting with me?" He arched a brow. "And what about swimsuits?"

A captivating pink smeared her fair cheeks. "Swimsuits can be purchased in the gift shop."

"You're sure about that? That guilty look of yours is telling enough."

She looked away, but not before the flush deepened.

"Come now." He reached to turn her chin back toward him, and fire flared in those dark irises. "No reason to be embarrassed. I was only playing."

She breathed in deep. "Are you still hungry?"

"Very." The word growled from somewhere primal deep within him.

"Don't tease." She hooked a finger around his pinkie and pulled him to her side. "I'm starving."

In the dining room, floor-to-ceiling windows displayed the river vista. "The spa overlooks the Natori River and is called *Akiu*," Ami explained as he held out her chair. "It is hard to believe, but this hotel is more than a thousand years old."

Whoa. His head jerked up, his hand trailing over onto her shoulder. "How is that even possible?"

Before she could respond, a uniformed waiter approached the table. "The lady is correct." The waiter flashed an easy smile as Keane took his seat. The guy poured fragrant amber tea into ceramic cups and eased back a step. "The Hotel Sakan is in the thirty-fourth generation of ownership."

Considering the historic structure's age, it was hard not to develop an appreciation for it. The Hotel Sakan pulled off an incredible balance of old and new. Stringed music sailed on ginger-scented air. The color palette and lush textiles melded with the tranquil view, the focus on balance and harmony.

"Impressive, especially considering my country isn't half that old."

"It is an extraordinary place." A fan of fine lines crinkled up the waiter's eyes. "Now, if I may, allow me to recommend today's special."

They ordered, the waiter vanished, and the electric charge returned. Keane tested a sip of tea to wet his mouth. It stung his tongue, running hot through his body, but failed to quench his thirst. He tugged to stretch out his collar, fighting off an urgency, compelled to know everything about her all at once.

"So, I'm not here for long." A dull ache settled into his chest. He could hope it didn't register on his face.

"I know. Not long enough at all, right?"

Lips pressed together, he only shook his head.

"Well, and it's strange." A wistful twist tipped her mouth.

"What?"

"How things can become strong. How an afternoon shopping trip turned into this bizarre arrangement. Like some earthquake, it has flipped my personal landscape upside down." She peered at the distant mountains. "That day at the train station, I pegged you as a typical fighter, but you might be more than I bargained for."

He let a grin unfurl. But what might she *not* be saying? She was slow to share, but their initial encounter—Was it providence? How had such an odd marketing arrangement come about? Was the attraction as intense for her?

"I know exactly what you mean." He scratched his jawline and folded muscular arms across his chest as he scanned the restaurant. Huh. More than one curious glance flicked away. "But I also want to know what's between you and Ichiro. And don't tell me I imagined it."

The tip of her finger completed a slow circle around the rim of her teacup, and she savored a sip. Her now-damp lips pressed into a grim line. When she met his eyes, she held her shoulders back and didn't flinch. "My father arranged for me to marry Ichiro when I was ten years old. 'Every passing day raises the stakes for a willful aging woman,' he tells me. 'How dare you disgrace the Ono name?

It would be a fall from grace.'" She gave a raw impersonation of her father, but it was hard to miss the glint of hurt in her eyes. "My brothers hope I'll comply and honor my father's commitment, but I won't—whatever the cost."

The lifeless words drained her, leaving a hollow space in her soul. In all the years she'd rebelled against her father's wishes, had some part of her resigned to marrying Ichiro? She shook off the unwelcome feeling. Keane was unexpected, and even then, she never imagined more than a fleeting companionship. That chance encounter no longer felt like a coincidence. It felt destined.

Time wasn't a luxury they had, and he was too good a man not to know the truth. Her composure nearly broke. But she'd withheld the whole truth once before and ended up regretting it. When Keane stood without uttering a word, her pulse pounded out a battle beat. She wasn't sure what to expect, but he rounded the table and sat beside her.

Was he *not* going to bail? He inched closer until their elbows touched. His hand drifted over hers, his fingertips tracing abstract designs over her palm. The sensation—the touch of Midas—felt like fiery magic, felt like gold.

Her lips parted, but before she could divulge more, he tapped her lips with a free fingertip. "You don't have to explain." His green eyes leveled on her with such an affectionate intensity that she didn't dare protest.

Keane propped an elbow on the table and stroked his jaw as Ami floored him with a wide smile that made the yearning in his chest swell to an ache. "Can I ask you something?"

"Ask me anything." He fiddled with her fingers.

"What was with the lady?"

Lady? "You mean at the park?"

Her head bobbed. "You didn't seem to know her, but I over-heard part of the conversation. I thought . . . Well, you have held back with me. Maybe because you're polite and being businesslike, or maybe you're not attracted to me, but—"

A sharp laugh ripped from his mouth. "How can you say that?" He leaned closer, tipped her chin, and spoke in a private whisper. "I'm a man. What man wouldn't want to spend every waking minute with you? Look, attraction isn't the issue. It's taking heroic efforts for me not to close the distance and kiss you right here, right now."

Fire flashed in her eyes before fading. "What is it, then? My brother?"

"Niko was a surprise. Ichiro too." He swept a midnight tress behind her ear. "But I don't care. I'm trying to take things slow and not screw this up. I've learned too many lessons the hard way. And truth is, I've not always been as good as I ought to be."

"Because you're being a gentleman? Or for religious reasons?"

Keane cleared his throat. The last time a woman asked about his beliefs, his openness backfired. In retrospect, it turned out to be a blessing. But faith wasn't to be denied either. "Both. It's easy to lose yourself in meaningless experiences. Let's say I'm ready for some-thing serious, something more, that can take root and grow. You?"

"Both." She flipped her hand and slid it under his, squeezing his fingers. "I hold my own beliefs too. In life, especially in my line of work where inexplicable patterns repeat in unlikely places, I'd have to be blind not to see evidence pointing to a greater design. I'd like to learn more about your beliefs sometime. And your *more*."

The connection rumbling between them intensified. When he shifted toward her, every inch of his skin hummed. His lips feath-ered up her cheekbone, inhaling her exotic perfume. He breathed warm words into her ear. "Don't doubt our chemistry. Or why our paths crossed."

Her head bobbed, their cheeks brushing, before she drew back and met his gaze. "I told you my mom died an untimely death." She rubbed her palms back and forth over her thighs. "It was an earthquake."

He sucked in a sharp breath and stilled her hands with his, pressing to keep the connection. "I'm so sorry." A heavy beat passed. "I already told you I fight for my mom. And you chose geophysics for yours, didn't you?"

"You could say that." She shrugged. "I couldn't save her, but our research will matter. Maybe another little girl's mother will live because of it."

Hope glistened in her eyes as faith swelled in his chest. Trying to heal through her scientific work, she had suffered a childhood both without a mother and with the stoic Ono men.

"Tell me about your project."

"It's been an academic scavenger hunt of sorts." The corners of her closed lips rose in a tiny grin. "Most of Japan—and this area in particular—is full of buried clues. We scoured the coastline, trekked mountains, accompanied drillers out at sea, and trudged through numerous rice paddies to collect ancient soil samples. We've even examined tree-ring data."

Keeping a hand wrapped around hers, he sat back. "And what does the data say?"

"It tells an untold story."

He cocked his head. "Meaning?"

"Data markers resurrect past events modern people don't know about. Earthquakes sometimes happen centuries apart. Our team pieces together dust from the earth's innards to comprehend when and where those events happened. If it happened before—"

"It could happen again." He sat up straighter.

"Exactly." Her grin broadened, and her eyes brightened. "The team discovered layers of coarse sand studded with marine micro-fossils buried miles inland below a rice paddy. Similar deposits in the mountains. There's superfine clay, slick as oil, hiding deep under the seafloor off Sendai's coast. All that micro-evidence has been run through the academic rigors of the scientific process and carbon-dated and analyzed."

"That's huge." He leaned forward, resting elbows on his quads. "Are the results finalized?"

"Almost." Her delicate shoulders lifted.

"Keep me posted." The project had promise, importance, but a nagging reservation poked him deep in his gut. "But regardless of what the results show, think you'll ever have peace about your mom?"

His gaze traveled from the column of her smooth neck to her narrowed eyes. "Do you?" She was watching him.

"Absolutely. I'll see her again in heaven." He threaded his fingers through hers.

Her gaze lowered, fixing on their joined hands. "Will you teach me about heaven sometime?"

He relaxed back, his attention homing in on her, even as a new charge raced through his veins. "Anytime."

"Good. But can we visit the *onsen* first?" A dark spark smoldered in her eyes.

"Let's go." And despite his posture, he was rearing to go when the check arrived.

A rushed trip to the hotel's high-end boutique. A scarlet sweetheart-necked swimsuit for her—Keane's selection. Burberry plaid swim trunks for him. Directions from the shop clerk to the open-air *onsen* overlooking the river. Ami left Keane by the men's lounge, headed into the hall to the women's dressing room, and changed. Then she meandered through the spa's expansive communal wading area until she found the side door leading to the private pool he'd rented for the evening.

A polished wooden pavilion edged by heavy curtains provided cover for the steaming pool, but the vista beyond drew her eye past the structure. Stunning. The air was chilly. A breeze stirred up the scent of pine, damp earth, and early plum blossoms. The river gurgled as it rolled by, and the coppery sinking sun silhouetted a mountain in a deep green.

Wrapped in a luxurious black velvet robe matching her own, Keane stood soaking in the scene, as regal as a king. "So, what now?" His gaze drifted over her. "What's *onsen* etiquette?"

"We plunge in." She managed a nervous smile and, from under her lashes, watched him ogling her.

A tug on her robe belt, and the covering slipped to a heap. His grin widened, and he didn't bother to hide it. She tiptoed across the cool rock floor to the *onsen* and dipped in a toe to test the silky water. But the sight of Keane wrapped in black velvet made her pulse thrum as she eased down a step into the natural hot tub.

He took his time. Undoing his belt. Folding his robe. Setting his sandals by the door. Making her wait.

And she eyed his every movement, the honed physique she'd dreamed about, flawless and golden-tan skin. "Come on, Midas. Aren't you getting in?"

It only took a single request. Then, like a lion giving chase, he leapt over the step toward her. Water sloshed out of the pool. His swiftness dazzled her senses. Enveloped by the roiling water, he captured her in powerful arms, taking possession of her, spinning her around. And then his lips landed on hers, stealing her breath until he inched back with a ragged gasp.

He stared at her as he stumbled back and settled on a submerged granite bench. "I've wanted that, but I gotta take this slow."

She followed, nestling up next to him.

"And I could get used to being close." She rested her cheek on his shoulder. "It's peaceful here, isn't it?"

"Very. And relaxing. Thanks for bringing me. It was the perfect choice." He pressed a kiss to her forehead, let his hands tickle down her spine, and guided her to sit sideways on his leg. When her breath hitched in response, he beamed.

She didn't dare tear her gaze from his striking jade irises. Though her hands itched to connect, Ami respected his request. She ruffled his golden mane, dislodging the fine beading of mist shimmering like amber crystals on his hair, and then she snuggled closer and watched the sun melt into the skyline.

Keane shifted to his hip, setting her to his side so he could face her, his elbow on the slate edge and his head propped in his hand. "When do you finish school?" he breathed.

"School?" The quick shift left her reeling. But he'd said he wanted to take things slow enough to get it right. Most men didn't have the self-control to honor such a commitment, especially given this . . . force of attraction. But how could she pass on a heart-to-heart with a remarkable man? "Well, in June, if the project paper is approved."

"And then what? Will you work?" His expectant look sent her stomach spinning. "Or travel?"

"Then . . . I'd planned to continue the research, but traveling is an appealing option. When I have time, I love to free dive and—"

"Whoa." He raised a hand so fast droplets shivered over her. "You free dive?"

"It's just a hobby." Her shoulders edged up, and her brows pinched at his astonishment. "It's crazy, but I've always wanted to dive in Greece. Maybe I'll go there."

The sunset burned on the horizon like molten lava. Dusk was deepening, and a speckling of bright stars now decorated the heavens. Butterflies frolicked through her stomach every time his jade eyes lit on hers, but the lingering nervousness melted in the therapeutic hot springs. She couldn't have dreamed of a more magical afternoon and relaxed back into the cocoon of his arms and chest.

"Well, aren't you full of surprises?" he crooned. "It's not crazy though. Greece sounds incredible."

"Mm-hmm." She leaned to the side, angling her shoulders enough to check his face. "What about you? Any hobbies outside of fighting?"

A guilty, boyish grin quirked his lips. "Collecting cars. Expensive vintage cars."

"Really?"

"Really. I enjoy restoring them more than anything. Rediscovering the magnificence in the mundane has kind of been my motto."

"I like that. You *were* talking about the cars, right?" She toyed with his mussed hair, trailing her fingers down his neck to his shoulder.

He only chuckled, but her show of comfort must have stirred something. His eyes darkened. His splayed fingers brushed by her waist as he looped his arms around her. "So, back to your plans." His lips murmured against her cheek, making it impossible to think. "Why not do both—research and travel?"

His fingertips stilled. Her head craned back to rest against his shoulder, and he lowered his mouth, placing a tender kiss on the column of her neck. His touch held an aching sweetness—a reverence—she'd never known before.

Relishing the scent and taste and feel of her, Keane listened for that telltale snag in her breathing. The bombardment of sensory delights stunned him nearly as much as it seemed to overwhelm her. He glimpsed pure joy. Only Ami's trembling in his arms stopped him.

"Wow." He shook the trance from his head and hopped up onto the pool's ledge, putting a fair cooling distance between them.

Lord, the connection is intense.

And he'd completely misjudged his resolve. "What are we going to do about this? About us?"

"Enjoy every minute while we can. And then my university has a sister research facility in California." She wove her fingers between his. "One day, I might manage a visit to the States for our project."

"It's very important to you—the project?"

She jerked up her chin. The passion in her eyes shifted into something unruly. Those bold expressions made his heart buck against his ribs. "It is—both important and necessary. My father cut me off when I refused Ichiro and decided to finish graduate school. The deal with *Silk* helps cover tuition and living expenses."

"You're a feisty little thing." He tightened his hold on her. She was more headstrong than he'd imagined, and he rather liked that. But would her fiery temperament complement his strength? Or burn him? They lingered in a blissful bubble, but nothing could be clean and easy about getting involved with an Ono. And their lives were a world apart.

Even as dark thoughts trickled into his thought-flow like joy-dulling anesthesia, Pastor Ray's voice crawled out of the depths of his brain. *Doors open and shut opportunely.*

The first time he'd heard those words, Keane had assumed Ray was referring to the brutal path that had drawn him to karate, his so-called gift. Now, he wasn't so sure. If she even considered letting their relationship further develop, she needed to understand his past. If he hadn't done so already, Mr. Ono would do thorough security checks. And Keane wanted to be the one sharing his history with Ami.

"What is that?" she asked, stilling his hand from thumbing over a white scar on his forearm.

Teeth clenched together, he stretched his neck from side to side and swallowed. "A family mark. Growing up, well, I already told you about my dad. My mom was his favorite punching bag, but sometimes . . . he picked fights with me. Then I was a troubled kid who needed an outlet." He tapped on the scar again and checked her face.

"You don't have to—"

He ran a finger over her lips and shook his head, hesitation storming through his mind. "You asked about religion earlier, but you need to understand more."

He skimmed a hand over the water's surface, finding comfort in its warmth. "I was bent on learning how to fight to protect my mom and myself. The only martial arts classes around were Tuesday and Thursday nights in our church gym. She signed me up, and I got hooked. Got to know some of the church kids. They became my family. I'm not what I always ought to be, but—"

Ami crowded in to silence him with a light kiss. "What you've shared explains much about the source of your passion and power."

He smirked. "Ray used to say the most powerful hands hold love. I'm trying to live like that."

"Smart man, your church friend."

"He is, indeed."

She caught his fingers, anchoring his arms behind her at the small of her back, and closed the gap between them. "I suspected you were as much lover as fighter."

"If you only knew, angel." The glance he gave her made her expression grow hopeful. But when he placed a tender kiss on her forehead, she looked as if she'd been cheated. Her all-too-alluring pout hinted at as much. And, truth be told, he felt cheated too. One swift movement and he could draw her against him, satisfying a desire that pained him. But he was trying to live right. Be a gentleman. Like his mom raised him to be. *I'm battling the flesh, Father. Help me resist this sweet temptation.*

Time stretched on, and his pulse hammered. He willed it down. Ami was an amazing woman, and he wanted to touch her, every inch of her, in due time. Was that what was gnawing at him? His ability to keep control where she was concerned? Or the certainty that their involvement would rip her family apart? Why should he even care?

But he did. His family situation was a disaster, and he sure didn't want to cause her more conflict with hers. With the tips of his fingers, he stroked a lock of her hair around her ear and thumbed her bottom lip. "I know right from wrong." His voice cooled. "I'll be gone soon, and I'm all wrong for you. Trust me. Even if we don't want to believe it, *us* is a bad idea. Maybe we should call it a night before things go too far."

Was she too shocked to speak? Or immobilized by confusion? Ami gawked as he pushed free of her arms, and the darkness of night diminished the flame kindled between them.

Chapter 9

It took sheer willpower—no, some otherworldly discipline—to peel himself away and retreat after dropping her off at her building. His subconscious scoffed, but parting ways was no mistake. And, for all his well-intended gentlemanly behavior, he felt unfulfilled to the core.

Her pouting echoed through his mind all night, monopolizing his thoughts at *the* singular time when he most needed to focus on fighting. But a new day dawned and repainted the sky a pale pink. Like her lips.

Keane threw his head back, scrubbed rough palms down his face, and tried to erase the ridiculous grin contorting his face. But grinning was better than aching. Surely, *that* was the byproduct of the serious spell she'd cast over him. *Sweet Jesus, is Ami going to be my undoing?*

A current of electricity strong enough to power the signs in Tokyo's brightly lit Shibuya Crossing underscored their candid conversation. When was the last time he'd enjoyed someone's company so much? Had he ever? Had he confided too much? She *was* Niko Ono's sister.

An angry voice boomed from the kitchen. Keane jolted to his feet and was in the living room with balled-up fists before he realized he was alone, listening to LL Cool J. "Mama Said Knock You Out" erupted from his cell phone. A glance at the screen confirmed his suspicion. A smirking picture of Mark flashed.

"Jerk." Keane laughed into the receiver. "You better be glad you weren't here."

"Why's that? Planning to unleash the Lion this early?"

Another chuckle. "Yeah, something like that."

"Keane Temple, you sound—I don't know—chipper. Are you happy?"

A long beat passed as he circled the room, absorbing the question and Mark's astonishment. "Happy?" The sentiment rumbled through his brain as Keane paused at the window overlooking the bustling street. "Nope. Actually, I'm a bit blue."

Leaving Ami bereft on the doorstep had been right, no matter how difficult.

Mark made a sound meant to convey sympathy. "Well, don't fizzle out on me before the fight. Got it?"

"Got it, coach."

"Good. Ya wanna take a stab at the headlines on today's gossip columns?"

Keane switched the receiver from one ear to the other and moved to the low couch. "Not really."

"First one is 'A. Ono Worships the Temple.' But my fave is 'Is The Golden Lion Preying on *Silk*'s Swan?'"

Keane sank back into the cushions, scratched over his stubbled chin, and let out a long breath. "Absolutely. I've been *praying* for someone like her for years, but it can't happen."

"Well, it's a publicity score either way, but word is Niko Ono is livid."

"Over his arrangement? Ha, guess he realizes his brilliant plan did, in fact, backfire." He smoothed a hand over the velvet. "If he wanted to keep tabs on Ami, he should've escorted her to the park or shown up himself. As far as I'm concerned, it'll make for one heckuva bout."

"That's what I'm counting on, champ."

Dawn found Keane still smiling like a schoolboy. He'd known happiness in the past, even felt some measure of success. But Ami had tapped into some sweet vein of life he'd never before discovered. Thoughts and plans long filed away now bobbed through his brain, competing with darker realities and doubts. When he was with her in that fantastical bubble, the mundane faded. He could write off Ichiro. Her feelings toward him were clearly arctic cold. But Niko Ono and her father, the infamous real estate tycoon, would be paying him a visit. It was a matter of *when*.

He did a Google search for video footage of Niko Ono's most recent fight, a nail-biting knockout. Ono was as callous as fighters come. The master of the double-leg takedown. His sharp eyes reminded him of Ami's, but lifeless and dark, lacking her inner fire.

Keane eyed the clock. Was she okay? Or was she already feeling Niko's wrath? And what could she be thinking about Keane's behavior?

He took a fortifying sip of coffee, fingered through his phone contacts, and found her name. It rang for seemingly forever. His frown deepened with each ring, and his palm turned slick against the receiver. Someone answered on the other end, but the voice was muffled. "Hello?"

"*Moshi moshi.*" Ami's voice came out in a shaky hush.

"Ami? It's Keane. Are you all right?"

"Yes, this is she. I'm sorry, Professor, the connection is bad. How can I help you?"

His grip tightened around his iPhone. A man spoke in the background. Keane couldn't understand Japanese, but he didn't have to, to know Niko was tearing into his little sister.

"You're not alone," he said.

"I have family visiting right now, but I could drop by the lab midday."

"Lunch?" Keane proposed. She seemed to be holding it together, but for the first time, he heard her fragility. Concern coiled around his chest.

"That should be fine."

"Lunch it is. Can I pick you up?"

"Yes. And thanks for the call."

The disconnecting click left him pacing. At least she wanted to see him again after he'd balked last night. But at what cost? He fisted a handful of hair and tugged at the roots. The anger sparking through him only stoked more worry for Ami, threatening to become a full-blown fire.

Maybe he'd pushed his luck, but now he was in and had to fix it. And once his heart was invested, it was all or nothing, with fighting gloves ready. He halted his pacing. After unleashing a good one-two into the back of the futon, he regained a glimmer of sanity, changed his clothes, and headed outside to run off the residual madness.

The sky was serene blue. The trees were wrapped in flapping spring-green leaves. With happy music streaming through his iPhone, he hit the pavement.

Ami stared out the window with her back to Niko. How long could he preach about her defiance? She'd heard it all and redirected her attention to a tabby cat across the street licking a kitten clean. The slight curve teasing her mouth expanded to a full-blown smile when a muscular man in a baseball cap sprinted by and disappeared down a side street. The wild patch of golden hair below his cap made her heartbeat rush, and the blissful pounding in her ears drowned out Niko.

Her psyche only returned to Sendai when a strong hand squeezed her shoulder. "Ami, did you hear me?"

She faced Niko, her expression conciliatory. "I always do." She tucked her chin and manufactured an apologetic grin. *I just don't obey.* "I realize Keane Temple is a predator. But give me some credit. Didn't Father teach us that the riskiest plays often yield the greatest returns? And in the entertainment business, drama sells. My being seen with him was unexpected and has already boosted buzz for both of you. It's a win-win."

Niko's jaw muscle stopped twitching, and his posture began to relax. Sure, her opinion held no value for him, but as one kneading putty into pliancy, she had softened him by using their father's wisdom as a reminder. His grumbling gushed out in a loud exhalation. "I'll call Ichiro and make sure he understands. He can arrange another joint event."

"You are so crafty." And she was so strategically silky. "The bout is already sold out, but if you continue to play this right, the pay-per-view buys will break records."

His head jerked up as he preened. Then he crossed the room to where Mika sat studying in a corner chair. He tugged her ponytail back and overwhelmed her with a kiss. Then he raised his head and winked. "Ichiro might even get a wedding bonus."

"You are too generous." Ami fought her smirk, checked her watch, and turned on a heel for a shower. Time was ticking on the Ichiro bomb.

True to his word, Keane eased the black Bentley to her front door the moment she stepped outside. He swept around the car to open her door, gripping an elbow to steady her as she slipped into the passenger seat. "How did you manage to sneak out under your brother's nose?"

She chuckled. The sound as sweet as honey somehow highlighted a considerable hole in his life. "He is preoccupied at the moment."

His gaze cut her way in time to catch a blush. "So, sneaking out was unnecessary?"

"Exactly."

"I'm not complaining. I've been worried about you all morning."

"Really?" She winced while pressing her palms against her lap. "You kind of left me in the cold last night, left me wondering. But *you* are worried, aren't you? I'm confused."

He captured her hand, swept his lips over the back of it, and rested it on the stick shift under his. The look he gave her should say it all. He squeezed her fingers as he shifted into first and then second gear.

"Take a right here and then an immediate left."

"You have plans I don't know about?" He arched a brow.

"Absolutely. Stay on the boulevard until you see signs for the Port of Sendai and then turn right."

After surviving her brother's wrath, Ami was beside him again, relaxing back in the seat with the ocean spread out before them. Given her contented expression, she must be enjoying the carefree moment too.

She directed him toward a dockside café, and they enjoyed a light lunch followed by a rich, *crema*-topped cup of Lavazza Blue coffee. The obsidian-eyed adventure sat opposite him.

He ran his thumb over her hand, delighting when her body shivered. "So why are we here?"

She tipped her chin. She had to know her sass drove him wild. Several long beats passed as she gazed over the gleaming sapphire water where a freighter crawled on the horizon. "Because I want you to *know* me."

She nodded down the shore to a metal industrial building and a connected pier. "The warehouse is the research facility where I work and study. We also use the hydrographic survey vessel right there." She pointed out a sizeable navy-and-white boat bearing the name *Sapientia*. "To conduct seabed and seismic studies."

He glanced over her shoulder to a noisy group being seated behind her, but his attention gravitated back to her. "Fancy boat."

"Very. Very high-tech." She swiveled in her seat and motioned inland toward a stone cathedral with four steeples. "And my mother was—" Her forehead puckered with something hard to pinpoint.

"Ami?" A voice boomed from the table behind theirs. "I thought that was you."

"Hiro." She turned and spoke with too much warmth for Keane's liking.

As she stood, Keane glared at the young Japanese man embracing his lunch date. Wearing a wet suit, his hair a spiky mess, the guy was noticeably fit. He aimed a megawatt smile at Ami. Apart from a much older Japanese woman, the company at his lunch table included a strange mix of foreigners, all in dark neoprene suits.

"Keane." Ami stepped away and patted Hiro's back. "This is my good friend."

"No need for introductions, Ami." Hiro laughed. "The second I laid eyes on him, I knew it was the one and only . . . Thor."

Keane couldn't help chuckling. "You found me."

"Thor with his thundering hammer." Hiro joked, miming a hammer toss.

"Have you already gone to dive?" Ami asked.

"We had a late start. The boat goes out tomorrow, so we're only hitting the aquatic center today. Care to join?" Hiro's bright-eyed gaze snapped toward Keane's face.

Ami began to respond, but her body stilled when Keane stroked a hand along her shoulder. He couldn't help himself. He was laying claim, absorbing her personal space. His proximity set off that pink flush. From such a savvy woman, her innocent reactions continued to surprise him. He nudged her, wanting to see her in her element. "I'm game if you want to dive."

Hiro seemed to gauge her blush, his lips converting into a grin. "It's decided, then. You have to come."

Ami rolled her eyes. "I haven't said yes."

"But I know you well enough to know you won't say no." Hiro ruffled her hair with brotherly affection.

Chapter 10

The pungent smell of chlorine and the echoes of the cavernous space dominated the aquatic center. An Olympic-sized training pool. Springboards and ten-meter platforms for the high-diving fearless. A pillar-shaped, multistory indoor dive tank for those preferring subsurface escapades.

An observation deck ran the full length of one wall, and from the spectator stands, Keane sat by Hiro, waiting as Ami changed into her wet gear. Keane nodded toward the massive tank. "How deep is it?"

"Fifteen meters. That's roughly a fifty-foot plunge for you, right?" Hiro relaxed back against the wooden bench. "You're quite drawn to her, aren't you?"

Keane tented his fingers and stretched forward, elbows on knees. "Drawn." He inhaled as he considered the word, then shrugged. "Yeah, you could say that. She's my ambassador, which is convenient since staying away proved a challenge."

"I'm glad." Hiro shot him a conspiratorial smile and pointed past the diving platforms to a steel ledge at the top of the tank.

Alongside the other free divers, Ami appeared wearing a

full-body wet suit, hair tied into a sleek ponytail. The older lady from the lunch party was helping her secure a thick weight belt around her waist.

"Mr. Ono is a hard man, and Niko runs off anyone he cannot control." Seriousness dimmed Hiro's bright eyes. "You stand the best chance of fighting for her, I mean."

Keane nodded and perked up as Ami slipped into the water. Three windows revealed progressively deeper levels of the dive tank. He lowered his gaze and watched for her to pass the highest window.

Ami appeared in the window. She sank deeper, her hands trailing along some sort of taut vertical rope. Floating there, she looked so at ease, almost angelic, with her porcelain skin and jet-black ponytail fanning up and out behind her. Keane peeked at a digital clock. Her time in the tank was clicking toward two minutes, and she pushed deeper still.

Sheer madness. He jerked forward on the bleacher. He'd never seen such in person. He sprang to his feet, his heart rate increasing as he raked a hand through his hair. "Is she okay?"

"Of course. Ami is a world-class diver. She can stay down a long time." Hiro waved, and Ami's splayed hand returned the gesture through the middle window.

"How long has she been doing this?"

Hiro chuckled. Keane had the distinct feeling he was being chaperoned, but Hiro was too cheerful a guy to care. "Since she was a kid. It started as a coping mechanism."

Coping mechanism? Keane spun to his companion. "What do you mean?"

"When she got fired up as a kid, Ami would hold her breath until she passed out. That morphed into this."

"She's a fiery little thing, isn't she?" Keane gave a hard laugh.

"That she is."

"Three minutes." He paced from the side stands. "So, you think she does it—what? As an outlet?"

"Her life is beyond complicated. Here, she can exercise control. It's *more* than an outlet. The water is the *only* place she finds freedom."

"I'm not sure I understand." He gripped the railing, leaning over as if he could join her battles. "For me, competition brings a rush of adrenaline. It's not like that in the tank?"

"Everything slows down in there. Time. Even the diver's heartbeat decelerates. The body relaxes. It is hard to explain, but if you ever try it, you would see." Hiro drummed his hands on the wooden bench seat. "If you *will* your body to surrender into an unnatural experience, let the water pull you deeper, you find this insane freedom. Ami seeks the freedom."

Haloed in water droplets, she broke through the surface, pushed up onto the ledge encircling the pool, and began toweling off. Keane stilled, unable to tear his gaze off her trim figure. She was panting. The clock stopped. The time blinked twice in electric red. Just under four minutes. Who could survive without drawing air for that long?

"Incredible. She's amazing."

"She is," Hiro said. For the first time since meeting him, Keane didn't feel like Hiro was his chaperone. "Tough too. She's had it rough, way worse than she'd ever admit, but I can tell she likes you. Unless you make yourself worth the risk, do her a favor and walk away now. And if you can't leave her alone, handle her with care."

Keane laid a hand on Hiro's shoulder and looked him in the eyes. "Understood, my friend."

Chill time in the tank followed by a steaming hot shower left Ami in a state of euphoria. But Keane was waiting, so she pushed through the happy daze and hurried to get dressed. What must he think of her free-dive habit? Would he find it crazy? Peculiar? At least, he now knew an important part of her. Free diving hadn't been a part of the day's plan, but neither was Niko's harsh tongue-lashing.

And once again, the water was a guaranteed, sweet escape. She closed her eyes, reliving it. Suspended in the tank for such an intense stretch of time made her feel the delicate balance between life and death. One wrong breath in too-deep water could be fatal, but long ago, she'd learned to control her breathing, rein in nervous tendencies, and listen to the water's resonant whir.

As Hiro disappeared to attend to his out-of-town guests, a sharp *ping* cut through the humid, pool-scented air. Keane slid his phone from his jeans pocket. A fresh group text from Hans lit up the screen.

HANS: Dinner at seven? Ella wants to go out.

Another *ping*.

PAULO: Definitely in.
KEANE: Will let you know.
PAULO: What does that mean?
KEANE: I'm with Ami.
PAULO: Then do NOT text right now. BAD idea.
KEANE: Let me rephrase: Just watched Ami hold her breath for four minutes during a free dive. Btw, you know I never discuss private matters.
HANS: Bring her with you.

Keane texted a maybe before Ami's velvet-soft voice called his attention.

She stood there, her hair swept into a low damp ponytail, her cheeks glowing hot-pink from the shower. She clasped her hands, but they still shook as she whispered. "Am I crazy?"

"Absolutely. But it's quite appealing." His teasing seemed to squash the trepidation straining her face. He snagged her hand, drawing her closer, his voice a rumble in his chest. "Ignoring Ichiro's existence, how is it you're still single?"

"Am I?" She inched closer, a fleck of fire glimmering in her eyes.

His pulse began a lively trot. He caught her waist, pulled her into a loose embrace, and nuzzled his nose up the curve of her neck and along her jawline before he remembered where he was. With a sharp breath, he stepped back. "No."

She flashed a coy smile. "Good."

"So, what does one do after free diving?"

"Tea."

"Tea? Would you be up for dinner too? Hans invited me— *us*—for dinner. It'll be his wife and Paulo too."

Ami shrugged her shoulders and pursed her lips. "Sounds perfect. One sec, and I'll text you a pin for the teahouse." Her fingers skipped around the phone. When his phone chimed with the incoming message, she slid hers into her purse. "Ready?"

"Then off we go." He extended a hand. "Do you want to tell Hiro bye?"

"Already did." She twined her fingers around his and followed him through the door.

The afternoon sun highlighted Keane's golden mane and turned him into an altogether glorious sight. He sauntered toward the parked Bentley and opened the passenger door with sweeping panache. Ami crossed the sidewalk and eased into the seat. It wasn't until the car door snapped shut that she stirred from her reverie. She found Keane smiling at her, his eyes aglow with some private laughter.

"What?" And why were they still parked?

"That's what I was asking. Your mind was elsewhere. What are you thinking?" He cocked a knowing eyebrow.

Mild embarrassment bubbled through her. "Hmm. Nothing specific. I guess I like hanging out with you." She waved between them, then turned her head to the window in hopes of hiding the heat flooding her face. How could she be so obvious? Was she even a tad apprehensive? By nature, free divers were wired to be aware of their breathing, but even now, she felt her measured breaths grow quicker and shallower, his clean masculine scent teasing her.

The mysterious command he held over her was thrilling, but in the vehicle's private confines, she felt its danger too.

"Is that all?" He touched her chin and turned her attention back to him.

She reached for his hand, her fingernails skating across its back before her fingers twined around his. "Honestly?" Growing up in a house of men, she'd had to be tough, but his patient nod encouraged her to share her private truths. "When you're around, it's like being high up in the Chilean mountains. The air is too thin. My head spins. No one has done that for me in a long time. No one in my family watches me dive—gets what it means to me. No one realizes the joy it brings. Thank you for going."

He lifted her hand and brushed his lips to the back of it, the contact sending ripples of comfort throughout her body until he let go to start the car. "Of course. Do you ever compete?"

"I used to. Not anymore." She gave a casual shrug as he followed the pin and drove to the teahouse. "Free diving is like leading a double life. I love geophysics. The research is satisfying and important, but diving is my passion. Hiro and the club—they're my people.

The sport can be dangerous, but we've developed trust and take care of one another."

"Takes crazy to get crazy?" he asked with camaraderie.

"Something like that." Her lips twitched as she failed to suppress a grin. His knowing chuckle rumbled straight down her spine. "The tank's different, but for open-water dives, I focus on the surroundings to relax and lengthen my dive time." She paused. "You mentioned God."

"I did." His grip on the steering wheel tightened as his gaze flicked her way before returning to the road.

"Diving muffles the world's noise. That forces me to zero in on the underwater world, filling me with a divine sort of peace that surpasses everything else I know. Does your faith bring you that kind of peace?"

"It sure does. And so much more." He loosened his hold on the steering wheel and rested back, a serene smile smoothing his expression. "I'm a fighter. Not every day is peaceful or perfect, but yeah, I know peace through my faith. Would you like to hear a story?"

"I guess so." She knitted her fingers together in her lap, and as their drive meandered through the city toward the teahouse, he began sharing about the beloved boy sent to save the world.

"He lived a perfect life. A life without sin before he died and was resurrected. The price of sin is death, but—"

"Wait." She turned in her seat and clapped her palms together. "Eternal life is a gift to those who confess their sins and believe." Whoa. Where had that come from?

His gaze swiped her way. Was it confusion or astonishment creasing the corners of his eyes? "You've heard the story?"

Hazy memories took shape. "My mother read the Romans Road to me as a child. She told me to start back there if I ever lost my way."

"Really?"

"Yes. How could I have forgotten that? Those verses were her favorites." Sadness squeezed her heart. "My father probably threw away her books. Goodness, she had a Bible, Keane. I was so young when she passed away."

When his phone beeped, his eyes flicked to the car's navigation map, and he eased the Bentley to a stop outside a simple wooden house. "Sounds like your mother was a seed-planter. You know, sometimes memories hang out until we're ready for them." He cradled her hand, giving it a compassionate squeeze.

Her attention veered to the teahouse. "It's a lot to think about." And she'd never been quick to believe and needed time to sift through memories of her mom.

"It is. But you'll know when you know. And when you do, you'll have the courage to take the next step."

She turned back to him with a nod. "Can I ask a favor?"

"Anything, Miss Ono."

"Think you could summon your driver for the ride home?"

Head tilting to one side, Keane looked amused. "Miss Ono, do you not trust yourself with me?"

She cleared her throat, giving her a moment. "Let's call it insurance."

He flashed a charming grin. "Ask and you shall receive."

Keane pushed out of the car in pursuit of his exquisite guide and, as they entered the historic structure, rested a hand on the small of her back. Tea was a serious art form in Japan, and the teahouse was designed not to detract from the traditional experience. Small windows. *Tatami* mat floors. Air steeped in an earthy-sweet aroma.

Ami bowed to the hostess, explained something in Japanese, and steered Keane out a side door into a quaint garden.

"This place is called the *roji*."

"The *roji*." He soaked in the peaceful experience. A palette of moss greens and gray rock washed under warm afternoon sunlight. The soft crunch of pea gravel underfoot. An ancient tree, maybe the great-grandmother of Sendai's vibrant treescape, stood sentinel over a lone limestone bench.

"Hans's wife, she is coming tonight?" Ami settled onto the bench.

"Her name's Ella. And she will like you, which means she'll make sure you like her too." Keane bent over, scooped up a handful of gravel, and sifted it from one palm to the other. He separated a brown object from his fistful, leaving only the pebble in his hand and holding it out. "What's this?"

Ami leaned over, her warm breath tickling his palm. "A seed." Her gaze flicked up to meet his. "One of the *zelkova* seeds. That's lucky. A good seed for a good man."

He shook off the compliment and said nothing as an elderly waitress delivered a bamboo tray containing an iron teapot, two ceramic cups, and a decorative bowl of flower-shaped candies in shades of pink, purple, and yellow. Keane slipped the tree seed into his pocket and sat beside Ami. "I've already told you—I'm not perfect."

She poured him a cup of tea and lifted it toward him. Her fingers barely brushed his, but at that feather-soft contact, electricity zipped throughout his body. "Who said I want perfect?"

Pinned with a look that made his mouth go dry, Keane sampled his tea. Slightly bitter and piping hot, but rich and satisfying. The corners of his mouth twitched up. No one else was in the garden, so he set the teacup on the tray and dragged his thumb across her shimmering pink lips. They parted at the touch to release a sigh.

He had a dominating build, but he was fast when he wanted to be. His mouth made quick work, anchoring her lips—velvet-smooth and warm from the tea. He lost himself in the delicious moment he'd longed for all day.

An intrusive string of cackles shattered the reprieve and jerked him back from his little trip to heaven. His lips ached as if he'd taken a dirty uppercut to the smacker. The waitress had returned and stood absorbing the scene, a hand over her mouth to screen her amusement and too-bright eyes. She had the happiest eyes and made no attempts to hide her gawking.

Cheeks aglow, Ami struck up a humorous conversation with the eavesdropper. He wished he could understand, but it must all be at his expense. After the exchange and an invasive once-over by the waitress, he recaptured Ami's attention.

He jerked his thumb toward the intruder. "What was that all about?"

She tucked her lips together, but a giggle still escaped. "Isn't it good to keep a man on his toes and wondering?" With an innocent look, she taunted him before clarifying. "I told her we were business partners."

He wasn't sure what he'd expected and there must be more she didn't translate, but being business partners sure wasn't it. "And she believed you?"

He glanced at the older woman. Every wrinkle on her face curved with joy.

"Not exactly." Another bubble of mirth escaped before Ami composed herself. "She said she was available to do business too if Mr. Temple likes an old tigress."

The waitress gave him an affirming nod and continued to try to hide her amusement by shielding her mouth with a hand.

He stood, approached the wrinkle-faced woman, and stunned her with a bear hug.

After taking turns doing far too much bowing, he tucked a wad of yen, more than enough to cover their beverages, under the cast-iron teapot and captured Ami's elbow in his hand. By the time they cleared the ancient garden and emerged into the modern busyness of a city street, he felt as if they'd stepped through a portal from some bygone time.

The evening sun angled spears of copper light through the city. Like its ambient glow, Keane's kindness toward the old woman warmed Ami's heart. Not one of her brothers would have spared a moment for the elderly waitress. With a contented breath, Ami reached for his hand. It was always toasty compared to hers, and his rough palm wrapping around her fingers felt nice.

The Bentley waited at the curb, but Keane punched out a message to the driver, passed the car, and tugged her along for a stroll.

Ami nudged him with her elbow. "Back to Ella?"

"Ella." He chuckled, his eyebrows lifting. "Ella is an experience you'll have to witness for yourself. Hans is sharp. Very sharp. Very witty. And Ella handles him like no other."

They ambled along to Fin, letting an hour slip away. Swank and sterile, the restaurant's furnishings created a complete contrast to the century-old teahouse. The slate flooring merged with the architectural bones of modern steel. An unobstructed column of water—an eye-catching central aquarium—connected floor and ceiling. And in that tank cruised an unconcerned shark.

Swathed in head-to-toe white, a hostess led them through a maze of bubbled glass tabletops to their waiting party.

"Ami! I'm thrilled to finally meet you." The Irish accent somehow fused the sweetness of honey with the sting of the bee, but the warm welcome engulfed her before she narrowed in on the speaker. A character, Keane had called her. And Ami saw it in her eyes. Ella was a fairy-sized firecracker with wispy red hair, crystal-blue eyes, and clothing as colorful as it was eccentric.

"Glad you could join, my friend," Hans remarked as they sat. His expression was neutral, but laughter glimmered in his eyes. "We thought you might have taken the wrong train."

"I've avoided trains as of late." Keane didn't elaborate. Instead, he shifted his focus to Ami. An electric tingle heated her as his fingertips grazed a track along the small of her back. He tugged her waist closer to him.

"Understandable. Yet I believe that uncharacteristic train trip delivered you into a pleasing predicament." Hans smirked. "Am I right? Or am I right?"

A long beat passed. What was she missing?

"Men." Ella sighed, crowding toward Ami for a tête-à-tête. "Why do men try to take credit for fateful coincidences? Well, I'll tell you. They like to *think* they're in control—ha."

Ami shrugged and shot Keane a searching look.

"Keane Temple." Ella's face scrunched as her head tipped to one side. She let out a low whistle. "You didn't tell her?"

Something like guilt—or maybe regret—rippled across his handsome face before smoothing into something more vulnerable. Ami's cheeks flash-heated. He reached out and twisted a lock of her hair around a finger. "The day we met at the train station? Me being in a train station at all? Hans had set me up, and then you picked me up." A smile softened his sculpted cheeks. He stretched and wrapped a muscular arm around her shoulder. "His trick became my gain."

"Or perhaps it *was* fate?" Hans paused as if to savor his words.

"Perhaps." Keane wagged his head. "Call it whatever you want. Whether life goes—or doesn't go—our way, the one thing we *can* control is our response. So, I went with it." He took a long pull from his water glass before returning it to the table. "And now Hans thinks he's a matchmaker."

Wow. This lighthearted Keane was manageable. It was the serious, sexy Keane that made Ami's soul somersault.

"Yes, he does." Ella tossed her arms out. "Men."

"Men, what?" Paulo's Brazilian bass cut straight through the restaurant clamor.

Hans and Keane got to their feet, gave Paulo side hugs, and greeted his date. Ami covered her mouth with her closed fist to stifle her amusement. Keane slid back into the seat beside her, nuzzled her neck, and whispered. "What is it?"

She let her gaze ease toward Paulo's date, a very thin, bottle-blonde Japanese woman. "I know her."

Keane sipped his water and narrowed his eyes over the rim of the glass. "And?"

"And . . ." Ami shrugged, flashed a this-could-get-interesting kind of smile, and then recast her attention. "Izumi, how have you been?"

Izumi's eyes widened. The young woman bowed and mumbled a rushed response in Japanese.

"I'm glad you're well." Out of politeness to their company, Ami kept with English. "It has been quite some time. Small world, right?"

No need to mention the girl had been one of Niko's flings. Discomfiture reddened her cheeks, and her sensual stance slipped for the first time since she'd approached the table.

"Yes, small world," Izumi remarked in an equally small voice. She settled into the seat opposite Hans.

Paulo relaxed back, tossed an oval-shaped sliver of bruschetta into his mouth, and draped an arm around his date. The way he touched her radiated raw physical possession, no trace of affection. "Keane swears off ladies before big fights. Always has, until you. And you are keeping our teammate busy these days."

Was he trying to accuse her? Provoke her, even? Or was his statement meant to be reassuring?

Whatever Paulo's intention, Ami smoothed on a smile. "Business keeps us both preoccupied."

"Ah, yes. Work and pleasure. Pleasure and work." He untangled his arm from Izumi and rested his forearms on the table. Then he cocked a thick eyebrow. "I also hear you have a thing for diving deep."

Keane bristled at the overt double entendre. He began to growl a response, but she squeezed his forearm, then winked. "I do. And I'm so glad I could share my hobby—it's a labor of love, really—with Keane."

Silence overtook the table. Their gazes bored into her until a sharp laugh erupted from Ella and Ami's taut muscles loosened.

"Well played." Ella threw a mock punch at Keane. "I like your woman."

"Me too." Keane brushed a warm kiss to Ami's temple.

And the conversation flowed until the waitress delivered volcanic rock platters laden with meticulously arranged delicacies. Slices of pan-seared Kobe beef. Medleys of spring vegetables glistening under a salty-sweet marinade wash. Bowls of mounded sticky rice. Sashimi wedges arranged like a flower. A bottle of glacier water.

Paulo replenished the crystal glasses around the table and swigged his own. "Temple, perhaps you met your match. You are a lucky guy. Do not screw it up."

He knocked a fist on the table as if finalizing his ruling. Whatever awkward tension there was at his and Izumi's arrival had faded.

"Indeed, I am lucky." Keane's eyes screamed sheer adoration as he tugged Ami to his side, superheating every cell of her being.

Just great. She ducked her head, trying to slink behind her hair as a flush surged up her neck and face to exhibit how he affected her. Her gaze roamed everywhere but his direction until his fingertips toyed with the hair at her nape, melting her nervous energy into a profound awareness that they now sat as a couple, a unified force for all to see.

Izumi grew quiet—too quiet—as she worked not to fumble her fork. With her thin red lips sealed together, one corner of her mouth turned up in a cruel twist. A nagging seed of suspicion wedged in some deep part of Ami's brain. Could it be a coincidence one of Niko's former flings had found a seat at this table?

Niko had a habit of stringing women along. Young, impressionable girls spellbound by fame and blinded by flashing lights. Keane shattered that mold. Niko would try to convince her otherwise, but Keane was grounded in a way her brother never had been. The two fed on different fuels. One consumed fame. One endured it. Was she right to think Keane fought for family? Still battled for reasons more noble than his own glory?

Ella slapped the tabletop. "Indeed, my fat fanny." She stood, gripped Keane's chin in her hand, and stared into his eyes like a mother scolding a child. "The world knows you as *The* Temple, even The Lion, but their perception is incomplete and twisted. Gloss. Glamour. Shifting smoke. It's easy to get swept up in that." Then she spoke to Ami, waving as if swatting away a cloud of smoke and a crowd of mirrors. "None of that satisfies for long. Keane is real. Raw passion inside the ring and out, but a good and humble man, Ami."

Ami broke eye contact with Ella in time to catch something flicker in Keane's expression. Embarrassment? How could this man *not* enjoy being the center of attention?

"Not always," he countered with a headshake. "But thanks for that."

"A good man with a lethal upper cut." Paulo angled himself to rest a hand on Izumi's thigh.

"Just a good man," Ella repeated. "One who wants to satisfy his woman and—what?"

Paulo chuckled.

With her lips still compressed, Izumi managed a smile.

"All right now. Calm down, fiery lass." Hans tugged at her arm, his bright eyes aglow.

"I am calm." Ella patted Keane's cheek and winked. "Fighting men need fighting women." Grinning, she drank her water and hushed up.

What an amazing atmosphere with such easy banter. But a serious undercurrent tugged on the conversation. Ami liked Ella a lot. And Paulo and Hans, blood or not, were Keane's brothers. Except for Izumi, this gathering was an unconventional family, and Ami had just been introduced. This was no small thing.

The rich meal comforted her, leaving her cheerful and warm. But one glance at the affectionate glow in Keane's jade eyes kindled her deep hope. Could everyone see how smitten she was? But he would be gone much too soon. How would life roll on then?

Paulo and Izumi lay low the rest of the evening, mumbling together, an island unto themselves, before excusing themselves for the night. Hans insisted on picking up the check. He and Keane had a side conversation while Ella cornered Ami.

"Fight for him," Ella commanded.

Confusion clouded Ami's mind. "Pardon?"

Ella stood and circled the table to sit beside Ami like her new best friend. "Keane needs you. He hasn't taken a serious interest in anyone in a long time. Relationships aren't easy for him."

Ami's gaze cut to Keane as he pounded out a text. "But he could have anyone."

"I've known him for seven years, and you aren't just anyone. He doesn't want to—look, fight for him. Publicly, if you have to."

Chapter 11

Outside the restaurant, a Bentley Bentayga SUV idled at the curb. Keane had handled her request, and a chauffeur, sporting a Burberry driver's cap and the formal glove-handed demeanor of another time, opened the door as they approached. He guided Ami ahead of him, giving her the distinct feeling he was trying to screen her from rapid-fire camera flashes and eager fans in the chic dining district. The driver snapped the door shut and circled the car. Inside the posh confines, the spark of desire smoldering over dinner roared to a full blaze.

"You okay?" Keane asked.

What had Ella meant? Ami nodded, but her gut fluttered. She never wanted to push too hard, especially not so soon. "Is it a safe guess we'll make the cover of some magazine?"

"Probably, and I hope that doesn't become too problematic for you."

She let him pull her back against his solid wall of body. She liked the way she fit into his powerful arms, finding comfort in his warmth as her back molded to his chest. Through the oversized moon roof, her gaze fixed on the star-studded sky as he leaned in to press a kiss to her temple.

"Me too." She tipped her head back to examine his face. A satisfied grin stretched out his lips before they sealed over hers, his steel-hard arms anchoring her. He deepened the kiss until the SUV eased to a stop. Her frenzied thoughts throttled forward. But when he thumbed over her bottom lip, his hand cupping her chin, his intensity immobilized her.

The tap of knuckles sounded on the privacy window followed by a ten-second lag, and then the back door opened wide. "Mr. Temple, we have company with cameras. Three cars back. Silver Audi."

"Thanks." Huffing, Keane straightened in the seat and stripped Ami of the heat she'd been enjoying. "It's been a good day, hasn't it?"

"Better than good."

A crooked grin worked on his lips, teasing her to wonder what he was thinking. Several beats passed. "I want to come in—just hang out longer. I'd planned to, if you'd let me. But . . ." He jerked his head toward the unwelcome company, his lips pursed.

"At least Niko isn't here. That's something." Not a trace of humor thawed her voice as she offered Keane his hand. "Will you escort me to the door, *my* Temple?"

His eyebrow rose, those jade eyes glowing like kryptonite. "My Temple?" He tried out her words, lifted the hand to his lips, and planted a kiss on the tender underside of her wrist. "I could get used to hearing that. And, of course. It would be my honor."

The walk to the front stoop was too short and quiet. Ami wasn't sure if that was because they were being watched or because the man had the confidence of a king. But whatever *it* was, it heightened her awareness to Himalayan extremes. His smell. His genteel patience. His dauntless possession of her hand. His matching her stride. And his lionlike way of circling her.

"I'm going to kiss you now." His eyes radiated such seriousness that she almost missed his gaze dart to the paparazzi's car before fixing on her lips. He caught her by the elbows. She shivered from the contact, knowing the camera was aimed in their direction and clicking away. Even that wasn't going to temper the moment.

"Yes, please."

With a swift tug, he cradled her body in his arms and crowded into her space. "I want to kiss you senseless. Until your knees tremble." His lips skittered up her cheek toward her ear, coaxing a moan from her mouth. "You're so beautiful, and one day—when the time is right and you're mine—we will have that. Just. Not. Tonight."

She drew back a fraction of an inch to check his face. She was lost in the wilderness of those green eyes. They spoke of disappointment. "Not tonight," she repeated. Even she could hear the dejection darkening her voice.

Keane placed a gentle peck on her forehead. "They *are* watching."

"So?" She let her lips curl into a playful grin. "Feels like you are about to cheat me."

"Does it now?"

For such a towering, muscular man, Keane could move lightning fast. With the grace of a dancer, he twirled her around on the front porch before closing in for a final kiss. All-consuming, it seized her body, mind, and soul.

Keane released her lips without moving away, mumbling against her skin. "Still feel cheated?" His voice husky, he donned a cheeky grin.

"No, not cheated. Expectant."

Salt-N-Pepa's "Push It" boomed through the pitch-black. At the first drumbeat, Keane bolted out of bed. It only took a few chords to realize what it was. Even at the brutal hour, seeing his pastor's face appear on his cell phone with the blaring rap music cheered his soul. Mark had outdone himself with that combo.

"Hello. Ray?" Keane yawned, his voice gritty with sleep.

"You couldn't give me a heads-up?"

"It's four in the morning here. My head shouldn't be up." Keane raked a hand through his sleep-mussed hair and cleared his throat. "So, guess news travels as fast as they say, huh?"

"Indeed. They say to keep your friends close and enemies closer, but you dating Niko Ono's sister is all sorts of beautiful twistedness. Look, as your old friend, I have to ask it. Are you sure—without any doubt—she's not a pawn?"

The swan was no pawn.

Still, his memory replayed their passionate PDA last night. He'd been delighted to see her eyes inviting more, even as the door clicked shut behind her. Ami was the fulfillment of his every fantasy. Scholarly passion. Kindhearted. Athletic prowess. Rosebud lips. A match made in heaven. Things had happened fast, but his mind was set. Finally.

"And who says candor's a virtue?" Keane chuckled. "You know I don't do flings."

"That, I know all too well. You're the most disciplined, thoughtful man I know. I've never seen you as much as blink without considering how it might impact your life thirty years down the road."

That was the truth. He spent too much time thinking and not enough time living. "And for the record, I'm trying to be on my best behavior, but man, the draw of the flesh is fierce. Pray for me, Ray. It's hard. Really hard."

"So, I can assume there's more than meets the eye with Miss Ono?"

Even on the opposite side of the globe, Keane could hear his friend's grin in that tone. His mouth had gone dry. "*More.* The word seems inadequate when it comes to Ami Ono."

Pale light greeted Ami as her eyelids fluttered open. Sunday morning started on a residual high following the best Saturday night—ever. No one had kissed her with such abandon. A silly grin tugged at her well-kissed lips. She yawned, stretched under the plush down comforter, and sat up.

Down the hall came muffled audio from the television followed by Mika's uncomfortable laughter. Ami wrapped in a robe and padded to the living room.

"Morning."

On her knees, Mika lazed against the sofa's arm, clutching the remote. She tried and failed to squash her nervous amusement.

"What?" Ami spoke too loudly, anxiety rising at her friend's stiff body language.

With raised eyebrows, Mika tipped her forehead toward the television. "You made the news again. And not just entertainment news. A headliner."

Following her roomie's lead, Ami stared at her televised profile. The paparazzi had landed a goldmine, catching her with Keane in a cozy embrace. "I sure did. Oh, my goodness."

Unfolding her legs, Mika stood and circled around Ami to check her face. "What are you thinking?"

"To be honest, I expected it. Has Father called yet?"

"No, but Niko has."

Ami steeled herself. "And he's on his way."

"Uh-huh. Need some tea?"

"That'd be perfect. *Mugi-cha*, please." Ami mustered up a look that—she hoped—conveyed something like gratitude.

As Mika slipped into the kitchen, Ami picked up the remote control and replayed the recorded footage. Entangling her in his arms, Keane had possessed every fiber, every dream, of her being. Seeing herself on television always felt surreal. Just watching brought a fresh flush to her cheeks.

"Come what may." A satisfying freedom accompanied the words as Mika handed over an earthenware cup.

"You are certain he isn't playing a game?"

"Positive. Ella, Hans's wife, even confirmed as much last night." Ami's heart softened anew at Ella's parting whisper. "*He's never been like this. The man is glowing, and as difficult as this relationship may be for you, he is worth the challenge. You are a lucky lady.*"

"So, you wouldn't rewind if you could?" Mika's eyes narrowed as she took careful sips from a Niko Ono memorabilia mug.

"Absolutely not. The connection is more than I ever imagined, even if I have to fight to have it my way."

The doorbell dinged her out of a daydream. Pulse humming, she hurried down the stairs to the foyer. No one lingered at the front door. She leaned through the doorframe and scanned the street before spotting a turquoise box a step beyond the threshold. She snatched up the gift.

Yes, *more* truly was inadequate for Ami Ono. During the wee hours of the morning, Keane had racked his brain, wanting to surprise her. If he was in for the long haul, then he'd lavish her with the best. Dinner wasn't enough. Time to step up his game and cull himself from the crowd.

As a favor, get-it-done Mark agreed to carry out the details while Keane pounded through a special sparring session with Hans.

Keane needed the workout. But more than the workout, he needed to prove his focus remained intact.

Six practice rounds. Sweat-slick skin. Battle-taut muscles. Thirty minutes of one-on-one sparring between friends proved to be telling.

Hans swiped a towel across his forehead. "She's affected your game."

"Seriously?" Keane choked past mild panic. "I thought it was good."

"I did not say the effect was bad." Hans tossed him a sly smile.

"We've been friends for a long time. Shoot it to me straight."

"It was better than good. That woman is your magic weapon."

Whew. Keane grinned. "Did Ella say anything last night? Women are so insightful about this sort of thing."

"What? You don't like my insight?" Hans pressed a hand to his chest, feigning a wounded ego, then chuckled. "Ella likes Ami. She said she'd kill you in your sleep if you found excuses to make this not work."

His grin stretched. "Sounds like her. Is that it?"

"Nah. She said you need to share with Ami. Open up. That will be a good experience for both of you."

Sounded easy, right?

The "immortal embrace" of Keane Temple and the Ono Swan graced news headlines. The astronomical ratings and ticket presales dampened Niko's fury. SkyPerfecTV subscriptions soared to an all-time high only three hours after the airing of Keane and Ami locked in a steamy kiss. Both Niko's and Keane's careers would benefit. Ichiro's calls had ceased, which was a plus, but Ami's future remained uncertain. And though it was a very bad sign her father had not yet called, Keane's curious gift made her forget her nagging concerns.

Sendai's high-end shopping district was a sensory experience. The storefronts dazzled. The occasional tree injected a healthy dose of nature into a corridor of glass, gloss, and haute-couture consumerism. A contagious harmony materialized from the clack of stilettos, shuffle of traditional sandals, screech of hangers dragging along clothes racks, and singsong voices of happy shoppers.

The morning left her wondering, but she wasn't sure *what* she should be wondering. The doorbell had rung just past eight. The bird's-egg-blue box was not from Tiffany's, as she'd first presumed. Inside the palm-sized package was a note written in an elegant hand: *Redeem your prize.* On the reverse of the thick linen card stock was an address. What adventure could he have planned? And where was he?

Now she found herself fidgeting at a streak-free glass counter displaying the Takashimaya department store's finest jewelry. When she presented the card, the salesgirl erupted in giggles. The jubilant worker dipped a bow and punched digits on a security pin pad, opened a storage vault concealed behind a mirrored wall, and retrieved a bundle of packages wrapped in velvety white paper.

Ami shifted the bundle in her hands and inspected it from all angles. Two larger boxes and one small. Should she tote the boxes home and open them there? Her brow twitched as she contemplated how to proceed.

"It is from your friend, Mr. Temple," the young attendant explained, pointing to a doorway in the store's back wall. "Please use our dressing room to change. A car is waiting outside for you."

Carrying the stack of packages, Ami made her way to the dressing room, slid the metal lock into place, and then tore off the wrapping paper and box lids with a gasp of delight. Keane had gifted her with a rather outdoorsy ensemble. How did he know what size she wore? And where could they be going? Her curiosity piqued, Ami changed and rushed outside.

A car was inaccurate. Outside of Takashimaya were three identical black Mercedes. They inched along the curb in single file like a parade of glossy black ants. Ami stared, clueless as to which car to approach. Then the first car's back door cracked open from within.

Keane never stepped out, but she spotted his unruly golden locks ducking away from the entrance. Hurried strides carried her across the pavement, and she was in, enveloped in his masculine scent. Like clockwork, the door snapped shut behind her, and the cars rolled off, jockeyed order, and then split into different directions to divert the paparazzi.

She'd escaped through some otherworldly wormhole and, given the getaway, intended to chase the sparks still smoldering within her.

"Where to?"

At her whisper, he floored her with a grin. "No doubt you underestimate how much I love it when you blush." He scooted closer and captured her hand in his rugged palm. "How is it you look as lovely in a flannel button-up and hiking boots as you do on that magazine cover?"

"The gold bracelet helps." She displayed her gleaming wrist for him to examine. "Thank you, by the way. It's beautiful."

"You are most welcome." He seared a kiss on the underside of her wrist.

"You're not going to tell me where we are going?"

"No need." He tipped his head toward the Miyagi Museum of Art as the car began to slow, seemed to confirm no one had tailed them, and exited with a gentlemanly hand extended to assist her.

They made a whirlwind trip through the museum, pausing long enough to explore the Van Gogh exhibition, the paintings more amazing than their printed counterparts. Thick layers of paint created bewitching depth and exposed new subtleties, even in the more familiar masterpieces. Keane appeared as in awe as she felt. She could spend hours hand in hand with him, strolling the art-lined corridors, but the man on a mission kicked into gear.

Tucking her arm under his and holding it against his body, he steered from the exhibitions toward a maintenance hallway, passed through a back door, and slipped into an idling oolong-gray Audi 8. The Audi carried them out of Sendai to the edge of Japan. Sheer cliffs stood like timeless watchmen guarding the secrets of the Pacific. With a swerve toward an overlook pullover, the car halted before the Sanriku Coast.

"Up for a hike?" His thick brow cocked, and he opened the door.

"Sure. I dove in the Blue Cave near here, but I've never hiked." Her mood lifted at the notion of tackling something new.

Keane popped the trunk, handed her a hiking stick and a water bottle, and pulled a baseball cap over the crown of her head. She rose onto her tiptoes to peck his cheek. Privacy was an underestimated privilege, and the kiss was her way of giving thanks.

"I am told it's no longer hiking season, so maybe we will have the day to ourselves."

"What more could a girl ask?"

That made him smile. His past acquaintances wanted him to buy the moon and stars, but Ami was satisfied with companionship. Keane had muscled through life as a single man and forgotten how nice a lady's company was. "Does that mean you want to take the easy trail or the advanced?"

Shooting him a look of feigned disappointment, she laughed. The sweet sound pressed in on him. "What do you think?"

"Advanced it is, then." He rubbed his hands together and ambled toward a narrow footpath strewn with white pebbles and shells. Gulls rode the steady whip of wind, only flapping their wings to shift directions. A pelican dove into the cobalt water and resurfaced with a twitching fish. A constant roll of waves crashed against a line of rock-bergs, sending spray into the air.

The ocean's roars and rumbles silenced conversation, and the path along the cliff required concentration on each footfall. After an hour of hiking, he gestured to a boulder where the trail widened. "Let's sit a bit."

She uncorked the water bottle, took a long sip, and passed it to him.

"It sure is something, isn't it?" He checked her face for a hint of her thoughts.

"What is?"

"The Pacific. That much salt water, in general. I had the same feeling when I visited the Alps. The ego gets taken down a notch when you land next to something so vast and grand."

"I know what you mean. It is humbling."

"What's it like to free dive out there?"

"The tank is one thing. The Pacific is a different beast. Every open-water dive is a new experience."

"How so?"

She leaned forward, hugging her knees to her chest. "It's mysterious."

"Mysterious?" Said the woman who kept his mind in a perpetual state of wonderment.

"Yeah, the ocean never fails to be unpredictable. Dealing with pressure on your body is a given, but then there's the current trying to pull you with it. Sometimes you're down there with unwelcome creatures. Jellyfish. Sharks. Sometimes you resurface and find a storm has rolled in."

Arching her chin, she stopped talking. "What? You look—"

"Intrigued?"

"Don't put words in my mouth. I was thinking *uncertain*."

"Not at all. But you, Miss Ono, are the most maddening woman I have *ever* met. I'm not sure what to do with you."

"*Moi?*" Her hand flew to her chest, but then her face fell. "You might decide to take a permanent detour when you meet my father. Katsu Ono is not a man to be ignored."

"Not a chance. Unless *you* decide you want me to get lost." His eyes locked on hers, but her spontaneous smile won him over again.

"Father has always been fond of fighters, so maybe it won't go too badly."

A glimmer of optimism brightened her eyes, but the way her forehead creased gave him pause, making him wonder.

He laughed. "I'm pretty sure that honor won't extend to the fighter dating his one and only baby girl." He leaned back against the rock and listened to the waves slurp up the shore.

Her cheeks glowed as a cautious grin rounded them. "It has been a long time since I've enjoyed a day this much. Hiking may be even more fun than diving."

He got to his feet and offered her a hand. "Shall we carry on, then?"

Keane wasn't wearing his Patek Philippe watch, and that dime-sized cross tattoo inked the underside of his wrist. If she had doubted the man's devotion, she didn't now. She nodded and curled her fingers around his upturned palm.

The trail climbed higher before sloping toward the beach. "*Jodogahama*," she mumbled, almost to herself.

Fingers still linked, he turned. "What does that mean?"

"Pure Land Beach. I'm surprised we don't have company." Could Keane have arranged *that* too? After the hoops he'd gone through to protect their privacy today, she didn't doubt it. A gift delivered on her doorstep. Three identical cars picking her up to play a shell game. A diversion through the museum. Now, a popular beach all to themselves. When had any man in her life made her feel so treasured? Such a priority? Her heart felt full.

"Too bad it's not warmer. A swim sounds nice." He arched his eyebrows.

Fifty feet from the shoreline, jagged white rocks rose out of the ocean like icebergs, sheltering calm blue-green pools. And at the beach's far end, a cluster of buildings promised civilization—a hotel, a restaurant, a gift shop—backed by a pine-studded mountain.

"How about a wade in the shallows?" She unlaced her hiking boots, toed them off, and bent to roll up her hems.

Just as she stood, he cupped her cheeks and surprised her with a tender kiss. "Works for me." He chuckled and peeled off his boots and socks.

She eased ankle-deep into the clear water, peering at the ocean floor. "There are so many fishes."

He stepped in, not taking his gaze off her. "Oh, it's cold."

"You'll get used to it. Just be careful where you walk. See that?" She gestured to a spiky purple creature.

"Yeah."

"That is an urchin."

He froze. "Maybe wading wasn't such a good idea." He hunched forward and, with the scrutiny of one searching for land mines, examined his direct path. One stiff-legged baby step at a time, he edged away from the shore until the water hit him midcalf.

"I've only seen that one. And nothing else will bother you." The cool water sharpened the senses and brought out her liveliness. Having Keane all to herself was an unexpected treat.

His mouth quirked. "You find me amusing, don't you?"

She shook her head, but her lips came undone. "Well, maybe a tad."

He stooped over and sent a playful splash her way.

She shot him an indignant look as she shook the water droplets from her shirt. She was calculating a revenge move when Salt-N-Pepa's "Push It" rang out from his back pocket and stopped her.

He fished the phone out of his pants and checked the screen. His face fell. "Hey, I need to take this," he said, turning to trudge ashore.

Chapter 12

"Hello?" Keane paced along the beach with the phone pressed to his ear.

"Keane. Hey, sorry to bother you."

"You're never a bother, Ray. What's up?"

"There was a break-in at the church's soup kitchen. No one was hurt, but the pantry was totally cleaned out. Everything stock-piled for the Easter meal is gone. Look, I've exhausted all my other options. I could use your help."

"Do the cops know who did it?"

"Yeah. They're pretty sure it's a woman, a single mother. She's been through the line a few times. With higher inflation and unem-ployment, times have gotten tough for a lot of folks. We aren't press-ing charges, but now, we're empty-handed for the regulars."

"Ray, you're a great giver of grace. You've helped me countless times, and it'd be my pleasure to replenish the pantry. How much do you need?" He paused, bridging the gap between himself and Ami with a smile, as Ray rattled off numbers. Since her movements had decreased to strolling-turtle pace, she must have been eavesdropping. "'Kay. I'll have Hunter transfer the funds today." Keane shuffled his toes through the sand. Life hadn't thrown him any silver spoons, but he knew how to make the most of the bones tossed in his lap. And for those, he felt blessed beyond measure.

"Thank you. You're a godsend," Ray said. "Before I go—how's training? Everyone's been asking."

"Incredibly well."

"And how's Miss Ono?"

Keane ran a hand through his hair and fixed his gaze on her, watching for a reaction. "Ami is amazing." Stating his feelings was freeing, and when her face lit, some unnamed level of seriousness unfurled within his core. He mouthed, "And you look amazing." Then he spoke to the phone. "I'm with her now. I need to drop off, but call me again if you need anything."

His gaze lingered on her trim figure before he shot her a pleading look. "One more sec?" With her nod, he punched the email icon and scowled at more unopened mail than he cared to read. The subject line from his business partner, Hunter Montgomery, piqued his interest—Closed Seventy Million Sale of King's Center.

His finger skidded to the reply button. "Awesome news. Let's share the wealth. Please transfer fifty thousand to New Hope Church and pronto. Thanks."

It was ten times more than Ray requested, but why not? Keane never thought he'd own a commercial office building, but he'd claimed some hefty prize purses. A lucrative sponsorship. Remarkable timing getting in on an alternative energy investment. *Whop, bam, boom.* He found himself sitting on a corporate board and being the silent partner of a real estate shark.

He didn't like dwelling on his rocky start, but sometimes success, even the security of wealth, seemed more than uncanny. And now Ami. She made him come alive and, for the first time, want to share the abundance with which he'd been blessed. *We could be everything.*

Ami is amazing. His words twined around Ami's heart. Her ears failed her for the rest of Keane's conversation, but hope carried her back to the shore. She located her boots, yanked them on, and wandered toward him, scouring the beach for treasures as she walked.

Once they stood face-to-face, Keane planted a too-brief kiss on her lips. "I'm silencing this thing, so you are my one and only distraction." He stowed the phone and devoted his full attention to her. "I don't believe I've ever seen anyone spend so much time scavenging a beach." He nudged her shoulder with his arm. "How do you plan to carry them all back?"

With her hands still cupped around a treasure trove of sea pebbles and pearlescent shells, she examined the assortment, heaped most on the rocky shore, and stashed her favorite in a pocket. "Just this one. Are you hungry?"

"Always. We have a reservation there." He pointed toward the hillside café, then offered his elbow. "And it should be about time. Shall we?"

Her mood lifted as she laced an arm around his muscular biceps. "Do you have all the bases covered?"

"Every last one. Every couple deserves their privacy."

Thrilling at the word *couple* and his forethought in pulling off such a day, she squeezed his arm and faced him. "Thank you." She paused at the base of the stairs outside the restaurant, tipped her chin, and waited until he dipped his head for a proper kiss.

"Does this mean you want to skip lunch?" He flashed a teasing smile.

"Not a chance."

She sprinted up the stairs, knowing he'd follow, and they whiled away the afternoon.

Sushi in the restaurant. A strong cup of Italian roast for dessert on the outdoor patio. Good conversation wasting away hours on the beach, sitting side by side on a driftwood bench to watch scattered clouds crawl across the horizon. The afternoon sun overlaid the water with glittering copper confetti as it sank through the sky. More than once, she was astonished she hadn't heard from anyone— Niko, Mika, or her father. The silence gnawed at her, but she shoved the feeling aside and nestled back against Keane's warm chest.

"You're getting cold, aren't you?" He tightened his arms around her.

"A little. I don't want to move though." She yawned, fully content.

"Let's watch the sunset and then head back."

"I don't want the day to end." A long beat passed. "Keane?"

"Yeah. Sorry, I kind of zoned out. Just thinking." The warm breath of his mumble stirred her hair.

"Thinking about what?"

"How good *this* is. The blessing of companionship. I've been missing out."

She smiled. "That is a good thing to keep thinking about."

"It's crazy." He paused, perhaps searching for the right words. "I came here to win. I'm as focused as ever. And you dropped into my life. No, not crazy—*uncanny*." He angled to the side, so they were eye to eye. "Have you ever felt some invisible hand nudging you through life?"

For an endless moment, she held his intense gaze. Her throat felt cotton-dry, and she had to swallow past it. "Exactly like that. Twice in one week that hand delivered you to me—first in the train station, and then when Niko arranged for me to be your ambassador." That disclosure cost her a blush, for sure. "*That* was like a golden ticket. But then hard things happen. You've experienced valleys in the past. I have too. The realities of life can be complicated to reconcile."

"And, all along, I thought *you* were delivered to *me*." He joked, making light of her thoughts, but his expression turned introspective. "Seriously though . . ."

"What is it?"

"I've been there—down that same path of thinking, I mean." He ran a hand over his chin and leaned forward, sandwiching her fingertips between his. "Come on and let's find the car. I have something I want to tell you."

Like being seared by a fiery brand, his worst memory brought an immediate, aching pressure to his chest. The pain overwhelming. The remembered panic never forgotten. The hurt unhealed.

"What about the Audi?" Ami scooted across the chauffeured Bentley's back seat.

"It's taken care of. Unless you want to hike back?" He arched his eyebrows, giving himself a moment to collect his thoughts.

"No, this is perfect." She relaxed into the toasty cocoon the car provided.

He reached for her hand and flipped it, feeling they'd reached some new level of comfort. With his fingertip, he raked abstract designs across her palm.

"You wanted to share something?" She reminded him in a soft voice.

Hans's suggestion—that opening up was a wise move—echoed in Keane's mind. He was trying to get to know Ami, but transparency wasn't his forte, especially when the tale lacked sugarcoating. He stretched his neck from side to side, clutched her hand tighter, and took a deep breath. *Lord, help me share some words of wisdom.*

"I already told you about my rocky upbringing—how my dad

was . . . abusive." Saying the word out loud felt like he was putting the lead ball he'd dragged his whole life on display.

He checked her face. Good. No trace of judgment as she squeezed his hand.

"One of my first karate tournaments away, my mom decided to come watch. She never got out of town unless my dad was with her, but she didn't want to miss it." He drew in another lungful of courage. "She was my rock, and I was just a kid. There was so much I didn't understand."

He bent forward with his hands clasped, his elbows resting on his knees as if he were about to pray. Ami's hand ran up and down his back in long soothing strokes. "Anyway, our team racked up trophies. I took home my first gold. The coaches took the kids out for pizza to celebrate. But when I got home, blue lights and tape surrounded the house." Why did his voice have to crack? He cleared his throat.

"She had never left before because he was prone to fits of rage. She knew he'd be jealous since she'd picked to spend the afternoon with me over waiting for him to come home. She knew he would beat her for leaving. And she still chose to go and cheer me on. But he took it too far that night. Do you understand what I'm trying to say?"

A heavy silence followed. While willing his breathing to steady, he watched her eyes and prayed the ugly truth wouldn't run her off.

At a loss for words, Ami stumbled over competing thoughts. No man had ever been so vulnerable with her. It was the most fragile of gifts. He'd already told her he fought for his mom, though she never fathomed the seriousness of that admission. His fighting was about honoring and protecting his mother's memory, and it wasn't a stretch to imagine his abusive father also played a huge role in his hesitancy to commit. But now that he'd opened his heart to her, she didn't want him to shut down. She wanted more.

She kept a firm hand on his back. "You blame yourself?"

When he straightened, relief loosened his taut expression. "No . . . and yes. For a long time, I did. I wanted to right a grievous wrong. I trained like a madman. Revenge fueled me. But that was dark and destructive—an imprisoning dead-end. Played out in my thoughts, I kept reliving the worst time in my life. But it's not who I am. What happened to my mom was out of my control. It took me a long time to accept that. And I vowed I'd *never* be like my father."

"Is that why you are slow to let people in?"

He thumbed over her bottom lip, his gaze dipping to her mouth before fixing on her eyes. "It's a huge part of why I haven't let *anyone* in. Until you."

She nuzzled back against his chest as he wrapped an arm around her shoulder. He wasn't the only one whose childhood wasn't picture-perfect. In the years following her mother's untimely death, Ami knew the pain and hardship of living at another's mercy. Her heart hardened just thinking of her father and brothers. Could she cut all strings and move on like Keane? Was she brave enough to try?

"You are your own man, Keane Temple, and *you* continue to impress *me*." Intense feelings cycloned through her. Her trembling hand skimmed up the curve of his neck and twined into his wild golden hair. She pulled his mouth down, and then her lips took a slow trek along his angular jawline, kissing a path to the tender skin below his ear, inhaling the fresh scent of his cologne as she buried her nose in his hair.

He swept her into his arms and cradled her. Then he pulled back a fraction of an inch, his eyes boring into hers as he searched her face. Some unspoken agreement passed between them.

He touched her face with the deliberate care of one charged with protecting an irreplaceable work of art, but when his lips reconnected with hers, his kiss held abandon. When the Bentley came to a stop, he backed away and blew out a sharp breath. "This is *so* hard."

As a safety precaution, Ami rarely entered her building from the back alley. Tonight was an exception. What girl needed to worry about personal safety when she was accompanied by a two-hundred-and-thirty-five-pound world-class mixed martial arts champion? And, given the paparazzi, the back door was the safest means to avoid attention.

She already had her key in hand when the driver opened the door. From street level, her second-floor condominium appeared to be dark. She peeked over a shoulder at Keane. "Mika must be out."

"So it seems." He arched a brow. In one hand, he toted the bag of takeout they'd snagged on the way home. With his other hand, he clasped hers.

Ascending the interior stairwell was a rushed blur. By the time they reached the upstairs landing, everything within her swayed toward him as if he emitted his own gravitational force, and then he swayed in, holding the take-out bag to the side, and placed a gentle peck on the tip of her nose. Her lips eased back into an irrepressible grin.

"Give me a second." Ami joggled the house key in the lock, kicked the door open, and fumbled to switch on the entry light. From the living room's far side, the knob of a table lamp clicked, and blinding light flooded the space. As she blinked her eyes to adjust, a man's wiry silhouette took shape. Keane stepped in front of her, but the stranger didn't move. Still, she felt him bristle, fists clenched in a fighter's stance.

"Svalbard, Norway, is the most northerly settlement in the world. There is a season when sunrays do not travel that far north— months called winter darkness. Can you imagine how intolerable that must be? It is hard to conceive of such from the Land of the

Rising Sun." The man was a soft-spoken storyteller. Words streamed out, a hush of English with a Japanese accent.

"Father, is that you?" She brushed by Keane, her cheeks flushed as she gave her father a respectful bow. "What are you doing here?"

But Father's stare never strayed from Keane. What possessed Father to wait in the dark?

Keane, always the gentleman, closed the gap and extended a respectful hand. "Mr. Ono, it's a pleasure to make your acquaintance."

Time seemed suspended until Father stood and shook hands, not once looking in her direction.

"Likewise, Keane Temple. However, under these *intolerable* circumstances, please excuse my lukewarm hospitality." At last, Father looked her way, his expression frosty. "My daughter is a beautiful woman, but perhaps you are unaware she has already been committed to a gentleman. I spoke with Ichiro today to reassure him of the integrity of our agreement. Niko maintains that this . . . this arrangement you have with my daughter is creative marketing, but I beg to differ. This charade will end. Ami will not disgrace our family."

Did Mr. Ono always manage his only daughter like a business transaction? Keane's right fist dangled at his side, but he breathed in through gritted teeth. He wasn't so easily baited.

Though she said nothing, rebellious fire ignited in Ami's eyes.

"With all due respect, Niko created this arrangement, not Ami. And Ichiro was apprised of the details. The creative marketing *has* been successful. Both sides will benefit, but only if this plays out." That the connection was real was *lagniappe*—a bonus, a little bit extra, as good Texans say. "Apart from your distaste for me, can you make a solid case for changing marketing strategies this far into the game?"

His expression dour, the old man gave the slightest shake of his head. "I do not like it." He held up a smooth outward-facing palm. "However, I concede it could be detrimental to ticket sales if we alter plans now. But sometimes, less is more. By limiting coverage to the prefight party and the bout, fans will await more maximizing publicity. And this scheme can go cold."

"Then I'll be gone?" Keane's gaze drifted from Ami to the old shark.

Mr. Ono's face softened with a conciliatory smile, mistaking the question for a promise. "A clean break—Is that not what you call it in America?"

After a competition of humbling bows, Mr. Ono remained with Ami. Keane took his cue and exited the building. The whole encounter stung him as if a body-sized Band-Aid had been ripped from his flesh.

How had Ami weathered her father's harsh words like a silent saint? While the Ono men built their empires, she must've constructed a fragile shell around herself to lock out their influence and protect her hopes and dreams. And he'd witnessed that shell pop into place. He hated it. Sure, she had enviable connections, but the woman was bent on making it on her own. Now he could see why.

He shouldn't have let the relationship progress. Despite his intense feelings, should he bow out and save her from more family drama? They could honor the business deal without the *extra*. At least he prayed he could. She was young. There was Ichiro, dull and detached. There'd be others, if she so chose.

But every time he tried to slam the door to his mind, she was there, peeking through, brilliant and beautiful. The determination of her heart. The shrewdness of her mind. The silkiness of her skin. The enticement of her laugh. He *should* leave her alone, but that decision had already been settled. So why was he so tempted to throw gas on the fire?

Chapter 13

After the brief ride back to the Westin, Keane had made it to his room when his phone began to vibrate in his pocket. Mark's ruddy cheeks filled the screen until Keane thumbed over the green Accept button.

"Aye, aye, captain."

"What. Is. Up?"

"I cannot imagine what you mean."

"Don't toy with me, Temple. I just got off the phone with Ichiro Wanta—Wannabe—for the *second* time tonight."

"Is that so?"

"Yes, that's so. They asked us for this ambassador-meets-the-American b—baloney. Then they want to call it off, and an hour later, it's all good again. They're. Making. Me. Nervous."

"No need to swear. Look, take a deep breath and relax." Edgy, Keane forked his fingers through his hair. Right. He needed the same advice.

"Easy for you to say. If you weren't so blasted charming—I blame you for this."

"Blame me?" Keane wheezed out those high-pitched words. "You're insane."

"This is your fault. She's got you twisted around her pretty pinkie finger, doesn't she? That's why their panties are all jacked up—"

"Enough," Keane boomed. "The deal remains intact. We'll do joint coverage at the prefight party leading up to Fight Night. I spoke it over with Niko Ono's father."

Mark huffed. "And where d'ya run into him?"

"At Ami's."

Several long beats passed. Voicing her name made concern clench deep within Keane's gut. He needed to call her. Soon.

"No wonder they're worried. They should be, especially given all the heat you've been throwing around the ring."

Ami sandwiched her face between her palms and dropped her elbows to the kitchen table with a thud.

"Are you okay?" Mika pressed a cup of steaming tea into Ami's palm.

She nodded twice, then tipped her head from side to side. "I don't know. Guess I'm confused. It was *the* most amazing day. Keane did everything to make it special and keep us secluded."

A curious grin twisted Mika's mouth, then fell away as her delicate brows crinkled together. "And what about your father? What did he say?"

"It was humiliating." Ami set her teacup on the breakfast table, tracing her thumb over the butterfly wings etched on the treasured earthenware piece. "Father's pomposity didn't intimidate Keane. Keane bettered him, but now I'm worried. I don't want the intrusion to distance us. With Father there, Keane ended up leaving, so I don't know where we stand. You don't think he's rethinking *us*, do you?"

Or could he have seen the relationship as a business deal from the get-go and played the part to perfection? As the what-ifs ricocheted around her skull, a hand went to her neck, brushing over the boulder-sized lump settled deep in her throat.

"Ami?" Mika fussed. "Do not second-guess yourself. Do not waste energy for a tension headache. Just call him and see."

Ha. Bravo. Ami sprang to her feet and hugged her roomie. "You're the best. And you're so right."

"Of course, I am always right." Mika ducked out of her grasp, sipped her tea, and settled back in her chair.

"This whole arrangement is so contrived, and I like Keane. A lot."

"I can see why. And he must be a good kisser." Mika winked, fishing. "I mean, does it feel the same kissing an American?"

Ami laughed and reclaimed her chair. She sealed her lips together to hide the unruly smile. "So good it scares me."

"Then don't lose hope. You like to appease your father as much as you seem to adore Keane, but your father is a man set in his ways. And the way you happened upon Keane, it's fate—without a doubt. Let yourself enjoy being with him. Now, here's the phone."

The phone's repeated vibrating on the stone counter stirred Keane out of a deep slumber. He rubbed his eyes, blinking as a star-studded, inky sky came into focus beyond the window. Though his brain was foggy, he stalked into the kitchen, anxious to find out why Ami had called again at such a late hour. It wasn't a missed call though. A text message brightened the screen.

> RAY: You came to mind when I read this today. Take care and enjoy. "Do you not know that in a race all the runners run, but only one gets the prize? Run in such a way as to get the prize (1 Corinthians 9:24)."

The onscreen clock displayed four forty. Too close to his scheduled wake-up time to go back to bed. Keane filled the Jura coffee machine with water. While it gurgled and hissed, his brain applied the scripture to his upcoming fight and to Ami.

What constitutional quality makes a man race to win—setting him apart from the crowd? Absolute abandonment of fear? Extraordinary drive? Both? Or could the crux be that it's as important to identify the right prize as it is to race to win?

The coffee machine beeped its completion song. He gripped the mug, savored the dark brew, and shifted his thoughts.

Mr. Ono was a slow-moving hurricane used to leveling everything in his path, and the man had not minced his words. Keane was unwelcome. While they might have arrived at a short-term business agreement, given that Keane had no intention of leaving Ami, the edge remained, nicking away at his plans.

When her father left her around midnight, she'd called to seek reassurance of Keane's affection. After the day they'd spent together, how could she question the extent to which she'd captivated him?

Women often baffled him, but one thing was clear—Ami Ono would live life on her own terms, not those of her father's choosing. As wicked as it was of him, her unexpected need for affirmation paired with her feistiness pleased him. But, when the reality of their ongoing relationship came back into the spotlight, Keane had better *not* underestimate the Ono men—all seven of them.

They would be a problem.

Three hours later, Keane stared down Paulo as the Brazilian shimmied around the ring, his impressive footwork rivaling that of a competitive salsa dancer.

"Hey, lover boy, where's your pretty lady?" Paulo sang the taunt.

Apart from an occasional jab, his gloves were raised to protect the silly smile slathered across his face. "How's it to stroke that pretty swan? I imagine her feathers are soft, her legs smooth."

Paulo was cheetah-fast, but the singing winded him. Keane conserved his energy and tried to keep his annoyance in check. Paulo always got chatty when he forgot his mouthpiece, but Mark likely put him up to the swan banter.

A fraction of a second was all it took. Keane's patience paid off. Paulo tended to talk with his hands. When his mouth parted to start a new string of personal attacks, the gap between his elbows widened. Keane landed a vicious uppercut to Paulo's chin. Blood drained from the corner of Paulo's mouth. He tried to talk, but the strike knocked his teeth halfway through his tongue.

The whistle blew. "Throw me a towel," Keane ordered one of the trainers. Her jaw dropped at the bloody beard running down Paulo's neck, but she snapped to when Keane stepped toward her with an outstretched hand. Armed with terry cloth, he went back to his teammate. "Stick out your tongue and hold this tight. Don't let go." He wrapped the towel around the mincemeat and clamped down until Paulo took over.

"Doc's on the way." Mark yelled from the management office, phone still pinned against his ear. "Does he need stitches?"

"Absolutely." Keane winked. "Weren't you saying you wanted to steal my girlfriend?" He laid a consoling hand on his friend's shoulder. "What? Cat got your tongue?"

"Leave him alone," Hans chimed in. "You know he's panicking, right?"

"Why? If he's mad, he only has himself to blame. Should've worn a mouthpiece."

"The jabs were Mark's idea." Hans arched a thick eyebrow. "And poor Paulo has a date tonight. Maybe you can hold her hand."

Hans shot Paulo an overly sweet smile as the doctor arrived to assess the damage.

Then Hans jogged to catch up with Keane. "Hey. Want to get some lunch while they fix him up?"

"Hang on." Keane threw an examining glance toward Paulo. "You really okay, man?"

Paulo lifted a hand in the air, signaled he was okay, and gestured for them to go on.

Keane headed to the locker room, showered off, threw on some microfiber running pants and a sleeved tee, and joined Hans at the eat-in kitchen. Keeping a professional chef onsite saved commute time, which meant more ring time, and helped teams adhere to their strict diets. A commercial range and griddle lined the far wall. Three Vitamix blenders, jars of protein powders, and tidy stacks of white plates claimed the long stainless-steel island separating the prep area from the eating area.

Keane sat at the table. The round oak table featured a spinning lazy Susan covered with family-style platters of grilled teriyaki chicken, mixed vegetables, and a bowl of brown rice.

"So how was the excursion?" With a knowing smirk, Hans spooned rice into his bowl. "You know, Ella's asked me a dozen times already."

"Pretty fantastic. We managed to avoid intrusions until we got back to her place."

"Paparazzi?"

Keane emptied his water glass and spun the lazy Susan to the chicken. "I wish. It was worse. The father, waiting in the dark. Creepy."

"What'd he say?"

"Basically—stay away from his daughter."

"Are you surprised?"

"Nah. But with the power of a little suggestion, he agreed it would behoove everyone to continue the marketing charade until the bout."

"Sounds like a terrific guy. So Ami gets to come to the press dress-up party?"

Keane smirked as he forked a bite of chicken.

"Very nice. Ella will be glad for the company. And speaking of, Mark chartered a flight to Tokyo, so we'll have enough room for guests."

Paulo approached, sporting a swollen pout. He grabbed a tall insulated cup off the island and stalked toward the table, trying to sip a cold protein smoothie through a straw. Keane pulled out a neighboring chair and squeezed his friend's shoulder as he settled in. "How bad?"

Paulo shrugged. "Bad enough." The words came out thick.

"Sorry, man. At least mouths heal fast."

"*Ja.*" Hans crossed his arms over his chest and rocked the chair onto its back legs. "If it makes you feel any better, Keane got it good from Ami's old man last night."

Paulo's attention whipped in Keane's direction.

"I handled it." Keane held up a hand.

"Should be interesting, though, when Ami and Keane meet-and-greet with Niko and Mr. Ono." Hans chuckled before shoveling rice into his mouth.

"And even more interesting if all of the other brothers come," Keane said.

"How many of them are there?" Paulo managed to get out before wincing.

"Including Niko? Six."

Hans and Paulo exchanged a look before erupting into laughter. "Are you crazy?" Hans's eyes turned into brilliant blue saucers. "Niko—you absolutely have him, but not the entire family." He rubbed at his forehead. "I'm worried, Keane."

"Keane has brothers too." Paulo met Keane's eyes. "In case of trouble, any kind of trouble, Hans and I have your back."

Ami faced the mirror, a dress dangling from each raised hand.

"The red one. You look amazing in red." Reiko threw Ami an approving nod.

"What do you think?" Ami wiggled the shimmery fabric at Mika.

"The red *is* exquisite, but the other one is one-of-a-kind wow." Mika pursed her lips. "I wish it fit me, but Niko told me to wear blue anyway."

Ami held it to herself and ran a hand down the floor-length dress of antique gold. A cascade of crystals formed a plunge neckline that shimmered down her body, gleaming like sun-kissed water. A serious attention-getter. "It *would* make a statement."

She eyed the dress. It covered everything. It met the "recommended attire" description for the preflight party, but so many considerations must be hammered out. Father, Niko, and more importantly, which dress would make Keane never forget her?

"Well, you're about to be on the cover of every magazine in the country." Mika jammed her little hands on her hips. "So, are you in the mood to make a statement or play it safe?"

Good question. Ami knitted her brow and pursed her lips.

"Get the dress." Reiko made a suggestive face. "Have you—you know—yet? Because in that dress . . ."

"Reiko, you're shameless." A deep heat flushed Ami's cheeks.

"Well, in that, you'll know what's on his mind." Reiko's naughty giggle rushed out.

"We have a business arrangement." Ami reminded her friends in her most demure tone, minimizing the relationship in case the paparazzi got their claws into them. "And the man's focus is on the upcoming fight. Not me."

"But he *is* a man," Mika chimed in.

Ami frowned. "One with the restraint of a priest."

"Maybe that woman did a number on him."

"What woman?" Attention piqued and head cocked, Ami tried to keep her voice neutral, even as cold panic gripped her.

Reiko and Mika exchanged hesitating glances before Mika shrugged. "Gossip column fodder. *Very* old news. They're desperate if they have to concoct stories scrounged up from stale, four-year-old material."

Reiko waved to hurry Mika up, then stepped in. "He dated a woman for a few months, and it ended with no explanation. Some people think he never got over her, hence the chronic bachelor status."

"I don't think it was ever serious." Mika rolled her eyes and feathered through her short bob. "But I *have* seen how he looks at you . . . all possessive with those hungry green eyes. Say 'business partner' all you want. I have known you since you wore pigtails."

Keane's ardent interest was obvious, but maybe the news carried a nugget of truth. He claimed his childhood environment affected him. But had the mystery woman played a role in messing him up too? Was that why he'd failed to mention her? The rational part of Ami's brain told her that giving the man a chance to explain was only fair. Keeping her imagination in check was a different story.

She was about to respond when her phone chimed. Her heart leapt into her throat.

"Is it him?" Reiko asked in her nosiest voice, crowding in.

Ami scrunched her nose. "No, just an email from Professor Newman."

"Who's Professor Newman?"

"The Brit." Ami and Mika answered Reiko in unison.

"Ooh." Ami let out a low whistle as she read. "We got an A-minus. He says, if the project team expounds upon a few points, he'll submit our paper for publication." She skimmed the rest of the message.

> We've missed you at the lab. There have been some strange and rather interesting readings. Aren't we always saying to expect the unexpected, otherwise we'll be surprised?

"Congratulations," Mika said. "So, do you have to go to the lab? Or do you still have time for coffee?"

"We are on for coffee. Then I'm going to the aquatic center for an afternoon dive. Maybe that will help me get out of my head. Keane's training schedule has been insane this week. I haven't seen him in two days, so we're meeting somewhere for dinner." Ami winced at the admission. "Please don't tell Niko, Mika. Swear to me you won't. It's just dinner, and I need to speak with him."

With Mika's promise secured, two hours later, Ami worked through several warm-up laps in the pool before taking a three-minute forty-three-second dive. She spent more time than necessary in a fiery hot shower to ground her buoyant thoughts. Using a disguise to escape, she hurried to a white Mercedes with no idea where she was headed.

Keane hugged her at the restaurant's back door, caught her hand, and ushered her through the tidy kitchen to a sumptuous dining room. A mouthwatering blend of roasted garlic and maybe basil scented the air. "Italian?"

While her surprise reverberated in the question, he held out a chair at a table for two, every table around them empty.

"Did you rent the whole restaurant?" She slid into her seat, Pavarotti streaming through the air. Then she nudged aside the red rose in its fancy silver vase, so it didn't distract from a better view—him.

"I did, and they all signed NDAs. So, relax." He smoothed his palms over the white tablecloth, his chin up with an I-do-things-my-way attitude as he dominated the scene, but the smile made her heart tango.

"You look pleased with yourself." She shook a finger at him. "And the nondisclosure agreements—you didn't really, did you?"

There was a silent shrug, his unveiled expression full of brooding affection. "I missed you."

Maybe it was just dinner, but alone time with Keane was priceless. He poured sparkling water himself. She took a sip, narrowing her eyes over the rim. "Same here."

A server appeared with an appetizer, but Keane's piercing jade gaze arrowed at Ami as if nothing else and no one else existed. "Mushrooms stuffed with a blend of herbed cheese and sausage." The waiter set a platter on the table and retreated.

"So, how was your day?" Keane reached across the table and captured her hand, sending warm comfort from her fingertips to her toes.

"Good. I shopped with some friends and then went for a dive. Oh, I also heard from the Brit about our paper. He's going to submit it for publication."

Keane arched an eyebrow. "Congrats. That's awesome. And you found a dress?"

She shot him a playful look from under her lashes. "I did. I hope you'll like it." Then she transferred a mushroom to her appetizer plate, cut it in two, and speared a savory bite.

Keane refrained from the culinary indulgence. "You're gorgeous in everything. And you're sure you want to go through with the public appearance? It could be awkward with your father there."

She fought the frown pulling at her cheeks until determination flared deep within her soul. "I love a challenge. How about you? Think you're ready?" She wanted to change the subject and ask about his past and the woman he had yet to mention, but the timing wasn't right. Seriously, should she dig up the past and put inconsequential images into her head? It was history, and while they still had time together, they should make history of her own. The tightness in her face eased as she absorbed how Keane's gaze burned back at her.

He chuckled, rubbed at the five-o'clock shadow roughing up his chin, and seemed to zone out. Then his jade gaze turned dangerous, and her pulse kicked into double time.

"Keane? I asked if you are ready . . . for the fight."

"Of course, I'm ready." With a cheeky smirk, he raised his water glass and saluted her, then poised it there. Radiating confidence, power, control, he lowered the glass. "Are *you* prepared to handle your brother losing to your boyfriend?"

The waiter's appearance bought her some time to think. She'd been wrapped up in school and the novelty of dating Keane Temple. But, all agreements aside, Niko didn't like to lose. What if Keane *did* beat her brother? What then?

"That sure of yourself?" She toyed with him before easing into a plate of shrimp and pasta. He'd done his homework on her taste preferences and taken the liberty of ordering ahead.

He started on a plate of grilled chicken and roasted root vegetables.

"I am. I leave no room for doubt. So, be ready."

His cool expression released a wave of goose bumps breaking over her skin.

When his phone vibrated on the table, his attention didn't stray from her. His lips parted ever so slightly as she took a last bite and set down her fork. The look he gave her was sinful. "Now"—he halted long enough to push away from the table—"come here."

Her mouth parched at his authoritative tone. She hesitated, forcing herself to swallow as she got to her feet. One step forward and he pulled her crossways onto his lap, her feet dangling alongside the chair. He caged her chin between his splayed fingers, held it, and spoke. "Your family is going to be hard. We'll handle them together. Okay?"

She tried to nod between his firm hands. But his fingers combed through her hair, and his mouth sealed over hers. At first eager, he kissed her with an unhurried thoroughness until the scent of rich Italian roast coffee gave them pause. She glanced at the silver coffee service and plate of almond biscotti, her cheeks burning hotter since the server had slipped in and away unnoticed. "How do you look so . . . so unfazed?"

Sporting a satisfied grin, he made a cup of coffee, arms still boxing her in. "Do I? I find it impossible to be unfazed around you. You suit me nicely."

She closed her eyes a moment while dragging in a deep breath, venturing to ask him the question that had been lingering in her brain since their day trip to the beach. And he was in such a good mood. "Do you . . .?" She dared to check his face, giving him a flirtatious glance from under her long lashes. "Do you want to come back to my place and hang out? Mika will be there."

One arm supporting her back, Keane lifted his coffee with his free hand. Regret lit his green eyes when they met hers. "Can't."

The answer tripped her up. Her gaze dipped, but his thumb snagged her chin. "Believe me." The intensity in his eyes pierced straight through her. "I would love nothing else, but I have business to attend to tonight."

"Who has business meetings this late?" Her face fell, and she grew edgy. "I–I . . ." She swallowed hard, then blurted out, "Is there someone else at home?"

"Do not assume the worst. You're the only woman in my life. I promise." He placed a kiss on her forehead and softened his tone, but the frustration smoldering in those fiery jade eyes didn't match the words. "And if you need to know, your father isn't the only one buying up prime property. It's still morning in the States, and I have a call to see how a bid fared." Lips pressed into a thin line, he gave her a think-about-it look.

Keane Temple made her want to be a better woman. Every bit as striking as a full-blooded gladiator with cover-model looks, he managed to exude both raw masculinity and sophistication. Still, his messy golden mane and adventurous spirit led her to believe he was working hard to contain a wild side. Equally golden sparks were zinging between them, and even if circumstances kept putting their romance on ice, no doubt he felt the heat too.

Surely, he hadn't prearranged a business meeting as a preventive measure, had he? While patience wasn't one of her strongest virtues, *that* would be answered in due time.

Though not a single blow touched his torso, an intense pounding rattled through Keane's rib cage and suffocated him. Putting Ami in that white Mercedes—alone—had been torturous, but her expression sent him to the inner ring of hell. For too long, he'd defied nature, and it was costing him. Why was he doing this to himself? What could she think?

They were both adults with off-the-charts attraction. The twinkle in her eyes hinted at a penchant for playfulness and passion. More than anything, he wanted time with her. There'd never be enough. But more time in private would lead to the bedroom. And his willpower in that arena was wavering. He wouldn't risk a rushed misstep to exacerbate family tension or invite regret. He'd been there and done that. He wouldn't make the same mistakes again.

Remembered words—*run to get the prize*—bobbed through his thoughts before his cell phone came to life in his pocket. A glance at the screen confirmed it was his real-estate partner and college buddy, Hunter Montgomery. Sliding into the chauffeured Bentley, he pressed the phone to his ear as the door sealed shut. "Hey, man. How's it going?"

"Crazy. Working too much," Hunter groaned.

Keane gave an easy chuckle. "Have you made time to hit the Gulf in your new Scout? Snapper season's about to open up, and I hear the grouper have been biting."

"I've taken the fishing boat out once. Let's get the guys—maybe Noble Thrasher and Rowdy Jensen—and plan a trip once you win and get back. 'Kay?"

"Yeah, I can't wait." Keane settled back, hooked an ankle over his knee, and toyed with his shoelaces as the Bentley merged into traffic. "All right, so tell me about the house."

"Well, the kitchen and master bath will require some renovations, but it's prime. Checks all the boxes for what women love. And the view is incredible."

"Excellent. How much renovating are we talking about?"

"To meet your standards? Considerable."

"And what about time to completion?"

"Give or take a week, a month and a half."

"Okay. Let's make it final."

"Um, you sure about this?"

This was about the only thing he was sure of lately. He nodded in the dark. "Just get it done."

Chapter 14

After eleven, the Mercedes glided in front of Ami's building. The night sky was starless, but every light in the house was on.

She scaled the central staircase and wiggled her key in the lock until it gave a release click. She hung her purse on a peg by the door, calling "I'm home."

The dull thud of a body against wood flooring in the back room stopped her. Someone scuffled back there, and then the soft padding of bare feet echoed down the hallway. "Hey, Ami." Mika's thick voice sounded before she appeared in the hallway. She hugged her arms across a gauzy tee, its hem inching up over pink underwear. Her face a twist of wide-eyed surprise and mischief, she tried to play it cool. "Didn't expect you back so soon."

"Who is it, babe?" Niko strode into the living room shirtless, smug, and shameless, albeit handsome with his lean, powerful torso on display, and a thin tracing of midnight hair running down his honed chest. His low-slung silky red pajama pants, embroidered with his trademark flying dragon, left nothing to the imagination.

Ami's eyebrows flew up. "Who else would it be?" Her hard glare zigzagged between the two of them before embarrassment took root. "I didn't mean to interrupt."

165

"Ami!" Despite her cool greeting, Niko's singsong was over the top, typically the case when he was getting his way. "How was the lab?"

Mika threw Ami a serious go-with-it look chased by a smirk. Her roomie had been going above the call of duty to occupy Niko's time. Though the distraction benefitted Ami, Mika's expression showed it wasn't too inconvenient a chore. But concern unfurled in Ami's core.

She cleared her throat. "Good. There's been a lot of seismic activity. I'm running an experiment and have to head back in a few. I need to grab a book and change clothes." She brushed by them before Niko had a chance to consider her dinner date attire and probe into her personal life. "Have a nice night."

Only after she was alone in her room could she breathe. Niko had that miserable chest-crushing effect on her, and after Keane's dismissive send-off, she felt emotionally chafed. She tore off her tailored clothes, tossed them onto the bed, and scoured the room for a comfy change. Black running tights, an ultra-soft yoga shirt, and a dark baseball cap bearing the Sendai Diving Club logo won out under some serious scrutiny. The hallway was empty when she reemerged. Car keys to a shimmering silver Audi 6 dangled on a peg beside her purse. She snagged both and headed to the lab.

When she parked, a brave moon wedged through thick cloud cover. The heavy drifting blanket alternately blinked and then blotted out the silvery light. The lab was dark when the moonlight evaporated. She punched in the security code, flipped a switch, and strode to her desk. Since receiving the note from the Brit, she'd had a hankering to swing by and check the seismic activity to which he'd alluded. His office light was on, but the door was shut. Atypical. So, she ambled to her desk, spent twenty minutes catching up on unanswered emails, and tapped into a shared network drive to examine the team's electronic logs.

Activity was an understatement. A flurry of tectonic events and inland geological findings lit up the logs. A bristle of annoyance rippled up her spine. Someone should've contacted her sooner. But then, she also should've been by. No one else to blame.

Time with Keane was a trade-off, a balance she had yet to master, but gosh, did he still simmer through her thoughts and tug at her heart. She was a tad too distracted to give work her best, and being in the lab alone at night made her uneasy.

She locked her computer, twisted the knob on her desk lamp, hitched her purse up her shoulder, and strode to the parking lot. It was nearly one o'clock when she made it back into Sendai proper. Restless, she let the deserted streets invite her to cruise block by block. The music streaming from the radio stirred her thoughts.

Intent was *not* part of the equation that led her to park on a side street and scale the stairs to Keane Temple's suite. Her better judgment clashed with whatever mysterious force of nature compelled her to take another and another step forward.

With the backs of her knuckles, she rapped on the door a seventh time before the heavy footfalls of a large man lumbered closer. The metallic snap of a bolt disturbed the silence followed by the soft whoosh of air as the door swung inward.

"I didn't mean to wake you," she apologized. Her moment of peace shattered, her late-night confidence vaporized at the sight of Keane in nothing but boxers. Her mouth went bone-dry while her palms grew sweaty.

"What are you doing here?" he mumbled, his voice rough from sleep.

"I don't know." She rubbed those sweaty palms against her gray tee. "I ran by the lab and wasn't tired. Call it a whim. May I come in?"

She shifted on her feet and threw a glance over her shoulder. No one else was around.

"Yeah, sure. I apologize. I wasn't trying to be rude." With a throaty chuckle, he ushered her through the doorway, his hand at the small of her back. The door locked shut. "I'm . . . stunned. Happy but stunned."

"Niko was with Mika when I got home from dinner. I couldn't be there and kind of freaked out." Disgust roiled her. "I went to the lab."

"At this hour?" His brows knit. When Ami nodded, he drew her against his chest in a tight bear hug, pressing his lips to the top of her head, providing the comfort she sought. "I'm glad you came," he whispered. "You should never be out alone like that, especially at this hour. I can arrange for a car to take you anywhere at any time."

In so many ways, she'd been on her own since childhood. That fanned her already independent nature. But caged within his rock-hard arms, she felt cherished and safe in a way she never had. And more than anything, when he wanted to take control of things, she found herself willing to let a man—a man unrivaled in power and might—lead her for the first time ever. A silly grin played on her lips as her fingertips skimmed up the slope of his shoulders. His outward stoicism seemed to melt with each feather-soft stroke. "I don't want to go anywhere."

How quickly Ami's sweet company had become the highlight of his days, but in recent days, remaining a gentleman where she was concerned had become a formidable personal demon. And he was now under immediate attack. It was too much. *She* was too much. A war raged within. *Father, help me stay strong.*

Keane eased back into a tender hug, tucking Ami's head under his chin. Her perfume's citrus note revived his senses, giving him a fresh zing of much-needed strength. He pulled back with a cool smile, scooped her into his arms, and carried her into the suite, setting her on the couch.

"Give me just a minute." He held up a finger to stay her and then headed to the bedroom to grab a shirt. By the time he returned, she had slipped out of her jacket and was nestled in the couch's corner in running tights and a curve-hugging shirt.

"Thought you being here was a whim," he teased, enjoying her beautiful figure even when he shouldn't. Containing his stunned grin was impossible. "But seriously, you're gorgeous."

Lord, this woman is heaven on earth. I want to know every inch of her. I want to give her everything. My body is strong, but my heart is so weak. Please help me honor you. And please make her mine.

"You're not so bad yourself," Ami said, her teeth worrying the swell of her pretty lip. "But Keane, I'm tired and still edgy after my run-in with Niko and Mika. I don't want to be like them, and I don't want either of us to have regrets. I want a relationship I know will last. Would you just hold me?"

Pale morning light inched across the living room. Keane peeled his eyelids open to find a sleeping Ami, lovely as ever, nestled beside him. Their attraction was electrifying, but underscoring that attraction was a quiet intimacy—a developing bond—that meant just as much, maybe more. Satisfaction spread across his face as her soft breathing came like a kitten's purring.

If it weren't for Niko, he'd take in that sight all day. But Keane prayed he could get Ami home before Niko was up. Nothing had happened, and everything had happened. Nonetheless, there would be difficult questions to answer—questions that would only exacerbate the family tension—if Ami showed up after a full night out.

With the tip of his nose, Keane drew a line along her jawline from ear to chin, nudging her nose with his until she stirred. Bending her back in a long graceful stretch, she slit her eyelids to meet his gaze. "Good morning, Mr. Temple. You're looking quite lionly." She pushed her fingers into his hair, ruffling it. He liked her hands in his hair—too much.

"*Silk* got it wrong. You're no swan."

"I'm not?"

"Most definitely *not*. You might, however, be an angel." He placed a quick kiss to her lips. "I am hoping you are, because we need to fly and get you home before Niko wakes up to find his one and only sister missing."

Her face fell. "I'm not worried about that."

"But I am."

"I could get used to waking up with you. What if I don't want to go?"

"As much as I'd love to spend the day with you, I have to insist. We don't need to pour gas on the flames where your family is concerned."

The ride home flew by. Too fast for Ami's liking. With a healthy dose of angst, Keane saw her through the back door. Upstairs, Mika was nowhere to be seen, but Niko was wide awake and waiting. His broad shoulders faced the room as he stared out the window overlooking the back alley, and he didn't turn when the door snapped shut behind her. Her heart sank.

"Niko?"

"Are you in love with him?" He spun around and leaned forward with his fists propped on the sofa back, his quiet intensity troubling.

She swallowed as she draped her jacket and purse on a peg by the door.

"Answer me." The muscle in his jaw twitched when she faced him. "You are, aren't you?"

"I'm fond of him." It was the truth. Attuned as he was to body language, Niko would see through anything but the truth. But that was all she was willing to confess.

"You have wronged Ichiro and shamed our family."

It felt as if he'd landed one of his powerful punches right in her gut, but she planted her feet in a combative stance, ready to take and give as he saw fit. "You think you rule over me, don't you?" Her voice low, she clenched her hands at her sides. "Do you think I enjoy you bulldozing over every inch of my life? Well, I don't. I have done nothing wrong. But I do have feelings, and they sure aren't for Ichiro. This is something you cannot control, but your greed is. *Your* greed, *your* philandering, and *your* bullying is a shame. If anyone shames the Ono name, it is you."

Niko's eyes turned into dark saucers bulging from the eye sockets. His fists balled, and she braced herself. She'd been on the receiving end of those knuckles a time or two. When barely contained restraint flickered over his ominous expression, she darted down the hall to her bedroom. The lock slid into place with a metallic snap.

And she sat in silence, willing her breathing to normalize, even as her ears sought the slightest indication of trouble. After a muffled conversation from the front room—nothing. Niko never knocked.

A shard of ice had lodged in the back of her throat. From a man notorious for getting in the last word and the last punch, Niko's abandonment of this family tiff was beyond distressing. Cold, raw fear amassed inside her like a growing, out-of-control snowball.

She spent the day tucked away, her mind traveling back to the moment she'd seen Temple in the train station before rolling through the string of mind-blowing days. And the words Keane had whispered in the pitch of night, tangling romantic hopes with inevitable challenges. *Time and patience can resolve anything. I've got your back. Trust me. And have faith.*

The words reassured her a mere ten hours earlier, but now, revisiting them alone for the umpteenth time, they left her deflated and baffled. What was he getting at? What had he meant? Was it code for something else?

Resolutions weren't always agreeable, and they weren't always what was expected.

At work that week, reviewing the most recent additions to the world's earthquake archives fascinated her, and the database continued to flash and beep like a PlayStation video game.

"I've been looking over February's entries again." iPad in hand, her teammate tapped a glittery nail at the numbers. "Look at this."

Ami rolled back her chair, scooting closer as Nan braced her hip against the desk.

"It starts with a magnitude 6.0 quake in Samoa on February 3. Then one after another in Chile. A 6.6 shaker in the Fiji Islands on February 21 chased by a 6.3 quake in New Zealand the next day—"

Ami held up a hand. "Sadly killing a hundred and eighty-five people."

"I know." Nan set the iPad on the desk, crossed her arms, and uncapped her water bottle. "Then, nearly two weeks later, a 6.6 earthquake struck the Solomon Islands on March 7. That's a crazy one-month period, almost as wild as your last weeks."

At Nan's waggling brows, Ami held up an interruptive finger like a lecturer. "Which, by the way, seem to have gotten more press coverage."

Nan giggled and pulled her lunch from her satchel. "Not these last days. Just speculation, not news. Seriously, everything all right with the Lion and the Swan, or has there been a seismic shift I've missed?"

Ami paused to dismantle her bento lunch box. Even this close to a fight, Niko remained aloof, and concocted news stories were running rampant. Keane Temple and Niko Ono's younger sister— not naming her made her laugh—had become a daily feature not only on entertainment television but also during the main news segments.

"Since our date on Monday, we decided to stay apart. Keane calls every evening." She plucked a morsel of glazed chicken, but just sat there with it dangling between her chopsticks and those talks dangling between her thoughts. Long, uninhibited talks about life experiences and loves and professional plans. Though he refrained from elaborating too much on his parents, it was a wonder the man had survived childhood. Getting out from under his father's thumb had been a major turning point, but could not erase the scars. "He's amazing, and his success couldn't have gone to a more compassionate person. Keane's a fighter in every aspect. Gritty, resourceful, led by noble ideals, and yet still tender."

Those were the nights. She tested the chicken, savoring the tang, then swallowed. "Getting back to work's been the welcome distraction I needed."

"Well, let's get back at it, then." Nan patted her shoulder, put away her now-empty bento box—how Nan had eaten hers when Ami had barely started, she had no idea—and moved to her neighboring desk.

While she snacked at hers, she continued to pinpoint the quakes, taking care to catalog specific attributes such as region, magnitude, distance, and site condition. The data would be fed into advanced models, refined using decluster and deblast techniques, and then sliced, diced, and analyzed ad nauseam. She was nearly caught up when an ear-piercing siren sounded with a strong tremble.

Since she'd been born and raised in the country experiencing 20 percent of the world's earthquakes, years of drop-cover-and-hold preparedness training kicked into effect. She dropped to the floor, took cover under her desk, and held on to its legs. From her metal cocoon, she glimpsed the digital Richter scale on the lab wall.

"Everyone okay?" the Brit yelled from his corner office.

A chorus of "okays" and "I'm fines" came in reply as she sat, texting Keane to make sure he was all right.

"Seven . . . eight . . . nine . . . ten." The ref's voice echoed through the building. Keane stopped his attack and moved away from the sparring partner he'd knocked out. The locker room was steps away when the ground shook. He reached for the wall to steady himself, but the strange feeling continued. A fresh spurt of adrenaline had his heart bucking against his rib cage. Earthquakes were unfamiliar to him. Was this a strong one? Should he head outside? Unsure, he backed up to the wall, covered his head with his forearms, and sent up a prayer as the locals responded.

As swiftly as it hit, it was gone. He exhaled utter relief but didn't move, taking in the scene. Metal racks had tipped, spilling sports equipment and branded water bottles. The lights flickered. But every face held shock and a newfound seriousness.

"You okay?" Hans asked, jogging around to check on potential damage.

"Yeah, I'm fine."

"Good. Ella and the girls are flipping out. A mirror broke, and they want to switch rooms to skirt potential bad luck. I need to head that way before she catches the next plane out of here. Want to ride with me? Check on Ami?"

"Ami'll be having a field day right about now. I need to give her a ring, but I'm going to stay."

With less than a week until fight night, the final countdown was on. The week leading up to the fight was as much a ritual of psyching up the mind as it was of honing the body. As much as he wanted to have Ami cradled in his arms, a break in the time-tested ritual could throw his game. He wasn't taking that risk.

He stretched his neck from side to side to shake off the earthquake jitters, swung by the locker room for his phone, and headed to the gym. He'd hit the weights hard one last time, work in a two-mile jog, and get a massage before leaving.

The phone vibrated before he could dial. Sweat clouded his vision and stung his eyes. With the back of a hand, he rubbed them. Then he checked the incoming text.

> AMI: First earthquake?

Even though it was a simple message, he could hear her concern smile through it.

He typed a quick reply.

> KEANE: Yep. How big? I know you know.

And he secretly relished having a girlfriend brilliant enough to know that fact.

> AMI: Significant. 7.3 on the Richter scale but epicenter far enough offshore not to worry too much. Glad you are okay. 😊
> KEANE: Sure doesn't take much distance to make the heart grow fonder, especially today. Can't wait to see you all dressed up tomorrow.
> AMI: Ditto that.

Clouds blanketed the afternoon sky like an endless stretch of gauze. Rays of honey-hued light pierced the occasional break in cover to warm the life below, as if nothing had happened. Thank goodness, quake damage was minimal. And the sun decided to shine on Ami and Keane as they boarded a Bell 206L4 helicopter. She hoped it was a good omen. Even though they shared the cabin with Mark, Paulo, and the pilot, a palpable excitement charged the air, offsetting the dread deep in her bones. Not only would Niko and Ichiro be present for the prefight press party, but her father would also be there. Fight week had always been a family business, a tradition. As domineering as Father and her brothers could be, they were still blood, and messing with Ono blood was inexcusable.

"Are you huffy? Or nervous?" Mark gave her a questioning frown.

Ami wobbled on her spiked snakeskin heels, having been trying to kick her Chanel carry-on into an under-seat storage compartment. The display was revealing, and she hated that. She gave up and rubbed her palms down her dark-rinse jeans. "Pardon?"

How many times had she lectured herself to contain emotions within? Maybe Mark attributed her anxiety to the flight, not family dynamics.

He nodded to her abused bag. "Are you a nervous flyer?"

"Oh, no. Flying's fine."

Paulo raised his brows and shot Keane a *look*. "Here, give me your bag. It can go in the empty seat by me."

"Leave it to Brazil's bad boy to make me look like an unmannered fool." Keane eyed him in a way that made her pulse jive.

"Watch and learn, Temple."

"Thanks, Paulo." Ami smiled, thankful for their lighthearted banter as she eased into the leather bucket seat facing Keane.

"Where's Hans?"

"With Ella and the twins. They came earlier today."

Once all seat belts snapped into place, the pilot covered the safety procedures and ran through the flight plan. By the time he wrapped up his spiel and turned to take off, Mark dove into the evening's order of events. The three men reviewed press questions and scripted responses. Though he was engaged in the conversation, Keane let his long legs stretch forward, a foot hooking her ankle as if he knew she needed the comfort of his touch to steel herself against the night.

Que sera, sera. She'd make the night unforgettable, and contentment swelled in her chest as she focused beyond the curved window. A series of volcanic mountains carpeted in lush pines gave way to the occasional village until the distance between villages shortened and a continuous string of toy-sized towns formed. Out of the suburbs sprouted Tokyo's twinkling lights and modern skyscrapers, but to the west, Fuji-san dominated the skyline. With a fiery-orange sun as its backdrop, the volcano turned into a silhouette, an old watchman, majestic in every way.

"Look," she urged.

"Mount Fuji?" Mark asked.

"The one and only."

Chapter 15

"Crazy," Keane muttered as his gaze roved over the horizon. "And humbling."

"What's that?" Mark cupped a hand behind his protective earmuff.

"The volcano. Tokyo. Even from the air, can't you feel the energy pulsing off the city?" Could any town boast the spectrum of modern marvels coexisting alongside such a collection of honored antiquities? Quizzing fighters on local trivia was always fodder for the reporters. And being duly diligent, he'd done his historical homework before arriving in the Land of the Rising Sun.

"Yeah." Mark grunted and continued checking his email.

But a jolt of appreciation hit Keane in the chest. Tokyo's roots fanned deep and wide through more than five thousand years of history—from the earliest farming and fishing villages to a powerful military headquarters to the nation's capital and into an international financial mecca. The Japanese showed an incredible resolve to rise out of natural disasters and other dark times in triumph. Like the bright lights of Ginza, Tokyo's famous shopping and entertainment district, the highlights flashed through Keane's mind. Renowned artists such as Toyo and Tōhaku and Korin. The poet, Basho. Skilled craftsmen. Sumo stars. Distinctive architecture. Extraordinary cuisine. Earth's most populous metropolitan area sprawled like a field of colorful flowers.

"No, there's definitely a vibe." Paulo flashed a lopsided grin.

"Wait until you see it from street level." Ami swayed toward Keane with a smile, lifting her chin toward the famed Mandarin Oriental Hotel. "We're here."

With the winsome grace of a dragonfly, the helicopter hovered over the city until it lit on the hotel helipad.

Paulo rubbed his palms back and forth over his thighs. "Let's get this party started."

The fighters exited the aircraft onto the rooftop, where hotel staff awaited. The two groups fell into a competition of bows before porters collected the luggage. The concierge offered polite instructions and escorted the guests to an elevator ride. Then golden-filigreed elevator doors unveiled the gleaming penthouse lobby.

"Very nice." Keane turned, waiting while Ami stowed her phone in her purse.

The cavernous lobby, with two giant men flanking the front door, made him feel almost Lilliputian. The duo wore stern expressions, matching black suits with pale gold ties, and semiautomatic pistols holstered at their hips. Their presence was a necessary intrusion in Tokyo, but Ami brushed by them without a glance and made her way to the alabaster vase of the flawless ballet-pink flowers resting on a console.

"Look—cherry blossoms. My favorite."

Keane plucked a twig with perfect petals and tucked it behind her ear.

"And you're mine." He looped his arm around hers, keeping her close.

"Alrighty." Mark clapped twice, glaring at him. "Time to get to work, boys."

The concierge brandished a metal key like a sword before unlocking the door to a central living space. Four bedrooms cornered the penthouse floor.

While the concierge updated Mark and Paulo on security measures, Ami drifted to a paned window in a dark room. She stood alone, inspecting the twinkling night.

As if by some sixth sense, her body tempo began a lively trot, and she knew before turning that Keane had shadowed her. Such was the man's power over her. With the turn of her head, his cheek swept over hers, and his fingers laced through the hair at her nape. His lips traveled feather-light along her jawline, pausing to deliver a murmur in her ear.

"Bewitched. That's what you've done to me."

His words touched her like the smooth caress of oil, easing into her ear and warming down through every cell of her being. "Really?" As nice as she felt, uncertainty slipped through her tone.

"I won't answer that." He gave her a reproving look, nipped her under her earlobe, and then stepped back. "I need to handle a few things. I ordered a fruit plate to snack on and will have the porters bring your bag. Take your time but don't take too long to get dressed, okay?"

"Okay. Better get to work." She managed a wink as a flurry of butterflies took flight in her stomach.

A lazy shower sounded nice, but there wasn't time to start the makeup from scratch. Once her luggage arrived, she set the timer on her phone and lazed on the bed for fifteen minutes. Just being still, staring out the window to collect her thoughts and will down the nerves she pretended not to have, did her good.

When the timer chimed, she fixed her face, twined her long hair into a chignon, and filled out the dress she intended to remember forever. Gliding like the swan for which she was publicly known, she sailed into the living room and interrupted the men's conversation. At their abrupt silence, heat stung her cheeks.

Mark stood and cleared his throat. "Seeing you, in that, I suppose it's time I went and got gussied up too."

"Ah, you have such a way with words." Paulo rolled his eyes. "And look at her. She doesn't bite. Well, I guess she might, but—"

Keane's frosty look stopped Paulo cold.

"What Paulo meant to say is the dress is absolute art. And you in it—a stunning masterpiece," Keane crooned, his expression radiant. "You look amazing. You are amazing." His hands fixed on her waist, keeping her close. Trying not to mess up her makeup, he placed a careful kiss on the tip of her nose.

"Paulo is still here." Paulo reminded them.

The spell broke, and Ami cast him her most winning of grins. "And Paulo needs to go get ready too."

Half an hour later, Ami and Team Temple boarded the elevator and began the descent to the third floor's Linden Conference Room for the prefight press conference. Nerves made her feel constrained by a corset. However, the anxiety transformed into an almost out-of-body daze at the first camera flash.

They'd both been to scores of press events, but this crowd's size and unruliness made her breath hitch. In addition to Japanese anchors, reporters from other countries milled about, chatting it up with translators and sponsors. Bright lights assaulted them from all sides, but her eyes adjusted in time to see hundreds of heads swivel in their direction.

People were seated. People were standing. Many were shoving.

Why did they all have to gawk? Heart in her throat, she resisted the urge to fold and kept her chin high. With a steady hand at the small of her back, he steered her straight through the gasps and whispers to the front of the room where Mark, Paulo, and Hans and Ella waited at the stage's side.

"Watch my girl," he clipped before drawing her close, pressing his mouth to her ear. "You got this."

"I do." She drew back an inch and met his gaze with a brave grin. "And so do you."

He brushed a tender kiss on each of her cheeks, followed Mark up onto the raised platform, and proceeded to take his designated seat. Team Temple sat ready, but Niko Ono and his entourage had yet to show. This delay only fueled the excitement, and the rumblings of the crowd rose.

The president of the Mixed Martial Arts Federation of Nihon mounted the podium, fixed his focus on the central camera, and with the stern strong presence of a starred general, addressed an audience of millions beyond that lens.

Ami didn't even hear what was said.

Then Niko emerged through a back door and interrupted the conference. All eyes cut to the rude intrusion.

Holding her breath, craning for a glimpse of Mika in her new blue dress, Ami stretched higher on her toes, the heels of the Louboutin stilettos leaving the floor. Had he not brought her?

Niko peacocked across the room with Ichiro and her father trailing. They hadn't spotted her yet. She inhaled in a shaky rush.

"You going to be okay?" Ella leaned into her space, gripping her elbow, and Ami nearly yelped.

Relax. No ruffled feathers tonight. "Of course. I'm looking for my roommate. She'll be crushed if he didn't bring her."

Liar. Like Mika was *all* she worried about.

Ichiro took to the podium. "Ladies and gentlemen, thanks for waiting."

His smugness brought bile to the back of her throat. She swallowed hard.

"Niko Ono needs no introduction. But know this." Ichiro's pointer finger hammered the glass podium. "The Flying Dragon came. The Flying Dragon *will* conquer."

Flexing her fingers, she pressed her back to the cool wall. Her attention cut from Keane to Niko, who glared at her with angry eyes. Betrayed eyes. It only lasted a moment. Maybe no one else had even seen.

As Ichiro settled into a chair by Niko on the left, the president stepped forward with a grin. "Two champions. Two kings. Facing off for one night. No doubt it'll be legendary, so don't miss it. The floor is open for questions."

Excess energy fizzled through her. She reached for Ella, leaning into her friend's shoulder as she continued to watch the stage. Keane and Niko sat behind tables draped in pristine white tablecloths resembling the altars of the grand churches Ami had visited while studying in England. "Yeah. Two legends in the world of fighting being offered up to the media moguls as living sacrifices," she mumbled to Ella.

"They're legends for a reason, sister. Breathe. Then blow out the bad. You're on show as much as them." Ella nudged her shoulder and jutted her chin in the direction of a woman taking Ami's picture.

Be smooth as silk.

Microphone static redirected her attention. "So how do you find Japan, Mr. Temple?" asked a nervous man from the *Asahi Shimbun.*

Keane nodded with his lips knit together, his fine camel cashmere suit bringing out golden flecks in his jade eyes. "Lovely. Diverse.

My time in Japan has been an unexpected adventure for which I will always be grateful."

When he spoke, his commanding presence did crazy things to the rhythm of her heart. He was at total ease, his posture inviting and his expression attentive. Just as he had drawn her in, he was about to win over the crowd with his genuineness.

"Sports commentators are calling this matchup epic. The battle of the century. A real bewdy." The new speaker dragged out the word with his Australian accent. "With your styles so matched, is strategy or stamina key?"

Niko chuckled and made a show of inspecting his left fist. "With a superior strategy, who needs stamina?" The flippant response rolled out like cold honey.

"And what about you, Mr. Temple?"

"Every fight has the potential to become epic. Given that Niko and I share more than one common interest"—Keane laid a heavy look on her—"strategy, both physical and mental, and stamina may play second fiddle to fighting with an invested heart." Only when he finished the comment did his eyes release her.

She blinked, taking in the sudden commotion of animated whispers and pens scratching on notepads.

A cheeky young woman sporting a purple ponytail and a nosy expression stood to voice her question. "There's been widespread speculation that Miss Ono is more than an ambassador. Are you fond of her?"

A sudden hush swept the room. Ami held her breath, watching him as seconds ticked by. At last, he met the young woman's eye.

"She has been an excellent ambassador—one who has kindled my great affection for Japan. Of course, I am fond. I must extend my gratitude to Niko Ono for his gracious hospitality."

His compliments were sweet validation, a soothing balm to her soul. Keane could discount strategy all he wanted, but so far, he was stealing the show. Even from a distance, Ami saw Niko's prominent carotid artery pounding in his neck. What could her big brother be thinking? Were his venomous thoughts directed at her or Keane?

She gulped. Time and patience would tell.

But as if she didn't have enough to worry about, she still hadn't seen Mika, and the press was determined to knock everyone off track. "Wow, it's a bloodbath out there." She crossed her arms over the tightness in her chest.

"They prep for these shindigs, but you're right. This exceeds rough. I sure wouldn't want to be out there," Ella said.

"My brother believes more drama yields bigger numbers and banks more for both fighting camps. But shouldn't the line be drawn at some point?" Some things were too personal and off-limits.

The Australian reporter stood again. "Niko, what do you think about your sister wearing a gold dress? Isn't that the color of Temple's fighting camp?"

"Oh no, oh no, oh no." Her hand flew to her forehead, rubbing as dismay hit her.

Niko's face reddened, and his eyeballs bulged out of the sockets. For the first time ever, she wore gold instead of red. Did he think the dress, her intentional rebellion, was the worst betrayal? Would he see she was happy with Keane?

Niko made eye contact with his father, but searching for his support was a waste. Father only tipped his head back, his face expressionless.

Niko drained half the water glass and cleared his throat. "Ami looks lovely in any color. Best in red, of course, but as his rather dedicated ambassador, gold suits her too." Not a bad sugarcoating. But his voice sounded tight.

A sharp sigh escaped her mouth when the federation president mounted the stage to give closing remarks.

"Thank you, Niko." The president then gave Keane a polite

bow. "And Mr. Temple. The federation and fans are eager to see this bout, but until then, all are invited to join the evening festivities in the Grand Ballroom."

"Well done." Ami thrilled, recovering from the deep kiss Keane had given her.

"The kiss or the press conference?" His brows arched until she swatted his biceps.

Lips tucked together, she let her gaze roam the now-empty conference room. "Both. That was nerve-racking though."

"Are you sure you're fine?" His fingers twined around hers.

"Better than fine."

"Then let's unwind at the after-party." He led the way down the hall to a set of oversized doors.

"This is impressive." She did a slow spin, taking in the vast space swathed in shimmering red and gold fabrics. A classy jazz ensemble. The scent of fresh-baked cookies. An all-female waitstaff snaked through the room, passing hors d'œuvres. Abundant candlelight. But the candlelight held nothing on the comforting glow Keane brought out in her.

"What are you thinking?" He slipped an arm around her waist and tugged her into the ballroom.

Her tight shoulders loosened as she savored the reassurance of having his hand back on her. Then her gaze narrowed in on Mark before flicking back to Keane. She didn't dare disclose the riot of emotions percolating through her brain. "I think you killed it."

Mark rattled the ice around his crystal tumbler, laughing. "Agreed. The fans are eating up this rivalry, and, Keane, you could *not* have played it any smoother tonight. There's someone I want you to meet." Mark waved over a reed-thin man. "Bob, come join us."

Keane extended his hand. "Hey, man. It's a pleasure."

"Bob's with *Fighters Only*," Mark said.

"And I'm a fan. Great to meet you."

So much for unwinding. Up close, everyone became a fan, and tonight, they all wanted a piece of him. But she understood his intoxicating appeal.

Bob turned to her. "And you, Miss Ono."

"Oh." That got her full attention. "You're very kind. Are you working on a special piece?"

Keane's fingers brushed hers.

"That I am. With his notable record, Keane's earned rivals' respect the hard way. Straight up." Bob turned, looking Keane eyeball to eyeball. "You are going to be a legend. An unblemished Greek god standing apart from the sea of weathered, tattoo-clad combatants."

"Midas." Ami chuckled and winked at Keane.

Bob swiveled her way and matched her grin. "Yeah. Midas."

Keane's head tipped back as he shook it. "Let's talk soon. As long as you don't call me that in print."

"I can make that happen."

"Sounds like a deal. Can I get you a drink?" Mark clapped a hand on Bob's shoulder and led him away.

"Ami." Her father's voice had the crisp edge of a drill sergeant.

"Hello, Father. You startled me."

She had spotted the dark-haired force earlier but always at a safe distance. Niko, Father, and Ichiro arced their way around the room's opposite side. But Niko stood out. His height, build, and black eyes gave him a dangerous, almost invincible appearance. A shiver shook through her bones. Her brother was a stark contrast to Keane's golden good looks. Keane and Niko became a sun and moon orbiting—never colliding—through the Grand Ballroom's star-studded space.

"I might say the same to you." Father kept his face one smooth, unreadable mask. His presence felt cold and detached, as if the shadow of death had arrived to seek her out.

"Mr. Ono." Keane jumped in, giving a deep respectful bow. "It's nice to see you again."

"Mr. Temple." Father returned a curt bow. "I wish you luck at this weekend's bout and a safe journey home. Have you decided to stay on in Japan? Or are your departure plans intact?" His brow arched, etching a series of parallel wrinkles across his forehead.

Ami's gaze connected with Keane's. Was that sadness welling up in his? Uncertainty? Was it hope he sought in hers?

"Your son is a formidable opponent, so your good wishes are welcomed. I have business to attend to in Texas next week. Our plane departs Monday."

"Very good. Please allow Ichiro to make arrangements to transport your team safely to the airport. It is the least we could do."

At Ichiro's name, a hiss, almost inaudible, escaped her teeth. Her father had nerve. From around the room, sets of eyes began raking over the Ono-Temple encounter with the heat and precision of lasers. Drama might be good for sales, but things could turn ugly.

"That is a kind but unnecessary gesture. I understand your message." Keane's steady, low voice showed his determination not to make a scene.

"Excellent. It pleases me to hear that." The muscles of Father's face worked to form the tiniest of smiles.

Fire flowed through Ami's veins. "*I* do not and will not accept your message, Father." Chin high, she managed to keep her voice calm. "Ichiro will never be a substitute for Keane."

Keane pulled her closer, pinned her to his side with a calming iron grip, and kissed her temple. Father wasn't the only one who could drop a subtle message. Ami was his. Laying public claim was a formality.

Father's strained smile vanished. "Safe travels." He threw a cool glance at her, nodded, and walked away.

From the fog of people into which Father disappeared, Keane's crew emerged.

"Why the long faces? This is your party after all." Flushed and animated, Mark hoisted his glass. "Liven up, kids."

Keane released Ami but caught her hand, then grinned at Mark. "What are you so amped up about? The deal with Bob?"

"More than that. Slight change of plans. Big plans, so hear me out." Mark paused to catch his breath. "I booked you for two guest appearances. One with NNS. The other with TV Tokyo. You'll need to stay the night, but it'll be great publicity."

Raking a hand through his hair, Keane ground his teeth together and ducked his head from Ami's gaze. Studying him so closely, she must know he was far from pleased.

She leaned toward him, her chin tipped up to speak. It made her look both stubborn and kissable. "Mark is right. That *is* a big deal. You need to stay, and if you're worried about me, don't be. I have to work tomorrow, and then I'll be back for the fight."

"I don't want Ami to fly home alone." His tone had better make it clear it was an order, not a statement.

"Hans already headed out with the girls, but I'll go," Paulo offered.

Keane rolled his eyes. "Not a chance."

"Paulo may be much more pretty than Keane, but Paulo does not want to make Keane angry." Paulo raised his right hand as if giving an oath. "And I promise, no matter how hard she begs, I will not teach your woman the amazing moves of a Latino lov—"

"Enough." Keane slapped Paulo's shoulder and eyed his friend. "I'm not sure I have another choice. You *will* take care of her."

"That's what I said." Paulo winked at her.

"Good. And now that that's settled, please excuse me. Ami and I need to dance."

Keane offered his hand and led her to the dance floor. Once there, he could avoid the queue of fans and reporters greedy for exclusive quotes and intrusive photo ops.

"Ah, we can breathe." Ami gave a breathy chuckle, the gentle reverberations tickling his chest.

Mmm, he liked it too much. "They're still watching us though."

"At least they can't hear everything I whisper."

"A nice change. Plus, I like dancing with you, which means I'm going to struggle returning to the States. I have to, but . . ."

"Duty calls?" Her head tipped up, one brow rising even as her lips slid downward.

He paused, his gaze landing hard on hers. "I was going to say we need to find a way to make this work. Not a half-hearted promise. A real commitment."

Her keen eyes flared wide, and her kissable lips opened before she closed them and swallowed. "What do you have in mind?"

He dipped a hand into his pants pocket, retrieved a trinket, and held his palm open between their bodies. A gold and diamond three-strand tennis bracelet glittered against his skin. She extended her wrist, letting him clasp the bracelet beside her simpler bangle, and he fumbled with the single heart-shaped Burmese ruby inset by the bracelet's clasp.

With the tip of her French-manicured nail, she touched the stone. Her finger shook. "Does this mean I have your heart?"

His gaze flicked up from her wrist to catch a fiery glint in her eyes. He swallowed and placed his lips by her ear. "It means you, Ami Ono, make my heart worth having."

Chapter 16

Keane startled awake. Sunrise slanted through the curtains, the angle slipping from the window across the floor to climb to the edge of the bed. He shook free from his sleep fog. Right. Still at the Mandarin in Tokyo. At six o'clock, he'd be able to work through his business emails before showering and heading to the television studio.

He reached for his smartphone and grinned at an unopened text from Ami.

> Ami: Thankful even the mightiest of men can fall. Especially thankful you fell for me. Sweet dreams, my Temple.

The postparty late night rushed back. Before boarding the helicopter, Ami floored him with a lingering kiss. Letting her go physically pained him, but true to her word, she called him the moment she and Paulo landed in Sendai. Paulo behaved the whole way.

As she was slipping between the sheets in her bedroom, she said how tired she was, the whole time mumbling into the receiver about the evening. How nice the party was. How he managed to trump Niko in his homeland. How she enjoyed dancing with him. How she'd never take off the bracelet.

He must've been worn out, too, because he had not the faintest memory of when the message pinged through. He started to call, but decided she must be getting ready for work. He typed a message instead.

> KEANE: Touché, angel. Fall is an understatement. Will call soon.

He opened his emails. Hunter Montgomery needed to speak about partnering with a private equity group on a massive class-A deal that hit the Phoenix real estate market. The drastic time difference made calling tricky. Keane proposed a meeting time via email, then hopped in and out of the shower.

The room phone rang, and he scrambled to answer with still-damp hands.

"You 'bout ready, champ? The car's been burning gas at the curb for ten minutes, and we've gotta roll," Mark grumbled.

"Be right down, sunshine."

A sand-colored Mercedes hummed beyond the Mandarin's front entrance. At his appearance, a waifish driver caught the door for Keane, bowed, and sealed him inside with the security detail and Mark. Mark had a cell phone pressed to his ear, so Keane admired the Tokyo sights, a morphing tapestry of modern architecture, illuminated digital displays, and busy people. Taxis and bikes jockeyed. In a narrow green space spliced into the cityscape, people stretched left and then right, saluting the sun from within the man-made wilderness.

Soon, the car stopped before a needle-shaped tower constructed of woven metal. An elevator ride delivered them into a sleek circular lobby in a palette of soothing creams and polished woods. Inset in the central wall, a television played the news with a scrolling

NNS logo. An enthusiastic assistant ushered Team Temple into the green room, prepped them for the morning show, and then left them to relax.

Keane stepped on set. A chipper anchor named Akiko made him comfortable during a commercial break, but when the on-air light snapped on, her energy translated into over-the-top intensity as she pelted him with gritty questions.

Most were basic. Some he pondered before responding. But when the conversation turned personal, he steeled himself against defensive tendencies.

His relationship with Ami Ono hatched in the spotlight, and he had no qualms about giving a glowing update on his softer side. Somehow, their out-of-the-blue relationship, rather than making him look weak or vulnerable, had endeared him to the public, catapulting his image. Or so Mark said.

"You nailed it, champ." Mark clapped a heavy hand over Keane's shoulder.

"Really?"

"Win. Gosh, even if you lost, which you won't, it's gonna be a windfall." Mark adjusted his snug pants around his midsection and planted his hands on his hips.

Keane chuckled. "Where to now? I need to eat."

"Me too. Already asked the girl in the green room. She recommended a place on the top floor, said it's quick and good."

"Excellent. Let's roll." He exited the office, punched the elevator button, and waited until the crowded lift arrived. He and Mark squeezed in. "What're the boys doing today?"

"Sumo session." Mark waggled his brows as the elevator began its ascent.

"Without me?"

"Nah." Mark laughed as they stepped into the chic restaurant lobby. "I talked to Paulo earlier. Told 'em to take the morning off after the late night, but they're planning to hit the gym this afternoon."

Keane nodded as they ambled toward the hostess.

"Welcome to Panorama." The young woman bowed. "Party of two?"

"Yeah. Window spot, if you can." Mark elbowed Keane as they trailed her to a table overlooking the business district. "Will you look at that?"

Tokyo swarmed with skyscrapers. The mirrored glass monuments winked back at the sun, and Keane blinked at the brightness. "It's something special. I'm glad we got to visit."

Mark roared with laughter. "Understatement of the year. No doubt that girlfriend of yours has sumpin' to do with it being special."

No doubt. And what might his girlfriend be doing? Was she also at lunch? "Hey, I'm going to make a call." He skimmed over the menu. "Will you get me the teriyaki chicken and buckwheat noodles?"

"Aye, aye, captain." Mark gave a playful salute. "Tell her hello from Uncle Mark."

Keane tried to shake the grin from his face. "Will do."

He headed to a lobby corner to call Ami, but it went straight to voicemail. He hung up and paced around the central space, planning to give her a few minutes before dialing again. But after the hectic morning, he welcomed privacy, and the restroom was the only option.

The door locked with a metallic click. He moved to the sink to splash cool water over his warm face. Why could he not stop smiling? In his reflection, the tightness around his eyes had smoothed. Had the spirited Ami Ono accomplished the impossible and calmed his restless soul?

He hit redial. Voicemail again. Disappointment jabbed him in the gut. He waited for the beep. "Ami. Guess it's a busy day for us both. Who knew missing someone could hurt more than any broken bone ever did? Call me soon, angel."

The waitress was delivering the meal as he returned to the table.

"*Bada bing,*" Mark chirped, giving his palms a greedy rub.

"And why are you so pleased with yourself?" Keane slid into his seat.

"Because I just got off the phone with el pres–si–dent–tay of MMAF-Nihon and you, my friend, now have a practice slot in the fight arena."

"Seriously?" His eyes locked on Mark's. "Well done."

"I try." Mark pretended to shrug off the compliment. "Better eat up. The arena is clear across town, and we need to be there by three if you want time to freshen up before going on *TV Tokyo Tonight.*"

Half an hour and a satisfying bowl of chicken and noodles later, Keane and Mark shuffled around the lobby, waiting for the elevator. Irritated by the delay, Mark hustled into the metal box, rolled his eyes, and jammed a pointer finger against the ground-floor button.

Keane shot him an amused grin and wiggled his cell phone from his pants pocket. The morning had gone well. He'd be able to practice in the fight arena, a rare occurrence. And his heart did a surging jig at a missed text.

> Aᴍɪ: Sorry I missed your call. Crazy day at work. Let's talk this evening. Does seven work for you?

The signal disappeared as the elevator began its descent, and he propped his shoulders against the back wall. The elevator halted on the floor housing NNS, and like the parting of curtains, the doors separated to unveil gut-wrenching pandemonium.

A riot of cries erupted from the studio floor. People rushed by others who had frozen in their tracks, hands over gasping mouths.

"What happened?" Keane asked a woman staring at the lobby television.

She pointed at the screen. "Big earthquake."

An urgent newsbreak streamed from the television. Keane couldn't understand the rapid-fire Japanese, but he could recognize the map of the Pacific coastline east of Sendai. An initial Richter reading of 9.0. A tsunami alert. More coverage coming.

One news snippet followed the next until he comprehended the magnitude. As if cold, heavy concrete set up in his gut, his stomach plummeted.

"Keane, did you hear me? I can't reach Hans or Paulo," Mark was saying. "The cell towers must be tapped out. Or down."

Blood, thick and hot, clogged Keane's ears, making him feel as if underwater. Sound was muffled, a distant thing. Ami was at work. *A crazy day at work.* She would be right on the coast.

"Dear Lord, let her be all right," he muttered before his thoughts darkened with what-ifs.

"Try Ami." Mark clapped Keane's face between stress-slick palms, making him look eye to eye. "Keane, do you hear me? Try calling Ami."

First came a tremble. But it wasn't just any tremble. The initial jolt struck before intensifying. With no time to think, only react, Ami dropped to her knees. She'd come home on her lunch break to get a sweater. She'd been cold all morning and had crossed the front-door threshold when the quake struck. The movement stretched on.

"Mika, are you here?"

Only the smash of dinnerware against the unforgiving Italian tile kitchen floor came in reply. Kitchen cabinets swung wide. Books shuffled off shelves. Her home groaned on rigid joints. Somewhere outside, a woman screamed.

The scientific part of Ami's brain snapped to attention. Deep below the earth's surface, along a subduction zone, the presence of slippery clay allowed one tectonic plate to glide a considerable distance over another. Terrifying sliding. If she'd gauged the time right, six minutes of bone-rattling shaking. The effects of such a record-breaking quake—bigger than popular geologic opinion deemed possible for the region—would roll around the world.

Her heart throbbed against her ribs. Where was Mika? Her roommate froze every time one struck. Ami checked her watch. There was precious little time with an earthquake of this magnitude. High eights. Could it have hit nine on the Richter scale? Tsunami sirens already wailed.

Unmistakably harsh things the sirens were.

Adrenaline fueled her footsteps. Down the stairs. Through the streets. Past fractured houses and a crowd of ashen-faced people on the move to higher ground. She tried dialing Mika, but the towers must have been down. No signal. So little time.

Against her better judgment, Ami sprinted toward the library where Mika worked, toward the ocean, hoping she could beat whatever might be coming and find her best friend.

The library was chaos. No lights. Books littering the floor. Abandoned satchels. A sudden ghost town.

"Mika," Ami called out, peering into the dim space. The books seemed to swallow her voice. "Mika, please. Anyone. Is anyone here?"

Only the hissing of a damaged air-conditioning unit. Ami wiped at the damp trails streaking her cheeks and checked her watch. Twenty minutes since the shaking stopped. *Where could you be, Mika?*

She had cataloged the library. But what about the break room? The restrooms? With care, she tiptoed through a literary minefield to the back hall. She was about to give up when the faintest of whimpers stopped her dead.

"Mika?" Ami shouted again.

"Ami?" The whimper came from the restrooms.

Ami's heart seized in her chest before pounding harder than ever. She pressed through to the ladies' room and found her room-mate crouched in a corner by the sink, a straight bloody scratch ran down her arm.

"What happened? Are you all right?" Ami stooped to help her friend to her feet.

"It's nothing. I fell into the doorframe during the quake. I am so glad you're here." Mika reached out to touch her. Mika's focus seemed to drift, the injury likely making her woozy.

"I'm glad I was home and could find you, but we *have* to move." Ami frowned at her watch again. Twenty-seven minutes. How long until the tsunami might hit?

"A tsunami." Mika spoke without emotion as if their true peril hadn't dawned on her. "And we're too close, aren't we?"

Ami gave her a nod, unable to muster up a dash of cheer. "You're going to have to walk. Put your arm over my shoulder if you need to, and let's hurry. There can't be much time."

"The danger—why did you come for me?" Some indiscernible emotion—maybe indebtedness—strangled Mika's voice.

Ami's spirit nosedived. But she drew in a deep mind-clearing breath, shook off any misgivings, and reminded herself about what mattered.

"Because you are the best—and only—sister I've ever had. Now, let's go."

They'd just made it outside when sound blasted their ears and overwhelmed other senses.

The sound of the tsunami was unimaginable. Transfixing. With the wild roar of a waterfall, it taunted Ami before it was visible. The song of destruction—breaking glass, clanging metal against metal, howling deliverance cries—made her blood run cold even as a sweat heated her brow.

Then the nightmarish rush of saltwater polarized life into *a before* and *an after* the tsunami.

"Leave me," Mika urged her, gasping for breath as they ran from it. "I'm slow, but you can make it home. Please."

Three blocks from the ocean, the water had hopped right over the city's protective seawalls, crushing and sweeping up everything. Fishing vessels from miles away were pressing inland. Cars bobbed and sank in the street behind them. Broken gas lines created infernos riding on patches of the water's oily surface. Two-story buildings collapsed like card stacks while daring souls tried to outrun it.

"Do not give up." Ami yanked at her, despite feeling powerless. "If I hadn't gone home at lunch . . . Well, look, we're lucky. Maybe we are inland enough. Maybe." Exertion burned her chest, and tears stung her eyes. "But we are *not* giving up now."

The world fell away as she reached fight-or-fall time. Charged by adrenaline, her feet churned. Her heart hammered.

They made some progress moving inland. But was it enough?

Chapter 17

Water, laced with debris and contaminated by unidentifiable substances, rushed over trees and raced around the buildings tall enough to withstand it. They sprinted several blocks and managed to get to the commercial district before that cold water began slapping against Mika's ankles. Why had they believed they could outrun an angry wall of water? Tried and failed. Disappointment crushed Mika. They weren't inland enough. They weren't high enough.

"There," she shouted, moving in hurried lockstep with Ami toward a nondescript door to their right. The fact it was unlocked was an incredible blessing. "We have to get higher."

Together, they scrambled up a metal fire stairwell. The water's pressure buckled the outer wall with a burst of jagged debris—damaged lighting fixtures, dangled wires, shattered glass, crushed wall plaster. Opened a patch to steely sky. The dreaded surge of water swirled in. And then stalled.

"It stopped!" Mika squealed. "We aren't going to drown. Ami?"

Mika glanced over her shoulder, and her triumph faded in a gasp. A four-by-four support beam had fallen. One end now wedged the door shut. The other end pinned Ami's foot to a metal tread under water. Had the beam hit her head on the way down? Ami lay partially submerged and unconscious. A gash ran along her left temple and disappeared into her hairline. Bright scarlet blood soaked her hair before trailing down her ashen cheek and neck.

"Ami, wake up." Mika sobbed, stroking her friend's cheek. Her hands were shaking, but from cold or fear, she could not say. "We are going to live. You need to wake up."

Sounds trickled in from beyond the wall. The incessant bark of a frightened dog. The tinkling echo of cool water sloshing on the metal stairwell. Her ragged breaths.

She slipped out of her jean jacket. Using a piece of loose metal and, at times, her teeth, she worked to tear off a sleeve and then wrapped the rough material over the worst of Ami's wound. "You're the tough one. Wake up. *Please.*"

As much as Mika did not want to leave her friend, she must. When the water began its slow retreat, she stood, worked to dislodge the beam, and ventured to the messy sidewalk.

With everything out of place, the stench of wet, sea-salted roadways was strong. An elderly woman wandered through the puddles. A boy sprinted down the street. A plush doll lay discarded without an owner. Who dropped it? Or did it wash out of a home? Where was the little girl who once held it? Her heart ached.

Mika swallowed hard, willing the bile to stay down, pushing sad thoughts away, returning to her task.

"Help," she cried out. "Can anyone help me?"

Minutes—white-knuckled, desperate minutes—passed before a blonde darted through the street. "Do you speak English?"

"Y–yes."

"Are you hurt?" The woman rested a hand on Mika's shoulder.

"No. It's my friend. Please hurry."

Mika spun on her heel and hustled back into the building. Still unconscious on the steps, Ami looked so fragile. Mika covered her with the jacket and stepped back, eyes brimming and throat clogging. "We were trying to escape the water, but the wall gave way." She made a motion toward the ground floor. "That beam caught her."

"Take a deep breath. You've done well. But tell me: How long has she been unconscious?" The woman brushed hair from Ami's ashen face to examine the cut.

"I'm not sure. Thirty minutes, maybe forty."

The woman nodded before her bright-blue eyes widened. "Oh goodness, I know her."

"You know Ami?"

"Yes, we met a few weeks ago at a fan event."

"Small world, I guess." Mika fiddled with her fingers, knotting them together. "Do you think we should move her?"

"I'm not sure. Give me a second. I can get some help." The woman rummaged through her cross-body messenger bag and pulled out a technical gadget. "Satellite phone."

She punched in numbers and held the receiver to her ear. "Mike? Hey, it's Mary. I have a young lady here in need of immediate assistance. Head injury." She paced the stairwell landing. "No, she's out cold. We need a neck brace and board to move her. Is there room at the hospital?" A long beat passed. "Okay then. We are in the back stairwell of the Chiyo Institute. See you soon."

As Mary took a seat by Ami, clasped a hand between her own, and began to pray out loud, Mika gaped, speechless.

"I don't care what it costs," Keane growled. "Get me there. Now." Palms pressed flat against the pane glass, he leaned forward and stared at that endless field of buildings gleaming like crystals in the twilight. The earthquake was torture, but what came after was different. How many hours had passed since he'd seen the initial footage of a massive tsunami wave bulldozing over the city?

From the depths of the earth, a life-changing monster had been released. His worry morphed into a scorching, consuming fear. Was she alive? Was she injured? Hell and high water had come together—Why? While Mark worked on arrangements, Keane lifted up countless prayers, but an unforgiving brand of hell ravaged his soul, leaving him ill. And he couldn't watch the news any longer. He slashed a hand through the air. "Why is it so hard to get a helicopter?"

"Because they're busy. Look, I still can't reach the boys but got word the tsunami didn't impact the Westin. The pilot who flew us here is Tokyo-based. I just got off the phone with him." Mark used the soothing tone one might use to reassure a child. "Now, if you would stop speculating and get moving, he said there's a Red Cross flight leaving in half an hour to deliver medical supplies."

For the first time in nearly five hours, hope soothed the knots in Keane's chest.

Mark jerked a thumb toward the door. "Go on. Get outta here. They said you can ride *if* you'll help unload."

An hour and twenty minutes later, the medical flight hovered over the outskirts of Sendai. The Red Cross medic beside Keane clamped a hand on his shoulder, jostling him from his daze. "You all right, man?"

"Yeah. I'm at a total loss. All of this." After a glance at the name *Jayce* embroidered on the medic's uniform, Keane waved to the wasteland of debris below. "I feel helpless, utterly helpless, and totally inadequate."

He sat back and raked his fingers through his hair. All the warm light seemed to drain from his day.

"I hear you," the pilot chimed in, his rich voice marked by a beautiful West African accent. "Mother Nature throws some wicked curveballs, but you showed up. That is huge. From up here, you see the broader path of destruction. It is a shock to the senses, for sure, but when we land, expect it to be a roller coaster. Pandemonium. Heartbreak. Sometimes relief when people find a loved one. There is no time to feel helpless when you face such suffering."

"It's a mess. Where *are* you going to land?" Jayce asked the pilot.

"There's a pad on top of the Westin," Keane offered. "It's been deemed structurally sound."

"Yeah?" Jayce arched a brow.

"I wanted to drop to street level, but it does not look like an option," the pilot boomed, head panning left to right, his eyes scouring the battered cityscape. He nodded toward a building several blocks away. "Is that it?"

Keane shifted forward and pointed. "There. That's it."

The pilot began snapping at switches as he spoke over the radio. Then the helicopter perched with the effortless control of a heron settling on a riverbank. A hotel employee appeared from the rooftop access door, clearly rattled as he approached Jayce to work out the logistics of unloading. As they spoke, Keane ventured to the roof's edge.

His heart plummeted to the pit of his stomach, unleashing a wave of nausea. A stray boat now rested outside the coffee shop. Several storefront windows bore fresh cracks or were shattered. Unattended cars had floated to a stop on sidewalks beneath battered trees, and seaweed bearded a nearby lamppost. The brine of seawater and the acrid smoke from ruptured gas lines soured the air.

"Where are you, Ami?" He whispered into the wind. The steel-gray sky was growing dimmer as dusk approached. She could've been anywhere. Work. Lunch. Diving. He ground his teeth, his hands fisting, but he had nothing to fight and no idea where to begin. A groan ripped free. *Why did I let her leave Tokyo?*

"Can you give me a hand?" Jayce called.

Keane pivoted. "Absolutely."

Forty-seven minutes and ten rolling freight carts later, dozens of boxes of medical supplies were available to the people of Sendai. Antibiotics. Saline bags. Painkillers. Gauze. A massive Red Cross flag now offered a beacon for the injured and suffering. The process had busied the hands but couldn't still his mind.

"Man, you're strong and driven but far too quiet. Your mind's heavy, isn't it?" Jayce laced his fingers behind his neck and stretched his back before letting his arms fall to his sides. "I'm not sure the best way to launch into this, but experience has taught me that, even though there are no guarantees, there's always reason to hope for a miracle."

He nodded toward the stairwell, then started down ahead of Keane, speaking in cadence to their footfalls.

"For ten years, I've served as a medical rescuer. Earthquakes, avalanches, massive wildfires on six different continents—I've seen it all. Despite the significant loss here, extreme events bring out the best in the survivors. Never underestimate a person's will to live." Before opening the bottom door, Jayce clasped Keane's shoulder. "And do not give up until you find her. I mean it."

He pushed through onto the street.

At ground level, the soul-shattering scene was unlike anything Keane had ever witnessed, and searching in dark unfamiliar streets was perilous. But he wasn't alone. Others shouted for loved ones. A displaced dog scurried by. For four hours, he focused on scouring the streets surrounding Ami's home. For four hours, he cried out her name. For four hours, he listened, making no discovery and growing desperate.

Depleted, he picked a new path back to the Westin, just in case. It had to be close to midnight, and until he cracked open the door, he'd forgotten he'd offered up the couch to the medic. But

208

both Jayce and Paulo were in the living room, waiting for his return. His heart began hammering as his gaze zigzagged between the men. "What's up?"

"Temple." Paulo stood. He closed the gap between them and gave him a man hug with a hard pat on the back.

"Man, I'm glad to see you in one piece," Keane said.

"And I'm glad to be in one piece. It's insane." Paulo shook his head. A new seriousness replaced his usual good cheer.

"I know." Slouching against the side of the couch, Keane couldn't bring himself to vocalize that he had yet to find Ami. Couldn't reach her. Had no idea where to target the search. "What's up, Jayce? I would've figured you'd still be at the relief station."

"I have been. I got here about ten minutes ago and met your teammate. As much damage as there is, getting workers in place has been a slow process, but news and updates are starting to roll in, even been some good news stories."

"Yeah?"

"Yeah," Jayce responded, matching Keane's weary tone. "A few hours ago, an interesting radio call came in from an American woman, a May—not May . . ."

"Mary. You said Mary earlier," Paulo interjected.

Keane straightened. "That sounds familiar."

"It should. Said she knows you," Paulo said.

Fragments of a memory surfaced in Keane's sluggish brain, but he couldn't pinpoint how he might know her. "And?"

"I made a special trip here, and do not get your hopes up because I'm not positive." Jayce held up a hand. "But word came in about a Japanese celebrity. Mary said you might know her. It could be Ami."

Pulse thrumming, Keane was on his feet in a heartbeat. "Where?"

"There's a makeshift triage center a few blocks away. I have to get back to my post. I radioed ahead, and Paulo knows how to get there."

Keane charged to the door, not waiting to hear anything else, not even listening to his brain warning him he'd already checked the triage centers.

The uncertainty. The possibility. Time, his feet, nothing moved fast enough. Everything between here, now, and the triage center became an obstacle. When he reached the entrance, a wiry man with a clipboard, a chirping walkie-talkie, and round metal-framed glasses blocked his path.

"We only have room for the injured." The man pointed toward the street. "The shelter is at the high school."

Paulo stepped forward. "His girlfriend is here."

"Name, please." The man wielded the clipboard.

"Ami. Ami Ono." Keane held his breath as the man shuffled through a short stack of papers.

"I'm sorry. I don't have an Ono listed."

"You're positive?" Paulo elbowed in front of Keane, his chin jutting in his I-mean-business expression.

Hooked to the volunteer's belt loop, the walkie-talkie buzzed to life. The man nodded as he stepped away.

How many hundreds of times had Keane taken a gut punch that knocked the wind from his lungs? Somehow those words, *I don't have an Ono listed*, felt worse.

Paulo got in his face and forced his mind back to the present. "This doesn't mean anything. Let's go get some rest, and in the morning, we can loo—"

"Mr. Temple?"

They turned to a relieved-looking blonde rushing their way.

Keane's spirits lifted a notch. "Mary, right?"

"I'm so glad to see you." She caught his hand, sandwiching it between hers. "Your friend, Ami . . ."

"I came looking for her, but the man said no Onos are here."

"I'm so sorry. I couldn't remember her last name." She squeezed Keane's hand and tugged him through a maze of people and treatment stations. Crying babies. Superficial wounds. Shivering old women wrapped in donated blankets. Through a tent and into a building. The power was out, but emergency lanterns cast a warm amber light.

"So, she *is* here?" Paulo confirmed as he trailed alongside them.

"She's here. Like I said, I couldn't remember her surname and didn't bother to ask her friend, so she's under Temple. Somehow, it seemed right." The woman silenced as if she regretted her confession, but Keane caught her up in a bear hug.

"Where?" Stepping back, it was all he could get out and not risk getting too choked up. That wouldn't be fitting for a fighter.

"End of the hall, but . . ." She grabbed his arm and met his eye with a glint of caution in her own.

He swallowed hard, willing the words past a desert-dry mouth, even as he dreaded the answer. "What is it?"

"She *should* be fine, but she's unconscious—has been for hours now."

Keane charged by her and navigated the pandemonium to the last room on the right. He knew a thing or two about knockouts, but nothing about being out cold for hours. *Lord, wrap her in Your powerful arms. Protect her. Please heal her, Father, and if it's Your will, bring her back to me.*

The aid station consisted of a makeshift tent connected to a suite of medical offices. In a private patient room, Ami lay on a padded examination table, her midnight hair fanned over the white cotton blanket covering her. Mika stood by her side, keeping watch. Her eyes were damp, and her face was covered in rose splotches.

He crossed to Ami's side, kissed her lips, and held her hand. "What did the doctor say?"

"She needs an MRI, but the hospitals are full," Mary, coming up behind him, answered.

Keane nodded, considering how he could get her airlifted to Tokyo. "Have you spoken with Mr. Ono or Niko?" he asked Mika. "They need to know."

"I tried. There is no cell coverage."

"Give me your number, and I'll try from my flat," Mary offered. "I need to check in and make sure my students are still okay, but I'll be back in the morning. I'm praying for her—and you."

With a solemn nod, Keane grasped her hands and met her kind gaze. "I appreciate that. Thank you for everything."

Paulo abruptly shifted. "Mika, let's give them privacy. Okay? I can help you get home."

Stifling a yawn, she nodded. "Okay, but I want to come back in the morning."

"'S fine. We will come back." He eased toward the door, leaning back so she could pass in front of him. "'Night, Keane."

"Thanks, man. See you tomorrow."

Enveloped in privacy, Keane exhaled. He slid a chair next to Ami's cot, leaned back against the wall, and cradled her hand in his. Held tight in her fisted palm was his *omedeto*, the watch. He'd forgotten she still had it. He pressed careful kisses against her forehead. "I found you, angel. Please come back to me. God, please bring her back to me."

The unimaginable day settled into stillness. He'd found her. But would she be all right? Fatigue of body and mind sucked him in.

No telling how many hours had passed before his eyelids opened. A yellow light hazed the room, and a racket was brewing in the hallway. Could it be midmorning? Ami's hand still rested in his. She looked as peaceful as an angel and as fair as the delicate swan for which she was known. But why hadn't the medical staff been by to check on her?

Irritation simmered under his skin. He laid her hand on the bed, swept his finger over her bracelets, and tucked the blanket around her legs before straightening his back to retrieve the phone from his pocket. The battery was nearly depleted, but a single coverage bar looked promising for the first time in twenty hours. A miracle. Would there be enough power to call Mark *and* Paulo? He opted to ring Mark first. It took six attempts before a call connected.

"You lousy—" Mark's bass voice greeted him.

"Whoa, is that how you treat your lead fighter?" Despite his manager's attitude, Keane chuckled.

"The phone has been burning up the hook. I've been worried sick."

"Join the club. At least you still have cell service in Tokyo. It's spotty here at best, and my phone is almost dead."

When Mark began to speak again, he was thoughtful. "Not ten minutes ago, I spoke with a tenacious lady who managed to get my number."

"Mary?"

"That would be the one. She's headed to see you now."

Keane's mind worked through that until he decided Paulo must've given her Mark's number. "So, you know?"

"Ami's unconscious and every hospital within a hundred miles is overflowing? Yeah, I heard that. I'm so sorry, man."

"Can you get a chopper here? Maybe get us back to Tokyo? Anywhere? She needs medical care."

Through the receiver, Keane heard Mark knocking on some piece of wooden furniture. "There was an aftershock or two early this morning. That got everyone worked up and put the damper on some flights, but I'll see what I can do."

"One more thing. Get in touch with Niko and her father. Please."

"Got it, boss man. But you're doing the best thing, just being there for her. Don't stop talking to her."

Shortly after he hung up, a double knock sounded on the door. It cracked open an inch. "Keane, may I come in?"

"Of course." When Mary's gentle voice drifted in, he unfolded his stiff legs and stood.

She edged the door closed. "No change, huh?"

"Nothing." He cleared his throat and wiped a hand over his tired eyes. "Not as much as a peep. And no one has been by."

Keane shuffled around the room, working life back into his legs and fuming like a penned bull.

"Hard as it may be to believe, she is a lucky one. The sun's up now, and . . . outside . . . It's bad, Keane." Tears trickled over her lower eyelids. "I've never witnessed such catastrophic loss."

He stilled. "You're right. We are blessed." The admittance was more for his benefit than hers. "I could've lost her. At least there's hope."

"You know there is, so bank on it."

"Think we can get her help?"

"There's a hospital nearby. The Red Cross is prioritizing cases and sending the worst." She swept a fan of black hair off Ami's cheek and secured it behind her ear. "Hey, there's a men's room down the hall. Why don't you go freshen up? I'll keep her company."

To prove the point, Mary turned her back and crouched beside Ami, caressing her sleeping senses with prayerful, healing words. Balm for the body, mind, and soul.

The night had been a black hole. Consuming. Powerful. Mystifying. And twenty minutes down the hallway and back was a dizzying drop, an emotional roller coaster shooting forward at the speed of light. Screams of pain. Unquestionable, unquantifiable loss. Tearful reunions. Controlled chaos. Selfless care.

In his absence, Paulo and Mika had arrived, but Mary broke

the heavy silence first. "You could've taken longer." Her too-cheery tone tried to lift the mood.

Keane gave a somber nod and, leaning against the doorframe, combed his fingers through his still-damp hair. "I took long enough." He mustered up half a grin for her sake, but the sharp set of his jaw probably said it all. What kind of human shows such extraordinary benevolence to a stranger? He'd forever be in her debt.

"We brought breakfast," Paulo announced. "You need to eat."

Mika lifted a shopper's sack as if on cue.

"Thanks." Keane accepted the bag, took a banana, and passed the sack on to Mary. "I spoke with Mark."

"Yeah?" Paulo laid a hand on Keane's shoulder, giving it a squeeze.

And that gesture snapped him out of his daze, rendering him ready to deal head-on with the day. "Yeah. He's working on the means to get us out of here. We need to contact Mr. Ono and Ichiro and . . ."

"Keane. Relax, man." Paulo punched both hands in a quick one-two gesture. "Those famous fists of yours—they can't control everything."

His mother's face flashed in Keane's mind before he refocused on Ami's. "You think I don't know that? I know *too* well. What I don't know is how to process all of this." He laid his vulnerability bare, throwing his arms wide open before turning and blanketing Ami's hand with his own. His heart plummeted. She lay so still.

"No one does," Mary commiserated. "Time *does* make things clear and brings healing."

"But why such suffering?" Mika shifted from her place as a quiet brace against the wall. "Ami's one of the most amazing of people. She has such positive karma. And geological research is like her baby." She palmed away a steady trickle of tears. But were they tears of heartbreak or self-reproach?

"I don't know so much about karma, but, yeah, it doesn't seem right," Paulo said.

Keane pressed his lips to Ami's forehead, breathing in her familiar scent, then faced his friends. "The world's a messed-up place."

"That it is," Mary agreed. "Some battles won't ever be won with fighting hands, Keane. Sometimes, you have to do battle on your knees. When the earth trembles and the ocean roars, *he* is our refuge and strength. Claim that—deep in your heart. Don't forget it. Have full faith that Ami is going to pull through this, stronger than ever. As unfavorable and foreign as it may sound, suffering serves its purpose."

Head cocked, Paulo crossed his arms. "Like what?"

"Have the events and the pain and the suffering over the last twenty-four hours not forced us to take pause, to redirect our time and attention with supreme urgency?" Mary pressed her hand to her heart. "Here's a simple example. If a grain of sand shimmies into an oyster, the sand chafes the devil out of the oyster. The poor creature suffers. It's disruptive until the oyster deposits part of itself to encapsulate that grain of sand. It keeps coating the grain of sand with part of itself, and over time, this accretive process protects the oyster and results in something beautiful, something valuable.

"Like a pearl, suffering can shape the soul. But it can also harden the heart. Unexpected events can unite the most unlikely of folks and remind us to love one another."

Everyone was watching Mary. Sharp and swift, she wore calm understanding like a comfortable flannel cloak. Her bright gaze lit on Keane's for half a second, seeming to check his mood. If he were honest with himself, he felt the firm pinch of self-examination as he contemplated into which camp he fell. Was his heart hard or turning into something better?

An authoritative shout from the hall broke the moment. After a booming rap at the door, it swung wide. A spry man, his white jacket speckled with medical grime, peered into the room, and they stood alert. "I am Dr. Takemoto. A bed has been secured for Miss Ono at the hospital. This team will transport her."

"I'm coming too." Keane's wave of hopeful energy seemed to enliven all.

"You come." A million crinkles formed around the doctor's eyes as he bobbed his head. "You help carry."

Chapter 18

Shards of sunlight cut through the morning clouds. In no way did the warm rays reflect the gray dealings of the rescue, recovery, and cleanup efforts. Dangerous, heart-wrenching, gargantuan duties. From the earthquake then tsunami double-punch to a shower of sunshine, how could Mother Nature be so temperamental?

Keane stared out the hospital window, one hand linked with Ami's. How much human loss would there be? And would Ami come out of this? He huffed, not wanting his thoughts to drift into such dark territory.

Hospital days were hell, the atmosphere alone taking an emotional toll. The wondering. The waiting. The sharp, sterile smell of alcohol, the slow drip of an intravenous line, and the incessant PA calls for doctors.

Three raps came at the door. Mark entered and stole a glance at the dark-haired angel on the bed. "Hey." He leaned against the wall. "The federation confirmed that they're postponing the bout. A new date will be set soon. The announcement could come as early as tomorrow, so you can't check out. You have to keep training. I spoke with Ella and Mika. They've both agreed to stay with Ami while you train."

Keane nodded but said nothing. He lowered Ami's hand and tucked it under the white cotton blanket. "I love to fight, but it seems so . . . trivial, in such poor taste, right now."

"Maybe. Maybe not. Hopefully, the delay of Fight Night will address that. But wouldn't some entertainment take folks' minds off the hard stuff?" Several beats passed. "Don't underestimate that. And staying at Ami's side, night and day, you're more of an inspiration to the public than you realize." From his back pocket, he pulled out a rolled-up newspaper and tossed it at Keane. Earthquake stats anchored the page. Time. Epicenter coordinates. Magnitude. Current death toll. He folded back the page. Amid a collage of images, a four-by-four black-and-white snapshot, Ami in a neck brace and him cradling her as he walked into the hospital, said it all.

He only shrugged.

"What's the doc saying?" Mark asked.

"The scans were clean. It's just a matter of time." Keane tossed the paper aside, took a seat, and hunched forward, elbows against knees as if he were about to pray.

"We can work out rotations. Have Ella and Mika stay so you can catch a break. And Mary asked if you'd swing by and move some heavy school desks damaged in the tsunami. But ya gotta get back in the ring, champ."

"Yeah, I hear you." Keane gave a slight nod. "But can you believe Niko Ono hasn't been by? None of her brothers. Not even once. Pathetic pieces o—" He cut himself off but not before exposing his utter disrespect for his opponent.

"Use that. Don't let the rage go. You hear me?" Mark prodded. "Niko may be MIA, but one more thing before I go. Mr. Ono is coming by again."

"Today?"

"Yes, sirree. He wants to talk to *you*."

"About what?" Keane fiddled with Ami's motionless fingers,

needing the tactile connection. But he looked up in time to catch Mark's gaze flick from her hand to the beeping monitor.

"Can't say, but think hard about getting out of here. She has to fight this fight, and you have your own to prep for. The gym is in decent shape. I'll give you until tomorrow. Did you hear that?"

"Yeah, yeah. Tomorrow. Line it up. Have Ella come by mid-morning, so I can train. And let Mary know I'm sorry I haven't already been by, but I'll be there in the afternoon to help out as long as she needs me. Make sure she has whatever resources and money she and her students need to rebuild. I owe her big."

Mark slipped into the hall to handle his requests, but the man was right. Keane needed a break. Hospital time, a time both idle and filled with the monotony of news-watching, was depressing him. At a quarter till three, the doctor dropped in with a patient folder and nothing noteworthy to share.

"No permanent damage. Strong vitals. Give her time to overcome the shock." He repeated the sentiments he'd shared during the morning rounds, proving doctors with their demigod degrees were just keenly trained observers. They studied the brain, but the structure's beautiful interworking remained beyond human understanding.

The doctor vanished, and the wall clock's hands snapped onward, the afternoon slipping through a rosy haze into twilight. Time became his companion. Constant, ever-present, sometimes it made choppy jumps forward. Sometimes it puttered along.

His hand swallowed hers, his body slumped forward, and his eyelids shut out the world. His desperate plea escaped again. "How long, Lord? Will she ever come back? If it's your will, please . . . please heal Ami and wake her."

Their meeting now felt like some cruel joke—given love only to lose it.

He shook off his bitterness and pent-up anger. "Forgive me."

Far too long had he basked in prosperous peace, living atop a mountain of blessings, the king of his own hill, taking every breath for granted.

A sickening self-loathing wrenched him in the gut. All those years of offering up comfortable canned prayers, rarely settling into a deeper, real connection. Was religion without the relationship even religion at all? Amid such widespread loss, how rote and shallow those prayers now seemed. Deep within his brain, his mother's voice surfaced. What was it she always said? *Valleys surround the good times.*

His two weeks in Japan had been good, an unforeseen adventure. A relationship, especially such an engrossing one, had never been on the agenda. Ami was, however, more than he could have hoped for. But the tsunami—a violent and abrupt *valley*—touched the nation and brought tears to the world.

He ambled for the dream that slipped through his hands. Praying for Ami felt selfish. And yet, believers were to pray over *everything*, so he dropped to his knees, bowed his head, and unloaded all the *heavy* on his heart. Could he hope his prayers would be answered?

Chapter 19

Keane sucked in a sharp breath, loving the stench of sweat as he raised his arms overhead in victory. "Here I am, boys," he shouted.

"Glad you're back. You belong in the cage," Paulo chirped, his voice thick with brotherly affection. Mock seriousness smoothed the Brazilian's face as he tossed Keane a towel. "I'll go easy on you."

Having spent thirty minutes pounding a sandbag into submission to reactivate his muscle memory, Keane felt primed for a knockout. He acknowledged the comment, his lips challenging Paulo with a slight smirk. "Are you sure you want to do that?"

Grinning, Paulo shrugged, his mouth guard still in his hand. "Who's watching Ami?"

"Ella, for now. Nice of her. Speaking of, where's Hans?"

"Ice bath. Sumo smashed him up good this morning."

Keane chuckled. "I can only imagine."

Mark materialized from the front office. "You lovebirds ready?"

"Yeah, let's do this." Keane knocked gloves with Paulo and waited while his friend slid in the mouth guard, lesson learned, apparently.

Five rounds of scrappy sparring. And with each landed punch, sensory snapshots from too much time spent watching the news flashed through the synapses of his mind. That tremble. The crushing wall of water. The fear-instilling sound—even on the television. The vast wreckage. The lives lost. The threat of a fractured nuclear plant. The life-altering events leaving forever scars on the region.

But then the sweeter memories. The feather-soft feel of Ami in his arms, her exotic scent, his unfulfilled dreams of a life with a plus-one. Dripping in sweat, he pounded through the bouts, fighting for her. The final bell sounded. He sauntered to the sidelines in search of a towel and the satisfaction held in a water bottle.

"I couldn't take my eyes off you two." Mark waved his hands to animate his words. "Paulo, you fought an incredible fight. And, Keane, you were extraordinary. Your instinct. Your passion. Your drive for excellence. If anything, the downtime reenergized you."

Mark shoved his notepad into a back pocket and thrust his lips into a grin. "Seriously, you're fighting on a whole different plane." He landed a jovial slap on Keane's shoulder. "I can't explain how, but my prizefighter's abilities have magnified to superhuman standards."

Keane squirted water into his mouth and wiped the sweat from his face. "Fighting in honor of those lost—and in hope Ami will come out of this—makes it real."

"Mr. Temple?"

His head whipped toward the familiar voice cutting through the gym noise like the sharp-edged blade of a katana. Mr. Ono stood observing him. Despite being stunned by the man's appearance, Keane gave him a deferential bow.

"You look ready to fight."

He dropped his chin to acknowledge the compliment. "I'm surprised to see you here."

"Yes." Ami's father assessed him. "While I—and Niko and Ichiro—have been engaged with work, I understand you have attended my daughter for many days." Ono brushed his chin with the backs of his knuckles and then folded his arms across his chest. "I offer my gratitude."

Even as the reality of Ami's condition and Ono's disapproval weighed on Keane, he sensed Ono was being sincere. "Your daughter is an amazing woman. I'm fond of her."

His face a mask of neutrality, Ono paced toward Keane and dropped his arms to his side. "Your relationship with my daughter is unusual. However, I was too hasty with my opinion of you. Your concern is genuine." He stretched his neck from side to side, perhaps buying time. "Ami is my only daughter, but her happiness is my happiness." The older man's jaw twitched. It must be as close to an apology as his pride would allow. "And so, I will take care of Ichiro, and you have my blessing to see her."

The words had to cost Ono face, but something in his expression softened. It was a good trade-off. At least Keane thought so. He offered a hand, and after a pause, Ono accepted it with a firm shake.

A string of electronic chirps sounded, redirecting everyone's attention. Ono retrieved a sleek silver phone from the inner pocket of his suit jacket and held it to his ear. "Yes?" The man listened, his eyes widening, his face revealing nothing.

Keane had slid several steps back to give Ono some space when Mark yelled from across the room. "You got a call, Temple."

He left her father to take it.

"Keane?" Ella's voice, thick with affectionate sobbing, coursed through the receiver when he answered. "She's awake."

That took time to sink in. There was a churn of emotions—a rushing ripple of excitement laced with deep-seated fear. He had to swallow before he could speak. "Is she all r—"

"She's asking for you."

"Then she's . . ."

"Perfect."

Letting the calm warmth of her tone relax him, he hadn't

realized he was walking to the locker room until he was there, phone pressed to ear, exchanging karate *gi* for clothes. He'd never known such relief or urgency.

"Tell her I'm on my way." He ended the call, dropped the phone into his back pocket, and paused, eyes closed and chin tucked, to offer up a prayer of thanks.

"May I give you a ride?" The cultured voice startled him.

Ono stood at the door.

"Then you've heard?"

"I have." A previously nonexistent sparkle now lit the old man's unyielding eyes. "The doctor is examining her, but we might catch him if we hurry."

Never would Keane have guessed he'd share anything with one of the Ono men, especially the stone-faced patriarch. Keane shifted and wiped his palms on his slacks, getting antsy. Given the state of the roads, a maddening path was necessary.

With cleanup efforts underway, the city buzzed. Emergency responders made daring recoveries. Volunteers sifted through debris. Homeowners swept stoops. Cell service improved. Like vultures angling for the best and bloodiest morsel, foreign news correspondents descended on the wounded city. Along with a captive news-watching world, the island nation had given its collective cry for the immeasurable loss. Known for its Festival of Lights and tree-lined streets, Sendai would forever bear the scar of the Great East Japan Earthquake, a dark mark in its history.

And yet, life rolled on.

"Have you heard about the nuclear plant?" Ono breathed out, breaking the thoughtful silence.

Keane felt as if his life had been caught in some powerful earthly hiccup. Quake became tsunami, and now tsunami became nuclear meltdown. The nuclear plant had gained priority in the news. "I have. The rule of three."

"I beg your pardon?" Ono cocked his head.

"Oh, I didn't realize I spoke aloud." Keane bent forward, elbows on thighs, scratching through the thick stubble covering his chin. "Superstitious people say bad things come in threes—the earthquake, the tsunami, and the threat of a nuclear disaster make three."

Ono gave a cheerless chuckle. "And four is unlucky in Japan."

Keane acknowledged this with a polite nod as the car approached the hospital.

"Are you ready?" New creases etched across Ono's forehead.

"I just want her to be all right."

"You and me both."

At the entrance, a woman heavy with child doubled over with a contraction before trudging in for assistance. Even in the midst of the unthinkable, babies were born, and others were delivered a second chance at life.

A mass of nerves, Keane mounted three flights of stairs. Down a hallway that smelled of alcohol-based sanitizer. Overly bright artificial light. And then two lines of pleased nurses formed a funnel into the room. Their focus shifted to him, but he only saw her. He would've filled the place with flowers, but such luxuries weren't possible with disrupted business operations. He'd do it soon, as soon as some normal was found again.

Ono entered first. Keane paused in the doorway, only a step behind. He glimpsed Mary, shedding happy tears and trying to fade into the wall. Ami was sitting up and, as if sensing his presence, lifted her gaze to him. An angel in a hospital gown perched before him.

"Hello, Father. Hello, Keane."

Even with her voice weak from disuse, those four words answered so much. Relief weakened Keane's knees as Ono went to pat her hand. Such was the old man's way. Distanced. Cool.

Keane lingered at the door, giving Mr. Ono space, wondering

if he could contain himself amid the crowd. He wanted her alone. All to himself. It was about to rip him apart not to pull her into the protection of his arms. Trapped in that reverie, he jolted when a pair of flimsy hospital slippers pelted him in the chest.

Angel Ami had been lying in wait and must've woken with a vengeance. That was a good sign, wasn't it?

"Where have you been?"

At her sassy urgency, he snatched up the slippers from the floor, eased them on her slender feet, and circled the bed. He sat beside her, his bulk dominating the bed. Then he reached to touch her, aware—and not caring—that his reverence would leave everyone certain he was undone by love for the woman. She swayed toward him with the first connection of skin on skin, but Ono broke the tenderness of the moment, flashing a kind of get-lost look that had the nurses crawfishing backward out of the room.

"Every day until today, and just hours ago really, Keane has kept watch over you, Ami." Ono crossed his arms over his chest and drummed a pointer finger against his chin. "Ten days."

When she raised her face toward him, Keane shrugged. "Guilty as charged. See, I met this woman who once claimed to take the unexpected by the reins, and I've been praying hard, wondering when she'd come back." Keane gave a dramatic huff, but joy must be evident on his face. "Your father is right. I've been here every moment until this very morning. You beautiful, stubborn woman, why did you wait for me to leave to wake up?"

He pressed his lips to the crown of her head and ran his finger-tips over her hand. When he became aware he was favoring the ring finger, he stopped and checked Ami's and then Ono's face.

Mr. Ono nodded with a grunt, his eyes redirecting from their hands. "Not one of my sons is half the man you are, Temple. Not one has even been to visit Ami. She picked you against Niko's wishes, but he failed as the eldest of our family. Given all that has transpired, it's beyond a professional fight, and he's too bitter to remember to protect and love his sister." Ono kept his face neutral, but was that annoyance below his composed mask?

Keane straightened, stunned by the man's change of heart. "Ono, you don't have t—"

"Let me finish. As disappointing as it is, it's true. Ichiro would never make her happy. I see that now," Ono said the last bit to Ami. "She is much like her mother was."

With a tempered smirk, he overlaid their hands with his own and gave Keane a meaningful stare straight in the eye. It could be interpreted no other way than the public giving of his blessing. After a pat on Ami's shoulder, Ono turned on his heel and left.

"Well, that was surprising. And awkward," she said.

"I thought it was amazing." Alone, Keane cuddled closer, his voice rough.

"Did you now?" she purred.

"I did. How are you feeling?" Cupping a hand on her chin, he examined her delicate mouth.

"I don't know." She nestled into his touch. "It's strange."

"What is?"

"Um, how can I say this and not sound crazy?" She smoothed the blanket covering her lap, and his hand slid down to rest over hers. "While I was in the coma, my brain was active. I have no idea what to make of it, but I saw things."

She blushed. Was she embarrassed by this disclosure or by what she saw? He couldn't tell. "Like memories?"

She shook her head. "The tsunami caught us. We were climbing a stairwell, and then cold water swirled around my calves. I panicked. I'd never been so terrified. And then everything went black."

When she checked his face, he sensed her hesitance and remained patient and attentive.

She drew up her knees, hugging them as her chin lifted. "It was so much like the tank."

"The tank?"

As his head jerked up and his gaze searched hers, Ami's heartbeat quickened. He sounded so surprised. How could she make him understand?

"Time drifted, almost like a dream, but I was aware of the water in a way I have never been."

"What do you mean?"

When she pursed her lips, weighing whether to share her experience, he laced their fingers together, somehow proving he'd do everything in his power to fuse them into one. "I've been so worried about you—praying all night and day. I promise you can tell me anything."

"Okay." She inhaled. "I felt I could sense what it touched—the water, I mean, like *I* was the water. Breathing in dew. Crying rain. Whispering through sand. Using a power both gentle enough to wash a pebble clean and strong enough to cut it in two. The ability to host life and take it." She halted and peered into his face, seeking confirmation she wasn't crazy. "I'm rambling."

"You're healing. People who have come through comas sometimes say they've had an almost out-of-body experience. Some believe they've had a divine encounter. So, what do you make of it?" He stroked her fingers with such tender interest her heart swelled.

"I know I did, Keane—have a divine encounter. What happened hurts, but even now, I have this sensation of sublime lightness. I am beyond humbled." Conviction fortified her. "We take so much for granted. We make things, build things, like Father's skyscrapers. We trust modern engineering marvels can withstand anything, even time.

"But it is not true. It's false hope. I've always leaned on science for answers, but it's nothing like the solid faith you have. You told me I would have courage when I was ready to take the next step. And I prayed, Keane. I believe."

He skimmed his hands up her arms, tickling her skin like the brush of a feather as his gaze met hers. Was it joy flashing in those jade eyes?

"Are you serious?" A note of hope lifted his tone.

She nodded. "One hour of one day, and so much was swept away. So much destruction. So many lives lost. Thousands of people are still missing." She cast a glance at the television. Tears slipped down her cheeks, stinging before they dropped onto the white hospital blanket. "I'm ready now. I believe and want to learn."

Thank you, God.

He pulled her into his arms and held her that way for a long time. "You're precious. My angel. Your anguish—the suffering of the people here—has become my own. If I could take it away, I would. But I can't. I am here, though, alongside you for the ride."

She wiggled from his grasp, her gaze narrowing in on his. "What Father was saying—is that what you want?"

Mild amusement flickered in his expression. Then he loosed a chuckle. "Ami Ono, are you asking if I want you?"

"I, um—" Heat rushed her cheeks.

He caught her chin between his hands and seized her mouth with his, kissing her with abiding love until she had not a single doubt. When he released her, satisfaction uncoiled his lazy grin.

Getting out of the hospital couldn't come fast enough for Ami. Once free of the incessant beeping monitors and constant nurse chatter, they burned through an entire month in mere days. He was back to training; she was back to researching. The little free time they had they spent together, aiding in the city's clean-up efforts.

Many nights after training, Keane and his teammates headed to Mary's school and a neighboring business to tear out and replace water-damaged Sheetrock, and she tagged along. In the tsunami's wake, so many people united in a shining display of what humanity *can* be. Immeasurable gratitude swelled in her chest.

But during the days, Ami had so much new data to sift through, and the Brit needed help. The tsunami had taken two coworkers, leaving the team with heavy hearts and bringing an even greater urgency to their work. They would dedicate the paper to their fallen friends. Though the lab was crippled, research continued at a satellite office.

There had been unusual marine discoveries found miles inland. Historical markers that skirted the boundaries of scientific opinion. If only the import of such findings had been understood, not under-estimated, earlier. That should never happen again. The naysayers would argue: Who can guess how and when Mother Nature will unleash her fury? But the project findings showed—if the scientific community continued to keep a close eye on the ancient evidence and signs around them—they might better locate the wheres and predict the whens.

Keane conducted his own research, devouring video footage of Niko's recent fights, and pushed through a wicked sparring sched-ule. Mark tried to get him to transfer to a Tokyo gym, something Niko Ono had already done, but Keane continued to train amid the wreckage near Ami.

"You look solid, my friend." Paulo stirred Keane from his post-practice daze. "Yeah, energized like you got new batteries."

Keane unleashed a hearty laugh, but a new rhythm did revitalize his fighting. "Thanks, man. It feels good to be back."

"Anybody hungry?" Hans shouted from Mark's office door.

"Always," Keane answered.

"Prefight meal—should we say at seven?" Paulo asked.

"Yes," Hans chimed in. "Ella is cooking at our place."

"That's good of her with how limited supplies are." Keane checked his watch. "Seven it is, then. I need to get going if I'm going to get Ami in time."

"And now Paulo is the fifth wheel." Frowning, Paulo spread his arms wide.

"Not really. You'll have Mark." Hans pushed away from the doorjamb. "But seriously, when have you ever had lady troubles?"

Paulo shrugged. "I have trouble keeping them."

"Because they leave you or because you fear commitment?"

When Paulo said nothing to Hans, Keane knew something gnawed at him. "What about Mika? Why don't you bring her?"

A flicker of interest ignited Paulo's eyes.

Chapter 20

A prefight meal had become the unconventional family's tradition. Ella. Hans. Paulo. Mark. Keane. And Ami was pleased Mika had been invited. Her longtime friend deserved more love than Niko was capable of providing, and Paulo had asked her out four times now. Keane suggested this was out of character for the fun-loving Brazilian, so maybe something hotter was simmering under her friend's warm expression.

Ella was Ella, as colorful and cheerful as always. The woman's frequent high-pitched bursts of laughter were contagious. While the others moved into the living room, Ami followed Ella into the kitchen. "Dinner was superb." Ami reached to hug Ella. "Thank you for everything."

"It was just spaghetti, but it was made with love—and electricity now that the power is back on—which makes a huge difference." Ella waved toward the lights, then nudged Ami. "Please don't get sentimental on me, especially after hardly making a peep all evening. Tell me the truth. Are you feeling back to yourself?"

"I am."

"But you don't want him to go?" Ella prodded, her brow raised.

"Of course not. We plan to keep seeing each other, but we haven't figured out how to make it work." Ami took a breath to steady her emotions. "Truth is, I don't like being separated from him. Even for a day."

"I know that feeling. That's why the twins and I travel with Hans." Ella backed up to lean against the kitchen bar, then spiked her eyebrows further. "Keane's better with you. He's still intense but not quite *so* intense."

"Are you saying I tamed the Lion?"

"Indeed, I am." Ella's laugh came out easy and loud, drawing Keane to the kitchen entry. He rested a shoulder against the doorframe, wearing the easy confidence of a contented man.

"Were your ears burning, luv?" Ella asked him.

"Please don't tell me all that girlish cackling was at my expense." He looked entirely too pleased with himself.

"I was telling Ami I'm sure you'll work out an agreeable way to see each other all too soon." Ella sent him a conspiratorial wink.

Though he tried to mask it, mild annoyance tightened his expression.

"It's complicated though." Ami crossed her arms over her chest, trying to make sense of the exchange.

He slipped up behind her, wrapped his arms around her waist, and nuzzled the skin below her ear.

"Always is, but doesn't have to be." Ella left that dangling as she turned with a grin to set a stack of emptied plates in the sink.

Keane's warm breath and tempting words tickled Ami's ear. "Ready to get out of here?"

When she nodded, he grasped her hand and led her out the back way. The quick trip brought them to his place where she snuggled with him on the couch before sliding to the floor at his feet.

Lazy-eyed, the Lion watched her roll off his socks and rub his feet. Soon, he was purring.

"You, Miss Ono, are a gifted woman," he crooned, relaxing on his side, propping his head in hand.

"Hardly. You're well aware how much I enjoy being around you. And there hasn't been enough of that all week."

But now she openly admired him. His broad body nearly covered every inch of the plush sofa. When he laced his fingers between hers and tugged her to stretch out in front of him, a wave of shivers rolled through her. Bodies aligned, face-to-face, he brushed his lips to hers.

She nestled her cheek into the crook of his elbow and let her fingertips drift up and down the muscled contours of his arm before stopping on his shoulder. She inhaled his scent, some heady blend of soap and sandalwood. His eyelids fluttered shut, and any trace of tension in his body melted away.

"Are you ready? I mean, do you get nervous before you fight?" With one fingertip, she traced the sculpted planes of his face.

"I feel ready." The Golden Lion let one eye open to a slit before the other joined it in a dauntless stare. "I feel like I've already won."

For a fraction of a second, his green eyes bored into hers with a searing power. Then he used his free arm to cuddle closer. What was it gripping her heart, pulsing through her? Could it be real joy? A satisfied smile tickled the corners of her mouth.

Ami Ono knew she'd captivated many men with her bold stares and proven poise, but once alone, she was at Keane Temple's mercy, powerless against his strength. And for the first time in her life, she found herself willing to yield to a man. With Keane, she lost nothing and gained immeasurable support, love, and care every time she stood beside him.

When she drew back, she found the courage to speak her heart. "Me too. But what are we going to do about us? We need to make this decision together, face-to-face, and we're running out of time to do that." She froze, her eyes trained on his face, not wanting to press.

Silence ensued, and she held her breath as he furrowed his brow and ducked his head. Her fingers twitched to stroke his lion's mane. What was he thinking? Was he giving up on them? Surely, no.

Then he raised his head, his jade eyes fixing on her with a warm glow. "We will be together as often as possible. I promise. Just let me get through the fight, and then we'll hammer out the details. Fair?"

She clamped her lips together. The sparkle in his eyes told her he was not putting her off, but he wasn't saying something. And she knew it. "Fair. Now, where were we?"

"The Nippon Budokan." Arms upraised and spread wide, Keane made a slow circle, relishing the moment as he inspected the venue. The industrial air conditioner kicked on with a steady whir, stirring up the scent of buttered popcorn—and legends. He *would* be one.

"Yes, sirree. Back in Tokyo. Finally." Mark practically squealed from the arena floor. He thumped Keane's back. "What d'you think, Temple?"

Letting out a low whistle, Keane met his manager's expectant stare as eagerness zipped through him. "I cannot believe I'm fighting here."

And that said enough. Built for the 1964 Summer Olympics, the cavernous martial arts hall played host not only to fighting competitions but also to scores of musicians and performers. Muhammad Ali. Kiss. The Beatles. Bob Dylan. Mariah Carey.

"I say let's win this." A smug grin carved into his face as Mark puffed with prideful hope.

"Please do," Paulo added. "I need a new suit in Santorini blue. Women like sharp suits, not scars. And, my friend, you ruined this face." He gestured to a scabbing quarter-sized scuff at the bottom of his chin.

"Looks impressive—dangerous, if you ask me." Ami dropped in the compliment, keeping the conversation balanced. "You're right about the suit though."

Straightening his stance, Paulo preened. "Thank you, Ami. And I very much like your swan dress."

"Whoa, hold up." Keane stepped in between them. "I didn't realize you like suits so much."

"Keane, you are irresistible in a suit. Throw in a crisp-pressed white button-down, loose at the collar, and some wing tips and—"

"Ah, I see." He seized her hands behind her back and rested his forehead against hers, the desire to possess and please Ami throbbing through him. "You aren't trying to distract me in the place I need to be most focused, are you?"

She pulled back a fraction of an inch. "No, but I am level-setting expectations for what you need to wear when you beat my brother. I want you looking sharp and strapping."

"I think I love this woman." Paulo cupped a hand over his heart and moaned.

Keane still held Ami close, but his eyes narrowed in on Paulo. "Bad idea. She's mine—and mine alone."

"Enough, boys." Mark waved to a hallway. "Let's head to the locker rooms and make sure everything was delivered from Sendai."

"All right, but then I need to get to the hotel for the night." Leading up to a fight, Keane adhered to a strict battle routine. A dinner formulated to fuel performance. A long bath infused with eucalyptus bath salts to relax. Specific bed and wake-up times. A quiet evening free of distraction.

Mark charged down a dim corridor that fanned into a well-appointed room lined with wooden benches and lockers on either side. In its center, a tidy stack of sports bags bearing the Team

Temple logo and an assortment of gloves and gear overflowed round discussion tables. Keane glanced from Ami to the suit bag hanging on the far wall. His eyebrows hiked in question, drawing an amused smile from her pretty lips.

"Hans, I'm glad you're here." Keane spoke when his friend walked through the door, flanked by four men. Their black cargo pants and long-sleeved black T-shirts showcased bulging muscles. Clearly, the security detail. "Is Ella ready?"

"Waiting, as we speak." Hans locked gazes with Keane to reassure him.

While Mark and Paulo inventoried the baggage, Keane pulled her aside. "I arranged for you to spend the evening with Ella at the spa." When she opened her mouth, he pressed on. "As much as I want to spend time with you, I need to rest and center my mind for tomorrow. Fernando and Alejandro will keep an eye on you . . . from a distance, of course."

"But I don't ne—"

"Look—indulge me in this. The other guards will trail me, but I need good rest tonight and will not get it unless I know you're watched over."

She jerked up her chin. Having been raised in a household of boys, including several fighters, she could handle herself. Each fighter had his quirky traditions, some to the point of being superstitious. As much as she hated to be separated from Keane, she was *not* helpless. But tonight was not the time to argue. So, she released a dramatic sigh. "Okay, it won't be the same without you, but I can endure some spa time."

A dark twinkle flashed in his eye before he swept her up in a full-body hug. "Okay." He spoke over her shoulder, addressing the bodyguards. The possessive edge sharpening his commands made her heart thrum as his gaze flicked from her face to the men. "I don't care if she begs. She goes straight to the spa and then to her room. Nowhere else."

"Yes, sir." The lead bodyguard moved to open the locker room door, holding it for Keane while keeping his focus on the hallway.

When Keane's gaze landed back on her, a shiver ran down her spine. Was it from that what-I-say-goes tone of his? Or her immense gratitude? Before she could decide, he captured her mouth in a sweeping farewell kiss, solidifying her deep love.

With the bold swagger of a pleased king, he made his way into the broad subterranean corridor connecting the locker rooms with the arena and the back exit.

"Have fun with Ella, and I'll see you after the fight. Deal?"

"Okay." Her heart beat an anticipatory tempo. "And then we will celebrate?"

"Then we will celebrate." He smirked, brightening the serious atmosphere.

But Niko's abrupt appearance at the mouth of the hallway cut the levity short. "Keane Temple and my traitorous sister." An eerily calm confidence showed in his strut. "How lovely to see you together."

Ami's mouth popped open, but Keane stepped forward, screening her with his powerful torso. And the bodyguards closed in. He cocked his head, rocking on the balls of his feet. "With such a warm greeting, how could it *not* be lovely to see you, as well."

Niko's face contorted. He ground his teeth and balled his fists.

From the arena floor, Ichiro approached Niko, phone pressed to ear, then lowered it as he assessed the situation.

When Niko said nothing, Keane carried on. "I haven't had the opportunity to thank you for bringing us together. After all, the ambassador arrangement was at your bidding, was it not?" He squeezed her hand and glanced over his shoulder, starry admiration glittering in his eyes. "I dare say she is one of the wisest, strongest, and most supportive women I've ever met."

How could she deserve this man? A bonbon-sized lump lodged deep in her throat until Niko's lavish laugh shook it loose.

"You are a fool, Temple. Tomorrow, I will end your conceit and enjoy erasing your legacy." Eyeball locked on eyeball, he stormed toward Keane with Ichiro fused to his heels.

Keane stiffened beside her. She held her breath, bracing for a brawl. But Ichiro shoved Niko toward his locker room across the hall.

As Keane turned to her, she released a pent-up breath. "I should go now."

"I think that's your cue." A warm smile broadened across his face. "Let me walk you out."

A sporty Mercedes idled outside the back exit. As the driver got the door for her, Keane enfolded her in his arms and rested his cheek on the crown of her head. She tipped her chin. "Kiss me good, Midas."

His chuckle ruffled her hair. Being in his arms, feeling his warmth made her reconsider her willingness to leave. "With pleasure." He slipped his fingers into her hair, bracketing her face, sealing her mouth with his. Her senses swam, and she wanted to stay.

"Hey . . ." What was it she wanted to say? A swirl of emotions claimed her, a pressure building in her chest.

"What is it, angel?"

"Just be careful tomorrow, okay?"

"I'll see what I can do."

"And win. You have to win."

"Count on it."

Chapter 21

Ami fluffed a silk pillow and relaxed back into the comfy spa couch. "I feel good about tomorrow."

"You should. I've never seen Keane like this." Ella set a glass of chilled green tea on the low coffee table and shifted sideways, tucking her legs under her. Her laughter pealed through the quiet. "You—Hans says you are magic. You changed Keane's entire mind-set in a matter of weeks. Never did I think that finicky man would find a woman who could meet his expectations. You have accomplished the impossible."

They were the only two patrons enjoying the spa's tranquility room, but Ami's face still flash heated. "While what you say sounds incredible, he's leaving. Plain and simple. It's impossible to enjoy these last days together when he will be on the opposite side of the world in a week."

"What if—" Ella's mouth made an *O* shape as she paused. Some undisclosed hesitancy snagged her friend's thoughts. Candor, *not* evasiveness, was Ella's strong suit.

Ami fixed a stony glare at her. "What?"

Ella reached for her glass and downed a swallow. "I was going to suggest you meet somewhere romantic between Japan and the States. That might be doable once or twice a month."

"That's not a committed relationship." Ami squeezed her eyes shut, willing away the uncertainty and frustration tangling around her gut.

"But it could be the next step toward forever."

Seated in the nippy Budokan stands, Ami rubbed her arms to warm up. The crushed-pearl exfoliation and rice-milk treatment had nourished her skin, leaving it smooth. She'd worn a becoming black sheath that managed to cover everything while highlighting her legs and toned arms. A sizeable stack of golden bracelets, including Keane's three-strand tennis number, shimmered under the event spotlights.

"You look keyed up," Paulo noted from behind her.

"I can't sit down." Her lip throbbed before she realized she was biting it.

"Try to relax. The fight doesn't start for another ten minutes." Ella's singsong voice brushed over her raw nerves.

Ami sucked in a controlled breath, released it in a whoosh, and tried to focus on the contagious atmosphere beyond her whirlwind emotions. As spectators shuffled to their seats, the fired-up announcer standing cageside raised his voice to echo throughout the arena.

"He has to win." She mumbled under her breath. "He deserves to win."

Ella gripped her forearm, her gaze reassuring. "He will."

"Ladies and gentlemen . . . This. Is. It." The announcer's booming voice called attention to the crowd, first in Japanese, then in English. Four spotlights chased each other around the arena before settling on the private hall leading to the Budokan's underbelly. A streak of red materialized out of the darkness and paused for effect before Ami's brother's form took full shape. He held up his arms to elicit a cheer.

"Give it up for hometown hero—Niko 'The Flying Dragon' Ono."

Niko, sporting shiny red shorts embroidered with a black dragon, pranced toward the cage.

Much of the audience clapped while a fan section chanted "O–no, O–no."

"And now, join me in welcoming the one . . . the only . . . Golden Lion—Keane Temple."

The roar threatened to bring down the house.

Head held high, Keane strode straight on toward the fight of his life. Black shorts with stripes of gold down the sides. The definition in his upper body a chiseled masterpiece of muscle that kept women ogling. Gorgeous. Powerful. His focus aimed at the cage.

Over the years, Ami'd watched her brother's relentlessness evolve into a dark, fearsome lifestyle. Keane's discipline would be tested like never before. *Epic* was the descriptor too easily tossed around in the press, but that's what the fight would be. And who would win and who would lose held epic implications for her. Though Niko was her brother and she wished him no ill will, Keane had tapped into an artery coursing straight to her heart. He'd invested the time to understand her private side and the woman she hoped to become, offering to be a true partner, offering a future.

"Gentlemen, let's have a clean fight. Now, touch gloves and back to your corners."

As the referee's instructions precipitated a familiar sequence of events, the knot in her stomach tightened. Trainers and water boys on both sides gave last-minute ministrations. Niko, eyes locked on Keane, psyched himself up by shuffling his feet and upper-cutting the air. Behind him sat two of her brothers and her father. One of her brothers stared at her with dark, fathomless eyes, and she winced at the sting of scornfulness—an outsider in her own family.

Then her gaze bounced to Keane. Apart from the rhythmic rise and fall of his chest, he'd become a statue cast in gold.

She zoned in on that minimal movement until the starting bell jarred her back to the spectacle. Niko hopped from foot to foot, skating from his side to the center of the cage. Keane skulked in a fighter's stance, his unflinching stare assessing her brother. Niko was the first to take a jab. Anticipating the action, Keane angled his torso to avoid the blow and took the opportunity to snap a kick. The ball of his foot connected with Niko's ribs with a *thwack* and whipped back.

Niko winced, and his scowl grew more severe. And like that, as instantaneous as the flip of a light switch, the charged atmosphere grew unbearably tense. The audience tuned in, yearning to see the beautiful brutality of a supremely matched bout. Darts of hatred, rapid punches, and bone-cracking kicks zapped from Niko to Keane and then Keane to Niko.

A counter left hook from Niko was chased by a solid right. A well-timed combination. Keane responded with a body kick that kept the action rolling. Niko's feet danced side to side before he lunged, but Keane was ready, connecting his knee with Niko's gut. They both backed up and circled each other around the cage. Keane rushed in, going for the body with swift shots.

The clock was ticking.

The exchange seemed balanced. One gave and then took the payback. But with such negative energy radiating off the two men, she could hardly drag air into her lungs.

"Ami?" Ella distracted her.

"What?"

"I asked if you're okay."

"I don't know." How true those words. "I care for them both, and they're trying to kill each other."

From the row behind, Paulo hovered over her shoulder. "Niko is getting tired. See his shoulders?"

The bell sounded, ending Round 4. Only one round to go.

"I know. But Keane's cut."

With Keane seated in his corner, the team physician worked to staunch the blood oozing from his right eyebrow. Mark was in his face, focused on pumping him up, while a young woman delivered a water bottle.

Across the ring, Niko aimed an unyielding, vengeful glare at Keane. Niko declined the water and continued the staredown. He was used to getting his way. But before converting to mixed martial arts, Keane had been a classically trained karate fighter too. Could it be that Niko had met his match and respected his opponent?

The referee settled in the center, waiting for the contenders to reconvene. With a clang, the call to action came. Fists up, Niko and Keane faced each other, teasing each other with the tips of their gloves and capturing everyone's attention.

The metallic tang of blood spread over Ami's tongue. She stopped biting her lip and tried to swallow her nerves, but her stomach clogged her throat.

In lightning-bolt speed, Niko struck Keane's jaw with his right fist, then popped him in the ribs with a left kick, seeming to knock the wind out of him. The fight had been a ping-pong match of blows, jabs, and kicks. Now, for the first time, Keane stepped back, assessing with patient experience while he refilled his lungs with air. Niko charged him again, but Keane anticipated his opponent's move and delivered a one-two-three of face strikes. There was a fumble in Niko's footwork, and—*pow*—Keane landed a spin back-kick to the side of Niko's head.

He went down. Following standard protocol, the referee

inserted himself between the fighters. Ami couldn't see her brother as the wild cheering rumble mixed with gasps. She glanced at the scoreboard. Five rounds. Nineteen minutes and seven brutal seconds of outright man-on-man war. And there at his feet lay the powerful Niko Ono. The Golden Lion had knocked out The Flying Dragon.

The announcer's animated voice bellowed through the sound system, but Ami couldn't make out what he was saying through the blood pounding against her eardrums. Ichiro and a trainer mounted the stage to tend to her brother. She wished Niko no hard feelings and exhaled when he stirred and sat up. Poor guy was clearly stunned when he realized the outcome. Keane offered Niko a hand to help him to his feet as the fight officials arrived to declare Keane the winner.

"Keane Temple!" the federation president cried out, clutching Keane's wrist and raising it overhead. "Speaking on behalf of millions of federation fans, this has been an incredible bout to witness. You have proven yourself victorious and worthy of the World Champion title."

A lovely model appeared with an enormous gold champion belt in hand and wrapped it around Keane's ripped waist.

"In the end, what gave you the winning edge?" The federation president thrust a microphone in Keane's face.

"It was a hard-fought battle against a fighter I respect." Keane paused, panting. "Start to finish, I did what I came here to do. Since childhood, I've trained for this, but along the way, I learned our fight isn't always what we expect. Let's say recent events hit home." His triumphant expression now thoughtful, Keane scoured the sidelines until his gaze landed on her. "And tonight, it's been a great privilege to fight in this extraordinary place in honor of my mother and those impacted by the Great East Japan Earthquake and Tsunami. I dedicate this win to them."

Keane yanked the title belt from his waist and held it over-head. A longing grin bridged the gap between him and her. Paulo was whooping, Ella bouncing as she shook Ami's arm. For Niko's sake, Ami tried to veil her reaction, but as the uncontainable joy seized her, she clapped hands on both sides of her cheeks, her astonished laughter streaming free. With unmatched strength, vigor, and the most persistent and kindest heart the federation had ever seen, Keane had snagged his moment to turn the tides, swooping in like the one-two punch of natural disasters to take the title and her heart.

There was a rushed shower in the Budokan's underbelly, fol-lowed by the donning of black pants, a black V-neck sweater, and a sharp camel hair sports jacket—Ami's pick. Facing the press for interviews on the way out of the locker room led to a crowd of wait-ing fans at least twelve people deep. Keane's job extended beyond the ring, and fan time had always been some of his favorite time spent. Hearing his name shouted was restorative, encouraging, and ego-stroking, especially when every throbbing joint in his body reminded him he'd been in a World Championship fight.

But, restless, he shuffled his feet. Where was Ami? He'd seen Niko, staring back with cold black eyes before he disappeared into the background. Mark and Paulo were halfway down the corridor toward the back door. But Ami had been missing in action since she'd left the stands. He aimed a questioning look at Paulo and mouthed, "Where is she?"

Paulo shrugged before turning his thumb toward a nonde-script door to the right.

Keane did a double take, strode in that direction, and cracked the door to a lounge of sorts. "Watch the door." He spoke over his shoulder to the bodyguard shadowing him. "No one comes in."

"Got it, boss man."

An overwhelming sense of triumph welled up within Ami, making her lightheaded. Her cheeks twitched from too much smiling. Keane had won. She had survived a tsunami, overcome a coma, and faced her family head-on to see him shine. With her focus trained on the door, she straightened the moment it cracked open. "Keane."

"Why are you hiding in here?" His gaze swept the richly appointed space before settling on her. Relief shone in his face until absolute affection pushed through—a look that made her breath hitch and her spirit soar. "I wanted you by my side for the interviews, but at least you've had company."

Hans and Ella stood and, unbelievable as it seemed, Ami swore Ella blushed. "And now she can have yours."

Ami raised a hand. "You don't have to go."

"We need to get back to the twins, and I hope our paths cross again." After a silent exchange between Ella and Keane, Ella smiled, then hugged Ami and joined Hans by the door.

"I'd like that. Same goes for you, Hans."

Hans knocked twice on the door, and a security guard opened it from the hallway. "Be good to my friend. He does not travel well." He gave Ami a mischievous wink.

"I swear . . ." Keane threatened as Hans disappeared behind the closing door.

She rubbed shivers from her bare arms, sliding back a step. "What was that about?"

He marched toward her, shoved his hands into her hair, and

proved just how much he adored her with his kiss. "You never answered." His voice came out gruff, its edge making desire swirl deep in her core. "Why weren't you by my side?"

How was she supposed to think straight when he took total possession of her? "I–I . . ." Great. Her tongue stumbled over a reply. "I didn't want to make a scene. It was your time. It didn't need to be about us."

His lips curled up at the corners. Between their bodies, he lifted her hand to his mouth, dragging it back to his lips.

"What did Hans mean about you not traveling well?"

"Caught that, did you?" he mumbled, almost to himself. "I was hoping you'd miss it. Hans is such a pot-stirrer."

"Well, I didn't miss it."

Delight smoothed over his face. "Do you trust me?"

"Yes."

"Do you love me, Ami Ono?"

She couldn't contain the smile pressing into her cheeks. "Yes. What are you up to?"

He tugged her hand, leading her toward the door. "You'll have to come with me to find out. I was thinking a change of scenery would do us some good. What do you think?"

The jolt of plane wheels on pavement startled Ami awake, and the evening rushed back to her. Keane's surprise. A private jet. An undisclosed location. She peered out a round window to a brilliant blue sea and a landscape of hills covered with gleaming white buildings. "Where are we?"

"I figured you'd guess."

"Greece?"

"Well done." His bright eyes heated her blood. He lifted her onto his lap and, with his chin nestled on her shoulder, looked out the window. "More specifically, Santorini. Didn't you always say you wanted to dive these waters?"

She nodded with a silly grin. Keane continued to amaze her. No one had ever listened to her so closely or cared much about her pursuits. "I cannot believe we are here. I've always . . . Thank you." She pulled his arms around her, loving the cozy security she felt nestled against his chest. Unexpected tears tickled the brims of her eyes.

"Hey now, what's that about?" He cradled her even more tightly and ran his chin up the side of her neck.

"You're too good to be true, and I feel *so* much right now. So many people lost loved ones, and sometimes I feel I don't deserve to be here and have you. I feel responsible. Like I owe it to them to make the most of life."

Keane pressed a kiss to her temple. "Good. I'm all about making the most of life, too, and figured a little distance would give us the freedom to explore this and figure out how to make us work."

"Sounds like a plan." She took a deep, fortifying breath. "Santorini—wow. The water looks amazing, but I seem to be sans swimsuit again." She glanced back over her shoulder to find herself pinned by his heated expression. "Perhaps we can stop by a store on the way."

"Who said you need one?" he joked, arching his brow before downplaying the suggestion with palms raised in surrender. "I'm only joking."

But was there a glint of truth in his jade eyes?

Her lips parted to speak, snapped shut without a reply, and curved as her mind fast-forwarded to entertain that idea. "You'll have to marry me first."

"I rather like that idea. Takes the guesswork out of how to make *us* work. Maybe it's fast, but so what? Sometimes you just know what's meant to be." His eyes softened, even as his hold on her—mentally, emotionally, and physically—tightened. "After all that we've been through together, how about it? Will you marry me, Ami Ono?"

Before she could reply, a rapping came at the cabin door and then a muffled voice. "Mr. Temple, your car has arrived, and your guests are already at the hotel."

Ami's gaze zeroed in on Keane as a gasp of surprise slipped through her glossed lips. "What have you planned now?"

The exotic view dazzled Ami. She lay on the bed propped on her side, attempting to memorize the sublime moment. Pure joy pulsed through her. Keane stood on the private terrace overlooking the Aegean Sea. In silk lounge pants and a fitted tee, his sculpted body appeared to be formed from hard rock. He was glorious— golden hair and golden skin outlined by a backdrop of sapphire sea. And that blue seeped into her psyche, beckoning her to the core.

But as tempting as the prospects of free diving in pristine waters and exploring the area caves might be, Keane's presence—powerful and pleasing—called to her. For as long as she could remember, diving had been her sole source of freedom and peace. But being with him, emerging to be by his side as her own woman, she'd found even sweeter still.

He angled his head toward the vista. "You like?" His eyes glowed like light penetrating translucent jade.

When had she ever felt such deep-seated contentment? "I like a lot."

"Mrs. Temple?" Keane gave her a slow grin and stalked toward her, every nerve ending thrumming. Her recovery after the tsunami and his final training preparations had kept them apart. Though a challenge, their patience promised a night of pure and unparalleled passion. And now, love, thick and sweet as honey, coursed through him. He hovered over her on the bed, hemming her in with his muscular arms. From under her long fan of lashes, her pupils flared and mirrored his longing.

"Why the frown? You should be smiling." He nuzzled the tip of her nose with his and leaned back to look at his bride.

"Do your bruises hurt?"

"Not much."

"My brother got in a few solid punches. He fought respectably." She traced gentle fingers over a tender spot at the base of his jaw before her lips tended to the injury.

"He did. He already wants a rematch." The huskiness in his voice filled his ears. Those leisurely touches . . . He would let her control the pace—for now.

"He might better you next time, though, when he hears we got married. He's likely fuming, but I'm glad you came out on top. And I still can't believe my father flew in for the ceremony. With Hans and Ella and Mika and Paulo—even Mark, it was private but perfect." She grinned, planted a foot on the mattress and, with a twisting thrust, attempted to flip him.

The quick move excited him, but he went with it, chuckling from underneath her. "I'm glad to hear that. Feeling adventurous, are you?"

A fiery twinkle played in her eyes as she leaned down and swept her lips over his. "Yes, I think now would be an excellent time to go for a dive." The corners of her mouth twisted with her tease.

Something integral to the strong beat of his heart softened toward this woman. "Is that so?"

"That's so." Her breath was a warm caress to his cheek.

With ease, he sat up. "You're sure you're ready?" His eyes did not stray from hers, even as she nodded, her teeth trapping her lower lip. "I love you, angel."

She released her pretty lip, allowing the corners of her mouth to curl into a shy smile. "I know. I love you too."

"Our paths crossing was unexpected, but no doubt about it, God orchestrated this—us. Ami, look at me." His gaze lit upon hers. "We've both survived rough times, and I feel beyond blessed you chose me. True victory does not come in the ring, and I will never take grace—or you—for granted. I promise to honor and cherish you in every way and can't wait to carry you into our new home. But tonight, I'll finish making you mine." He tipped his forehead to hers. "Tonight, let's celebrate life and love."

The sun was sinking, and golden-orange rays angled through the terrace door, gilding their bodies in a warm glow. There was the rhythmic roar of the ocean and his spoken vow. What he'd committed to her by mouth and in ceremony, he sealed with his whole body—touching, taking, savoring, uniting as one until the round silver moon spilled the last of its glittering light over the water and completed its turn through the sky.

If you enjoyed this book, will you consider sharing the message with others?

Let us know your thoughts. You can let the author know by visiting or sharing a photo of the cover on our social media pages or leaving a review at a retailer's site. All of it helps us get the message out!

Email: info@ironstreammedia.com

    @ironstreammedia

Iron Stream, Iron Stream Fiction, Iron Stream Kids, Brookstone Publishing Group, and Life Bible Study are imprints of Iron Stream Media, which derives its name from Proverbs 27:17, "As iron sharpens iron, so one person sharpens another." This sharpening describes the process of discipleship, one to another. With this in mind, Iron Stream Media provides a variety of solutions for churches, ministry leaders, and nonprofits ranging from in-depth Bible study curriculum and Christian book publishing to custom publishing and consultative services.

For more information on ISM and its imprints, please visit
IronStreamMedia.com